American Sneakers in Palestine

A Palestinian Saga

Book 4

Donn Hutchison

Cover photograph by Lisa Marouf

ISBN: 978-0-9970990-8-9

First Edition

Lovingly dedicated to those Palestinian students who brought joy to teaching.

With much love for Rana, Ramzi, and Kahlid, who, for me, represent the best of what it means to be both Palestinian and American.

Acknowledgements

Heartfelt gratitude to Rana Hutchison Copeland who continues to prompt, encourage, reread, and question. It is through her determination and work that this Palestinian family saga no longer slumbers in a bottom dresser drawer, but is awake and lives!

Continued gratitude and appreciation for Carol Hutchison Vago, who read the chapters as they were written and gave *instant* feedback: often critical, always insightful, and always supportive.

Credit is due to Lisa Marouf for the cover photo of the Friends School in Ramallah.

The Mansur Family

Sitteh Hasna: The blue-eyed, red-haired grandmother who lived with her son Omar and his wife Nijmeh in a refugee camp after fleeing a massacre in their village in 1948. She was a great story-teller. Her own story is told in the first book of the series.

Omar & Nijmeh: Illiterate yet wise patriarch and matriarch of the Mansur family. They managed to raise their ten children in a refugee camp and pushed them to be educated and successful. They have many grandchildren and great-grandchildren.

Mansur: The eldest of Omar and Nijmeh's children. He is a doctor, married to **Zaleena** who is of Circassion/Russian decent and works as a translator. They live in Amman, Jordan and have three children; Omar, Nijmeh, and Ahmad.

Hasna: Omar and Nijmeh's eldest daughter. She lives in the camp with her husband **Imad.** They have 7 sons including Saleem (the eldest), Sami, and Saji (the youngest). They have several grandchildren including Saleem's son **Imad**- named after his grandfather.

Khalil: Omar and Nijmeh's third child is a lawyer who lives in Amman. As a teenager, he was arrested for demonstrating against the occupation and served time in an Israeli jail. There, he met his best friend (and partner) **Amr**, who is a stock-broker and is looked on as another son by Omar and Nijmeh. He is a father figure to his younger brother Mohammad.

Manal and Mona: Mohammad's sisters who live in California with their Palestinian grocer husbands (who happen to be brothers).

Ahmad: Omar and Nijmeh's ten-year old son who was killed while watching a demonstration.

Najla and **Azeezeh:** Mohammad's sisters who live in the Emirates with their families.

Mohammad is the ninth of Omar and Nijmeh's children. He falls in love with and marries an American-Christian, **Sarah**. They have twin sons named **Khalil** and **Mansur** after his brothers, a daughter, **Yasmeen**, named after her mother's Palestinian friend, and a little son, **Amr** who is named after Mohammad's "foster" brother.

Issa: The youngest of Omar and Nijmeh's children is an artist and is married to Sarah's good friend **Yasmeen** (who had originally been chosen for Mohammad by his mother Nijmeh). He has red hair like his grandmother Hasna.

Kareem: like Mohammad and Sarah's children, Kareem has been raised in the States and is brought back to Palestine to learn religion, language and culture. He and Yasmeen find a common link.

Basim: A boy who works in the market to support his mother. Sarah and Mohammad take him under their wing.

The Goldman Family (Iowa farmers)

Dave Goldman is a non-practicing Jew and Sarah's father. He is caught between his wife's stubbornness and his desire to have Sarah and her children in his life.

Emily Goldman is a devoted Methodist; is married to Dave, and is Sarah's mother. She is unhappy about Sarah's choice in a husband.

Sarah: An agricultural engineer who falls in love with and marries Mohammad, a Palestinian man she met in college.

Ken and Martha Goldman: Sarah's Uncle and Aunt and surrogate grandparents to Mohammad and Sarah's children after Sarah's estrangement from her own parents.

Chapter 1

"We need to talk to the kids about the move," Sarah said as she set a cup of coffee down in front of Mohammad, but far enough away that one-year-old Amr (who was called *Andy* at Day Care) could not reach the cup. "They won't be excited about the prospect of living in the West Bank for four years."

"It's a great job offer working for the UN," Mohammad said taking a sip from the mug. "We both get to use our degrees; get to do some real service in the West Bank, and the kids get a chance to really pick up Arabic, to get to know some more about Islam; get acquainted with their extended family; get to travel and *see the world*. Those sound like *positives* to me," he smiled.

"I'm afraid the kids won't see it that way," Sarah said sitting down at the table with him.

"The boys will be coming back to the States for college in two years, and Yasmeen will finish high school there, removed from some of the distractions teenage girls are exposed to here. The school there offers a good education and she'll be better prepared to return to the States for college. And this little guy," he said kissing Amr on top of the head, "will pick up the accent and fundamentals of Arabic. He'll be speaking like a native!"

"The boys and Yasmeen aren't going to be happy about leaving their friends. The boys will argue that they want to finish their last two years of high school here. And, frankly, I can't blame them," Sarah said stirring a little sugar into her coffee. "They won't want to give up all their activities to begin again in a new school six thousand miles away. As for Yasmeen, she will really resent moving to a conservative society where her activities will be curtailed."

"It will be hard at first, I grant you, but this is such a great opportunity! It will be a once-in-a-lifetime experience for them!" Mohammad said excitedly. "They'll love the idea!"

"I *hope* you're right," Sarah said unconvinced.

He wasn't.

The twins were upstairs preparing for school. They were in their sophomore year of high school and loving life – except for the fact that they looked *identical*. It wasn't that they didn't love each other. They did. It was great being brothers, and sometimes great being twins; they just wished that they weren't *identical* twins. It had been great when they were five; they could *pretend* the other one did it, and sometimes even their parents couldn't really *be sure* who it was. They would look up at their parents with those deep, dark eyes and in all innocence say: "*Who? Me?*" It had even worked to their advantage when they were in elementary school until the principal had decided to put them in different classes. It began to be slightly annoying when they were in junior high and continued to get worse as they stepped into high school.

They wanted to be seen as *unique,* not as a Xerox copy of the other.

They were both on the football team, the wrestling team, the basketball team, and the swimming team. They had even, *both of them,* been in the debate club and on the newspaper staff. Even though they didn't *dress* like twins, their friends and teachers had a hard time telling them apart.

At home, they were *Khalil* and *Mansur;* at school, they were *Ken* and *Matt.* At home, they spoke Arabic (with an American accent) with their father and English with their mother. Six days a week they were *Moslem,* on Sunday they were *Methodist.* Their parents had the erroneous opinion that if exposed to two faiths, they would be able – when adults – to choose for themselves. With each other they spoke English ninety-nine percent of the time; on those rare occasions when they got angry with each other, they spoke Arabic. *F-you* and *a-hole* didn't seem quite as colorful as: *I will break your legs and drink your blood.* Cursing in English was really *quite* limited but there were scores of imaginative curses in Arabic. (Sometimes they would use them during a wrestling match, basketball tournament, or football game. Their opponents had no idea what they were saying.) *There were advantages to being able to curse in another language.*

"It's almost time for school," fourteen-year-old Yasmeen hollered as she knocked on the bedroom door. "You better get moving."

"We're coming. Keep your britches on," Khalil called from the bathroom, scraping the whiskers off his upper lip. He had wanted to grow a mustache, but it was against school policy.

Mansur ran a comb through his curly hair and straightened the collar on his shirt, as he tried to look around Khalil's head at his image in the bathroom mirror. "By the way, I'm driving to school today."

"It's *my* turn to drive, *ya zel'la'me,* (man)" Khalil said giving him a playful punch in the stomach.

Ever since the boys had gotten their driver's licenses it had been a continuous battle over *who* was going to drive the pickup to school.

"It is definitely *not* a chick-mobile," Khalil joked. "No back seat!"

"We don't need a backseat. You know Baba would kill us if we dated." Mansur said. "*Though* it *does have* a flat-bottomed *bed...*" he laughed.

"Dream on little brother, dream on!" Khalil smiled as they headed down the stairs.

"I'm only the *little brother* by three minutes," Mansur said poking him in the back.

Mohammad had agreed to Uncle Ken's giving the twins an old pickup when they turned sixteen *if* the boys kept their grades up, didn't race, and never got a ticket. "The first ticket either one of you gets," Mohammad had said,

"I'm taking the truck back to your Grandpa's. You'll be without wheels for six months."

It was odd that the kids had *three* sets of grandparents. They had Palestinian grandparents – a *Sidi* and *Sitteh* whom they had only met through pictures and stilted phone conversations; they had a *Grandpa Ken* and *Grandma Martha* whom they loved dearly and who were really their mother's uncle and aunt, and then they had maternal grandparents they had never *officially* met, though they had a farm adjoining Grandpa Ken's farm. *That* had been the most difficult situation to understand. Their mother had told them that her parents had been unhappy about her marriage and had decided to have nothing to do with her. "Even after sixteen years?" the twins had asked. "Haven't they ever wanted to meet us?"

"I am sure they have wanted to meet you," Sarah had said. "But I think it is hard for them to back down since they took this stand. I have tried over the years to go and see them but your Grandma Martha advised against it. She said she had talked with them and they were intractable in their stance."

The kids also had a number of paternal uncles and aunts, as their father had been the *ninth* of ten kids! They had over the years frequently seen their aunts and their cousins who lived in California. They also knew three of their uncles: Ammie Mansur, Ammie Khalil, and Ammie Amr; the three had come to visit from Jordan every two years since the twins were two- the year that Yasmeen had been born.

Their parents, unfortunately, had never returned to the West Bank. Their father had lost his West Bank ID card and needed to wait for his American passport. When he finally had it, there was always an excuse: the kids were too little; there was a new baby; they didn't have sufficient vacation days. It was hard to believe that *sixteen* years had been allowed to lapse.

Their dad, whom they called *Baba,* was pretty easygoing most of the time, but when he *put his foot down* it was like he stomped in fresh cement. He was immovable. Of the two, the boys thought their mother was stricter. Their dad tended to overlook things because they were *boys;* their mother thought *being boys* had nothing to do with anything.

On the other hand, their father was way too strict with their sister. She would argue with him, "But, Baba, everyone is going to be there!"

He would smile and say, "Everyone but *you.* You are not going to a party if there are boys there."

"Mom! Help me out here!" Yasmeen would say.

"You get to see plenty of boys in band, in chorus, in the youth group at church. You are much too young to date," Sarah would say.

"Date? Who said anything about *dating?* There *is no dating!* Not you, and not your brothers," Mohammad said. "You can date *after* you are engaged."

"It's like living in a village forty years ago," Yasmeen sighed. "We are living in *America,* Baba. *America!*"

"You don't want to date, do you, Baba?" Mohammad asked tickling little Amr who was sitting in his lap. Amr smiled at his father and patted his cheek before resting his sandy-colored curly head against Mohammad's shoulder.

Mohammad and Sarah watched their strapping sixteen-year-olds walk out to the red pickup, their fourteen-year-old sister in tow.

"They get to look more and more like you every day," Sarah smiled. "As your *Sitteh* Hasna would have said, *that just proves that I loved you more than you loved me.*"

"What would she say about the next two," Mohammad grinned. "According to Aunt Martha, Yasmeen is *you* at fourteen, down to the very *independent* spirit! And this little guy, this *little surprise,*" he said tickling the squirming Amr until he giggled, "has sandy-colored hair with a touch of red, just like yours."

"Yes, but he *looks* like a fair *you!*" Sarah laughed. "Our sons certainly take after their father, their Uncles Mansur and Khalil, and their Grandfather Omar. Three generations all cut from that same bolt of cloth. I had hoped that Yasmeen would have taken after your mother."

"Instead," Mohammad said grabbing Sarah's hand and kissing it, "she turned out just like *her* mother – *bet'jen'in* – an Iowa Beauty!"

Sarah smiled but her thoughts were on a different matter. "Now that we are thinking about accepting this job offer- moving away for four years – it's made me think more of my parents. I can't believe that in *sixteen* years they have never *once* made an overture to see me or to meet their grandchildren."

Tears threatened to fall as she stirred her coffee. "All the times that we have gone home to visit and stayed with Uncle Ken and Aunt Martha, not *once* did they call or come over to see us. Anytime I suggest going to see them Aunt Martha kindly says that it is best that I didn't. I am especially surprised at Dad."

Mohammad reached across the table and took Sarah's hand. "I don't understand it. I thought for sure they would come around. You're their only child, and these are their only grandchildren."

"The move makes it all seem so *permanent* to me; *permanent* in the sense that we will never be reconciled. It makes me so *sad,*" Sarah said wiping the tears from her eyes with the back of her hand. "Maybe I should make one last attempt," she said.

"I think you should, *habeeptee,*" Mohammad said rising from the table and going to stand beside Sarah. She rested her head against him and Amr reached down and patted her hair.

That night at dinner, Mohammad informed the kids about the proposed move to the West Bank at the end of the twins' sophomore year. Three sets of adolescent eyes looked at him in disbelief. Finally, Mansur said, "You're not serious are you, Baba? You are not thinking of taking us away our last two years of high school?"

"Yes, *habeebee,* I am serious. This is the chance we've been waiting for. It's a wonderful opportunity for you to travel, to live in the West Bank, to connect to your roots! You'll be able to learn about your religion, your culture; you'll become fluent in Arabic. You'll get a chance to get acquainted with your grandparents, your uncles, and cousins," Mohammad said, a little disconcerted at the shocked disbelief on the faces of their children.

"But, Baba," Khalil interjected, "we've been in the same school since first grade. We'll be leaving all our friends. We'll be going to a new school where we don't know anyone, and where they'll think we are *foreign!*"

"*Foreign?* You are Palestinian!" Mohammad said.

"We are only *half-Palestinian,*" Mansur murmured. "Through Mama, we are half-American."

"We're *all American* by birth," piped in Yasmeen. "I'd like to go for a vacation, but I don't want to go and live there!"

It wasn't going as Mohammad had hoped.

"We're only talking two years for you boys," Mohammad argued. "You will naturally come back here for college or university."

"But you're talking *four years* for me!" Yasmeen said starting to cry. "You'll probably try to get me married off to some man I don't know from the camp. How can you let him do this, Mama?" she said turning to Sarah. Pushing back her chair she ran upstairs to her room in tears.

"Weren't you going to discuss this with us *before* you made your decision?" Mansur asked.

"We always used to discuss things as a family before making any decision that was going to affect us all," Khalil added. "It sounds like you have already made up your mind and are just *informing* us that we are going to move."

"I want you to get exposed to your roots while you are still young," Mohammad said in defense. "It is my fault; I should have taken you back to the West Back when you were still children. I realize it is hard to uproot you when you are only two years away from graduating. But that is where your *true roots* are."

The boys were unconvinced.

"Your father really wants what is best for you," Sarah said. "He is not doing this to *punish* you."

"We *know* that Baba doesn't want to punish us, but it *feels* like a punishment," Mansur said.

"Can't we just go for the summer, and then come back and live with Grandma and Grandpa?" Khalil asked.

"I want you to try it for a year. If at the end of an academic year you are really unhappy about being there, I will speak with your grandparents about spending your senior year with them," Mohammad said, trying to reach a compromise. He loved his sons but was disappointed in their failure to see this as a great opportunity.

When he went up to bed he noticed that the lights were still on in the twins' rooms. He opened the door softly and peeked in. They were both asleep; the lamp on the table between their beds still burned.

Mohammad went over and straightened the blankets over their sleeping forms. He ran a gentle hand over the two black, curly heads. Bending he kissed each head in turn. *Ba'hib'bak* (I love you) he whispered. Mansur rolled over in his sleep, "*Anna ba'hib'bak (I love you too), Baba,*" he sleepily said. "*Ou, ana (me too), Baba,*" Khalil mumbled in his sleep. Mohammad switched off the light and left the door ajar as he left the room.

There was no light under Yasmeen's door. He went in and she was still awake; her face was still wet with tears.

Mohammad sat on her bed. "I don't like seeing you so sad, *bintee* (my daughter)" he said to her in Arabic. "You'll see that it will all work out."

"Oh, Baba," she cried in Arabic throwing her arms around him. "I know you think you are doing what is right for all of us, but it *feels* so wrong here," she said putting her hand on her heart. "We've never even been to the West Bank. Please, Baba, *please* don't make us move."

Mohammad put his arm around her. "You've grown to be such a big girl, Baba," he said. He kissed her sandy-colored curls and patted her hand. "It's going to be alright. You will see. It's going to be just fine."

"I hope so, Baba," she whispered. "But I still think you are wrong."

Chapter 2

Aunt Martha, when she wasn't basting the turkey, checking on the rhubarb pies, and pushing a fork into the boiling potatoes to see if they were done, kept pushing the lace curtains aside to get a clear view of the road.

"Looking down the road every five minutes won't bring them any sooner," Uncle Ken said.

"I know it won't," Aunt Martha smiled, straightening the lace panel so it hung just so. "But I haven't seen them for weeks and this surprise visit is such a treat."

Three days earlier, when the kids had brought home a notice from school announcing a long weekend due to in-service training, Sarah had said, "Let's drive up and spend the weekend with Grandma and Grandpa."

The whoops of joy had been deafening. Even Mohammad had joined the chorus. "What a great idea!"

"Can we drive up in the truck?" Mansur asked eagerly.

"We'll take turns driving and follow right behind you," Khalil added hopefully.

Mohammad smiled at his two sons and said, "I think that can be arranged. You can even take Kalb along," he said, scratching the ears of the mongrel they had picked up at the pound the year before Amr had been born. "He'll enjoy romping freely at the farm."

"Chasing Aunt Martha's geese, you mean," Sarah said. "I think at the farm he dreams that he is a fierce wolf hunting prey in the wild. It is only when the geese nip at him that he realizes he is only a mongrel and comes loping back to the house with his tail between his legs."

Yasmeen carried Amr out to the car and buckled him into his car seat. "There you go, Amro," she said to him in Arabic handing him a plastic car to play with. It was interesting that she, Mansur and Khalil only spoke Arabic with Amr when they primarily spoke English with each other.

"I think it's because he can't comment on our accent," Khalil laughed.

"Or correct our pronunciation," Mansur added. "You are an uncritical audience aren't you, habeebee?" he said ruffling Amr's sandy-colored curls. Amr just looked at them and grinned.

That they adored him, and he them, was obvious. The twins had been fifteen when he was born, and Yasmeen thirteen. He had been doted on and carried around since he was a newborn. Sarah used to joke that he never had a chance to cry; as soon as he opened his mouth – even if it was just to yawn, there was someone picking him up and carrying him about. "It's like he has five parents," Sarah would laugh.

It had been the twins and Yasmeen's suggestion that the small storage room between their bedrooms be made into a nursery for Amr when he was moved from Sarah and Mohammad's bedroom. They had carried the things stored in that room to the attic; the boys had repainted the nursery furniture that Mohammad had found at Goodwill; Yasmeen had made the cartoon-character curtains that covered the one window in Home Ec class.

"It's perfect, Mama," she said. "He is right between our two bedrooms; right where he should be."

The drive to the farm was lovely. It was early October and the leaves that were going to turn had already turned. Even though they would be coming up again in November for Thanksgiving; and then again in December for Christmas, they loved the farm and any extra visit was a real treat.

"They're here!" Aunt Martha exclaimed as she spotted the car and the red pickup turn onto the dirt road. She and Uncle Ken were waiting at the gate when the two vehicles pulled into the driveway.

"My, we're glad to see you," Aunt Martha gushed throwing her arms first around Sarah and then Mohammad.

"How are you, Pop?" Mohammad grinned, grabbing Uncle Ken in a bear hug.

"Fair to middlin', fair to middlin'. A sight better since you all came," Uncle Ken grinned. "Now, where are my grandsons and granddaughter?"

"Right here, Grandpa," Yasmeen smiled, kissing and hugging first Ken and then Martha.

"Here we are, Granddad," the twins said in chorus, hugging Grandpa Ken.

"When're you boys going to stop growing? You're already taller than me," Ken laughed.

"Each time I see you, you are an inch taller," Martha said hugging them both and kissing them loudly on both cheeks.

"Where's the little guy?" Aunt Martha asked. Yasmeen handed Amr to her. Amr looked at her, patted her cheeks, smiled and nestled his head against her shoulder as he slipped a well-sucked thumb into his mouth.

"My, it is grand having you all here. Just grand! Come on in, dinner's practically on the table. I made all your favorites."

"No one can cook like you, Grandma," Mansur said as he slipped an arm around Sarah's shoulder and winked at her.

"Not even Mama," Khalil laughed as he slipped his arm through his mother's, "though she does try."

"I know your mother can cook circles around me," Aunt Martha laughed, "but it is generous of you to imply I'm the better cook. You just have to look at me to know that someone enjoys my cooking. Me!"

"All the more to love," Mohammad smiled and put an arm around Aunt Martha.

Over dinner, Mohammad told them that they had told the kids about the proposed moved to the West Bank.

"We wanted to tell them early enough that they would have plenty of time to adjust to the idea," Mohammad said.

"It will take some getting used to," Sarah added looking at the three older children. "We realize that they will be giving up some things in exchange for some others."

Uncle Ken looked at the three sober faces before him. "If I was a tad younger I would come right along with you. Think of all the adventures you are going to have! Of course, you will be giving up some things; there is no argument there, but the benefits – why – they are almost too many to list."

"And, of course, you three will be coming here and spending the summers with us," Aunt Martha chimed in.

"And we'll be coming to spend Christmas with you," Uncle Ken added. "I've always had a hankering for travel, never had the right incentive. Now with my grandkids living in the Middle East, I'll be visiting so often you'll get tired of me."

"We may have to buy two seats for me," Aunt Martha laughed spreading her arms wide to accentuate her girth.

"You can share part of mine," Uncle Ken grinned.

"Summers Grandpa will work you so hard that you will be marking off the days on the calendar until you go back," Aunt Martha said. "He will keep that old pickup in running order, and by the time summer rolls around that old mutt will be right friendly with my geese."

Mohammad and Sarah glanced at Ken and Martha and both silently mouthed: *thank you.*

After rhubarb pie and coffee and milk, Uncle Ken said, "I need to run in to the feed store, why don't you two boys show me how well you can drive that old pickup?"

"I think that this little guy and I could use a nap," Mohammad said picking up Amr.

"Aunt Martha, Yasmeen, and I will do up the dishes and then have another cup of coffee on the porch," Sarah smiled.

"Mansur, you drive to the store, and Khalil, you can drive back. I'll just sit in the middle and appraise your driving skills. Come on Kalb, you can ride along in the back," Uncle Ken said leading them out to the pickup.

As they were putting the food away, washing and drying the dishes, Sarah broached the subject of her parents.

"Have you talked to Mom and Dad lately?" she asked Aunt Martha.

"I speak to your mom on the phone occasionally, and of course I run into her at church and sometimes at the grocery store. It is pretty much hello how are you. Oh, it's all very cordial – a cool cordial. They don't come to visit, and we stopped going there," Aunt Martha replied.

"It makes me sad to think that it has gone on now for sixteen years. I thought for sure they would come around, especially Dad," Sarah said.

"Oh, I think your dad would come around – wants to come around, but your mother is so stubborn and I don't think she knows how to get out of it," Aunt Martha said. "I've talked with her; tried to reason with her; begged her even. It is just a no go."

Yasmeen stacked the dried plates in the cupboard and listened. A plan began to formulate in her mind.

"Now that we are thinking about going abroad for four years, I feel terrible that things are the way they are between us," Sarah said. "I hate the fact that all this time has passed and she has never met her grandchildren."

"What do *you* think about this new job offer?" Aunt Martha asked.

Sarah hurriedly glanced over at Yasmeen and gestured with her eyes at Aunt Martha, "It's a wonderful opportunity," was all she said.

When the dishes were washed, dried, and stacked in the cupboard, Yasmeen said, "I think I'll go for a walk and walk off some of that delicious food," she smiled giving Grandma Martha a hug.

"Let's you and I take a cup of coffee and go and rock a bit on the porch," Aunt Martha said to Sarah. "This is a perfect chance for us to sit and have a heart-to-heart."

"So, what do you boys really think about the move," Uncle Ken asked.

"We don't want to go," Mansur said. "We understand it is a great opportunity for Dad and Mom, but it is our last two years of high school."

"We'll be leaving our friends, and football, and basketball, and swimming," Khalil added.

"We'd like to meet our West Bank family but it seems so unfair," Mansur said. "Mom and Dad are asking a lot of us, Grandpa."

"Look at it from your dad's perspective. He has lived in the States for almost seventeen years without visiting your other grandparents. This is his chance to show you that part of your heritage. You are really lucky to be such a blend of cultures. You should take advantage of this opportunity. We're only talking a few months here. You'll be back each summer; I'll be sending you boys and Yasmeen the tickets to be sure it happens," he smiled, clapping both boys on the back. "Even though your dad can afford it, and would object, I want it to be my treat. I think it is a grandpa's right to spoil his grandkids."

He went on, "Your dad told me that he only wants you to give it a year and if at the end of the year you really aren't happy, that he and your mom will send you back to finish your senior year here. Now pull up over there," Uncle Ken pointed.

The boys went into the feed store with their Grandfather. "You remember my grandsons," Uncle Ken said to the clerk behind the counter.

"Sure. How're you boys doing? You sure are the picture of your dad," he said.

The bell over the door rang as another customer came into the store.

Ken turned to look and there stood his brother, Dave.

Chapter 3

Dave stood still, frozen in place, when he saw the two teenagers standing with his brother, Ken. *They are the spittin' image of Mohammad,* he thought.

"Why don't you boys run down to the grocery store for me?" Uncle Ken said, handing them some money and a list. "You grandma wanted me to pick up these things for her. I'll meet you out front in the truck.

"Thanks, Grandpa," Mansur said.

"See you later, Grandpa," Khalil smiled.

Dave stepped aside as they reached the door. "Excuse us, Sir," the boys said going out the door.

The clerk looked at Ken and looked at Dave. "I have something to do in the storeroom," he said excusing himself.

"They called you *Grandpa,*" Dave said so softly that Ken wasn't sure he had heard him.

"Yeah, they call me *Grandpa,* though they *know* I'm not their real grandpa," Ken said. "They know they have grandparents who don't want to meet them."

Dave looked at his brother and there was pain in his eyes. "You know I wish it was different, but *Sarah...*"

"Stop right there," Ken said raising his voice and his hand, "over the years Sarah has *wanted* to come and see you. She has *wanted* you and Emily to meet your grandchildren. You could have made it different if you had wanted to. You're a grown man and Sarah is your *only* child!"

Ken walked over and laid his hand on his brother's shoulder. "It's *not* too late. Sarah, Mohammad, and the children are spending the weekend with us. Why don't you and Emily come over? If it would be easier, I can ask Sarah to go over and see you first. This has gone on way too long. What do you say?"

Dave looked out the door. The boys were no longer there but in his mind, he could still see them. He hesitated. "I'll see what Emily says," he finally said.

"And if she is still adamant that she doesn't want to see them?" Ken asked.

"Then maybe, just *maybe*, I'll drive over by myself."

"You don't know how happy that would make all of us!" Ken said squeezing his brother's shoulder.

Yasmeen came out on the other side of the woods and saw the neat farmhouse surrounded by a white picket fence. She hesitated and then crossed the field and approached the house. There was an aluminum mailbox fixed to the picket fence. On the side, it read: *Dave Goldberg*. This was the house in which her mother had been raised.

Again, Yasmeen hesitated, and then making up her mind, she pushed the gate open and walked up the stone path to the porch steps. There was an old-fashioned wrought-iron bell that she rang. She could hear footsteps approaching the door. The door opened, and a woman who looked like an older version of her mother stood there.

"Yes? What can I do for you?" the woman asked wiping her hands on her apron.

Yasmeen took a deep breath and steadied her nerves. "I'm Yasmeen. I'm your granddaughter."

Emily raised her hand to her heart. "My *granddaughter?* I don't have a granddaughter."

"I'm Sarah's daughter. My parents, brothers and I are spending the weekend with Grandma Martha and Grandpa Ken. I thought it was time we met."

Emily was at a loss for words. She just stood there staring at this granddaughter she had never seen.

"I know my mother wants to see you. And you *must* want to see her!"

Emily finally found her voice. "I think you better go," she said closing the door. For a long time, she stood with her back against it. She didn't trust her legs to move. She was shocked at how much the girl looked like Sarah when *she* had been fourteen. It was as though she was *seeing* Sarah – the Sarah who had been so dear to her heart. Emily's lips trembled and she felt tears wetting her cheeks.

Yasmeen just stood there staring at the closed door then slowly turned and walked down the wooden steps, over the stone path, through the gate, across the field, and into the woods.

When she got back to her grandparents' farm, she saw her mother and Grandma Martha sitting on the front porch rocking.

"Did you have a nice walk, love?" Grandma Martha asked.

"I walked over to see your mother," Yasmeen said looking directly into Sarah's eyes. "I thought it was about time we met. She looks a lot like you, Mama," Yasmeen said absently. Then she started to cry. "She told me she didn't have a granddaughter and she asked me to go," she sobbed, sitting down in Sarah's lap as though she was a toddler. She rested her head against her mother's shoulder.

Sarah put her arms around her and rocked back and forth. "There, there, *habeeptee*. It doesn't matter," Sarah said as her own tears dropped off her chin.

Mohammad came out onto the porch carrying a wide-awake Amr. "We had a good nap, didn't we, Baba?" Mohammad said tickling Amr under his chin. He raised questioning eyes to Aunt Martha when he took in the scene.

"Yasmeen went over to see her grandmother," Aunt Martha said through clenched teeth. "You can imagine how it went."

Mohammad walked over to Aunt Martha and placed Amr in her lap. "I'll be back," was all he said.

"Mohammad, where are you going?" Sarah called. He just waved at her, too angry to speak.

He took long strides down the path to the pond, across the field and into the woods that separated the two farms.

"Yasmeen, go up and wash your face and then come back down and keep Grandma company. I'll be back," Sarah said hurrying down the steps after Mohammad.

Yasmeen looked at her grandmother, "What's going to happen, Grandma?"

"Something that should have happened sixteen years ago, love," Aunt Martha said.

The red pickup turned onto the dirt road, drove up the driveway, and came to a stop in front of the two-car garage. Mansur, Khalil and Ken bounced out.

"Was that Sarah I just saw heading into the woods?" Uncle Ken asked.

"Yep, she's going after Mohammad who is on his way to see Emily," Aunt Martha grimly replied.

"What!?"

"Yasmeen went over earlier and Emily told her she didn't *have* a granddaughter and asked her to leave. When Mohammad heard that, he went tearing over to see her and Sarah went tearing after him. I'm afraid there is going to be hell to pay – and *about time too!*"

"We ran into Dave at the feed store," Uncle Ken said. "He saw the boys with me. Heard them call me

Grandpa. I think it shook him up. I talked to him a little and it seems like he would like to see Sarah and to meet his grandkids."

"Was that man at the feed store, Mama's father?" Mansur asked incredulously.

"Yep, that was your real grandpa," Uncle Ken said.

"*You* are our *real grandpa*," Khalil said. "That was just Mama's father."

"He didn't even know who we were." Mansur asserted, sitting beside his brother on the front steps.

"Oh, he *knew* alright," Uncle Ken said, "And it pained him a great deal that he has let all these years pass and he didn't get to know you, or you to know him. He's your grandpa. Oh, *I'm your grandpa too*," he smiled. "And don't you ever forget it!"

Sarah caught up with Mohammad just as he was exiting the woods and in sight of the farmhouse.

"Wait, Mohammad. Wait!" she gasped out of breath. "What are you going to do?"

"I'm going to say what I should have said sixteen years ago. This has gone on *way too long*. I have stood by and have seen how this situation pained you and I kept quiet. But hurting our daughter is the last straw. I will have it out with her once-and-for-all!"

"You are right," Sarah said slipping her hand into Mohammad's. "I don't want you facing her alone. We will face her together."

Mohammad raised the clasped hands to his lips and kissed the back of Sarah's hand.

Emily and Dave were sitting on the front porch rocking when Mohammad and Sarah walked up the path. Dave had just been telling her that he had seen the twins.

"I understand that you have met our daughter, Yasmeen," Mohammad stated still holding tightly to Sarah's hand and staring at Emily. "She came home in tears," he continued.

Emily opened her mouth to speak, but Mohammad raised his hand in protest. "Please let me say what I have come to say. I have understood your unhappiness over our marriage. You were convinced it wouldn't work. It *has* worked. We have been married seventeen years and have four beautiful children, praise God. Over the years Sarah has *wanted* to be reconciled to you. She loves you and this has been very painful for her," Mohammad paused.

"I have stood by too long. I have stood by and kept silent for seventeen years. No more! Hurting Yasmeen was the last straw for me. Sarah is an adult; Yasmeen is a child. I will not stand by and see our child hurt."

Emily looked grimly at Mohammad and Sarah. Dave looked grimly at Emily.

"It *has* gone on too long," Dave finally said. "I ran into your two older boys at the feed store with Ken. They called him *grandpa* and that hurt," he said with a noticeable mistiness in his eyes. "I don't want to *replace* Ken. He *has* been their grandpa, just like Martha has been their grandma. But I would like to get to know them. We...we were wrong," he choked out.

"Speak for yourself," Emily said grimly.

Dave glared at Emily. "We are grandparents, and I want to get to know my grandchildren. This is our daughter, our only child," he spat pointing a finger at Sarah. "She has to know, that in spite of all, we love her – have *always* loved her."

"Oh, Dad," Sarah said. Letting go of Mohammad's hand she rushed up the steps and hugged her father.

"Emily, I want you to make-up with Sarah. And *that's an order!*" Dave said.

Emily reluctantly allowed herself to be hugged. "Well, I suppose what is done is done," she said.

Just then a red pickup pulled into the drive. Ken was driving and Martha was in the front seat holding onto Amr. Mansur, Khalil, and Yasmeen (along with *Kalb*) were in the pickup's bed.

Ken got out and helped Yasmeen out of the back. Mansur and Khalil clambered over the side. Yasmeen went over to the side of the truck and took Amr from Aunt Martha. They made their way up to the porch.

"We thought it was about time that you two met your grandkids and that they met you," Aunt Martha stated.

30

"Let me introduce you," Uncle Ken said. "This is Mansur," he said placing a hand on Mansur's shoulder. "And this strapping young man is Khalil; you have met Yasmeen," he said turning to Emily, "but you have not," he said to Dave. "And this little guy is Amr. Kids, these are your mother's parents."

There were some moments of awkwardness. Finally, Mansur and Khalil went up and shook hands with their mother's parents. Yasmeen went up, still holding Amr, and also shook hands. She said to Amr in Arabic, *"Ha'dole Im ou Abou Mama."* Emily visibly bristled.

"I was just telling him that you are Mama's parents," Yasmeen said in defense.

"I don't know about you, but *I* would like a cup of coffee and the kids would like some milk. I even have two rhubarb pies in the truck – if they didn't get crushed by you three," Aunt Martha said smiling at the three older kids.

"We'll get them, Grandma," Mansur and Khalil said in chorus.

'Grandma'? For a moment, Emily felt as though someone had stuck a knife in her heart.

Chapter 4

Martha was just wiping out the old farmhouse sink, when Khalil and Mansur came into the kitchen. "I thought you boys would be glued to the TV," she smiled.

Khalil and Mansur came up to her and wrapped their arms about her ample form. "We just wanted you to know," they both said, "that even though we have met Mama's parents, *you* are our grandma."

Martha hugged them to her, too choked up to speak.

"You two!" she said swatting them on the shoulders even as she hugged them, "Making your old Grandma blubber like a baby. Go on. Go and watch the game."

She looked out the kitchen window. The sun was just setting and its brilliant reds and yellows were mirrored on the pond's surface. *I have been richly blessed* she thought gazing at the setting sun through misty eyes.

Later that evening as Mohammad and Sarah lay in the old spindle bed in the farmhouse bedroom that had been theirs for the past seventeen years, Mohammad whispered into Sarah's hair. "I'm so glad that you have seen your parents, that they have finally met their grandchildren. It seems like a dark veil has been lifted."

Sarah kissed Mohammad's chest. "It *is* a beginning. It has been such a long time in coming, but I am so glad that we have finally sat together in the same room. I was so touched by Dad saying that they had *always* loved me," Sarah said, choking a bit on the tears in her throat.

"Uncle Ken, the boys, and I are going to chop wood tomorrow," Mohammad said. "*Pop* says the boys need to exercise those growing muscles and that he needs a stack of firewood to use in the fireplace this winter. Why don't you and Yasmeen take Amr and walk over to see your mom and dad? I think they would like that."

"You mean especially if you and the boys weren't along," Sarah said raising her head from Mohammad's shoulder to look into his eyes.

Mohammad could see her eyes in the moonlight that was streaming through the window. He smiled as he kissed her on the nose. "We should take this slowly. Yasmeen and Amr don't *look* Arab. Let them get used to the idea of four Palestinian grandchildren gradually. It may be a little too much to foist upon them two sixteen-year-olds who look like Arab *sheiks.*"

"I happen to *like* Arab *sheiks,*" Sarah smiled kissing Mohammad's lips.

A farm over, Emily and Dave lay with their backs to each other; they were far enough apart that they didn't touch. "Well, we can be thankful for one thing," Emily said. "At least the two younger ones don't look Arab. The girl looks very much like Sarah did when she was fourteen," Emily said wistfully. "Though why she had to speak that gibberish to the baby is beyond me."

Dave got out of bed and thrust his feet into his slippers.

"Where are you going?" Emily questioned.

"I'm going to sleep in the spare room. You'll *never* change," he said closing the bedroom door behind him.

"But I *have changed,*" Emily said to herself. "I'm willing to talk to Sarah and to acknowledge the two younger ones. I can *almost* forgive her for marrying that man and for these seventeen years of estrangement. Oh, if she had *only* married Sam," she sighed. "He *is* divorced and back on the farm with his parents. I wonder..."

Ken and Martha were also wide awake. "It has certainly been an eventful day," Ken said as he pulled Martha close. "We finally got Dave and Emily to meet their grandkids."

"I'm glad," Martha said resting her arm across Ken's chest. "They have missed out on seventeen years. Life's too short for them to have been harboring this resentment. They have missed so much of the kids' childhood."

"Do you remember when the twins were about five, and how they insisted on dressing just alike so we wouldn't be able to tell which one was which? How they would try to fool us, and look so innocent and say, 'But Grandma, it wasn't me. It was him!'"

"You sure cured them of that quick enough," Ken chuckled. I can still hear you saying, *Well I guess that means that both of you need a swat on your backside with the fly-swatter.* And then Khalil would cry and say, *Oh, Grandma, it was me, don't hit my brother.*"

"And Mansur would pipe up and say, *No Grandma, it was me, don't hit my brother,*" Martha laughed. "I ended up hugging them both and no one got hit with the fly-swatter."

"How did your conversation with Sarah go this afternoon?" Ken asked. "How does she feel about the proposed move?"

"She's looking forward to it. Working for the UN will open all kinds of doors for them professionally. She *does* have some concerns about the kids' adjusting but she thinks it will be a good experience for them. They had been applying for a UN job for several years, and finally, this opening came. The couple who have been in the job will be retiring, so the positions have been offered to Mohammad and Sarah. They don't feel as though they can turn it down."

Martha continued. "She wants the kids to have the chance to know their other grandparents and to get acquainted with their roots. She thinks once they are there, that they will love being there; that they will *love* the experience."

"The boys aren't too eager to move," Ken said. "I talked with them a bit about it when we drove into town. I told them that we would send the tickets for the three of them to come and spend the summers with us, though I know Mohammad would be sending them anyway. I just wanted to assure them that they would be coming. A year can sound pretty long, while *nine months* sounds manageable," he laughed.

"They'll be fine," Martha said. "They are bright kids, adaptable kids, and *good* kids. And, they have Mohammad and Sarah as their parents. The kids will always be the most important thing to them."

"We should be getting some shut-eye," Ken yawned. "I'm taking Mohammad and the boys out to the woods tomorrow to chop wood. Can't turn down free labor," he smiled as he kissed one of the curlers crowning Martha's head.

After breakfast, Mohammad and the boys armed themselves with hatchets and followed Uncle Ken into the woods. Yasmeen and Sarah helped clear off the breakfast table and do the morning's dishes.

"Yasmeen and I are going to take Amr and walk over to see Mom and Dad," Sarah said.

"What a good idea," Aunt Martha said. "You run along. I've got plenty to do around here. We'll expect you back around lunchtime. Uncle Ken and the boys should be ready for a break about then."

Mother and daughter talked as they walked.

"Are you feeling any better about our move next fall?" Sarah asked.

"You *know* how I feel," Yasmeen answered. "I *want* to go for a visit, but I *don't want* to go and live there. You *know* what it will be like, especially for me! Mansur and Khalil, being boys, will have freedom to come and go as they want. For me, it will be *home-to-school, school-to-home.* I won't have any freedom at all. It *really* isn't fair."

"I know it will be hard at first, *habeeptee.* I worry most about how it will affect you. Just give it a chance. You are important to Baba and me. If we find it is too difficult, then we will make whatever arrangements are necessary. No job is as *important* as you and your brothers. Please always remember that." Sarah put her arm around Yasmeen.

"We're here," Yasmeen said looking at the neat farmhouse surrounded with its well-tended garden and newly-painted picket fence. "How does it feel coming *home?"* Yasmeen asked.

"It hasn't felt like *home* for a while now. Grandpa Ken's and Grandma Martha's place *feels* like home. I have some wonderful memories of my childhood here but they have been clouded by the events of the last seventeen years. But," she added smiling, "I am glad we are at this point. It is good to be talking again."

"Your parents *like* us better because we look more American than Baba and the boys," Yasmeen said perceptively.

"They will like you and Amr because of who you are not because of how you look," Sarah stated placing her hands on Yasmeen's shoulders and looking directly into her eyes. "And frankly," she grinned, "*I* think you *both* look Arab in spite of your light colored hair. Remember, your great-grandmother Hasna had blue eyes, red hair, and freckles! Maybe you really take after her!"

Emily was on the porch shelling peas when Sarah, Yasmeen, and Amr came up on the porch. "Let me help you with that," Sarah said taking a handful of peas from the basket and shelling them. "Where's Dad?" she asked.

"He's already down at the barn doing the milking," Emily said.

"Is it okay, Mama, if I take Amr and walk down to the barn?" Yasmeen asked. "He'll get a kick out of seeing the cows."

"Go on down, and let Amr walk a bit," she smiled. "He needs to be exercising those legs. He is getting spoiled by being carried everywhere."

"How old is the baby?" Emily asked.

"He was one in August. He goes to daycare five mornings a week and loves it. He is such a good natured little guy. Even though his brothers and sister spoil him he doesn't act the least bit spoiled. Sometimes it is like he has *five* parents each vying to take care of him."

"I see you gave your kids all Arab names," Emily said.

"We use their Arabic names at home, but they have Americanized names for school," Sarah said choosing to ignore her mother's tone. "Mansur is *Matt* at school; Khalil is *Ken;* Amr is *Andy,* but Yasmeen is Yasmeen-that one is easy enough to pronounce. We named them after Mohammad's three brothers, and Yasmeen is named after the friend I made when I went to the West Bank. She is married to Mohammad's younger brother, Issa."

"What was that gibberish that your daughter was speaking to the baby yesterday?" Emily questioned.

Again ignoring her mother's tone, Sarah said, "Yasmeen and the boys speak Arabic to Amr. I find it interesting, as they pretty much speak *only* English with each other. It is something they have chosen to do."

"Did Martha tell you that Sam is back in town? He had married and moved away for a spell. Now that he is divorced, he is back working on the farm with his father."

"She never mentioned it, but then why should she?" Sarah asked beginning to feel the hairs on the back of her neck stirring.

"I always thought that he would have been a perfect match for you," Emily sighed.

Sarah returned the handful of peas she had in her hand to the basket. "Sam is one thing that I will not discuss. You know what he did." Sarah said. "I never even think about him. I think I will walk down to the barn and see Dad."

I can't believe how irritating that woman is, Sarah thought as she walked down the well-worn path to the barn.

The sight that met her eyes warmed her heart. Amr was sitting on the back of a complacent jersey cow while Dave was instructing Yasmeen how to warm her hands before pulling on the cow's teats.

"That's it. Now you're getting the hang of it. You're a natural, just like your mother was," he grinned at his granddaughter.

"I see that you are teaching her the *skills* necessary for milking," Sarah laughed.

"She's a fast learner; just like you were," Dave smiled. "And this little guy is fearless. When I put him on the back of *Bessie*, he just straddled her and said *Giddy-up*. Didn't cry at all, didn't even pucker up."

"How have you been feeling, Dad?"

"No problems at all. There's been nothing since that brief heart spell seventeen years ago. Must be this good, healthy farm living," he joked. "And *seeing* you is the best medicine a body could have!"

"You can't believe how *much* I have *missed* you," Sarah said with a catch in her throat. "Not a day has gone by that I haven't wanted to pick up the phone and hear your voice."

"You can't imagine how many times I got in the truck and headed down to see you, and then, well, your mother..." Dave said not completing the sentence.

"I know," she said. "Unfortunately, we need to be getting back," Sarah said to Yasmeen as she looked at her watch.

"I'll walk back to the house with you," Dave said reaching for Amr who went willingly into his out-stretched arms.

"I'm so glad you stopped by. Why don't you and the boys stop over this evening? We'd love to have you," Dave said hopefully.

"That will be nice. We'll look forward to that," Sarah said.

"We'll see you tonight, Mom," Sarah called to her mother on the porch.

Emily only nodded.

Chapter 5

"Dad invited us over tonight for coffee," Sarah said to the group around the kitchen table.

"Well, that was nice of him," Aunt Martha said. "Why don't you, Mohammad and the kids go? Uncle Ken and I have a program on TV we have really been waiting to watch. It would be nice just for you- as a family- to go."

"You have to work on your *excuses*," Sarah smiled placing her hand on her aunt's. "You just think that you and Uncle Ken would be in the way. Of course, you wouldn't be, but I can see how Mom might take it that way."

"I think," Mohammad said, taking another slice of pie, "that your folks would really appreciate seeing you and the kids alone. After all, there *is* that program I have been waiting to watch. What's the name of that show again, Pop?" He smiled at Uncle Ken.

"You are another one who needs to work on his ability to prevaricate," Sarah said. "But perhaps you are right, Mom and Dad, especially Mom, might feel more relaxed if it is just the children and me, but *only this once!*"

"Didn't you want to see that show?" Mansur asked Khalil.

"Yeah, I have been looking forward to it all week."

"That is enough," Sarah laughingly said, "You, my two handsome Arab princes, are going. Mansur can drive us over and Khalil can drive us back. We'll take the pickup. Even though there is no car seat, it is only a mile to the farm on a back country road. Two of you can ride in the bed, and Amr and I will sit in front with whichever one of you is driving."

The stars were just coming out when they drove over to the farm. "What shall we call them?" Yasmeen asked Khalil sitting next to him in the bed of the pickup.

"I suppose we will have to call them *grandma* and *grandpa*," Khalil said.

"We already have a grandma and grandpa. I guess we could call them *grandmother* and *grandfather*, or Grandma Emily and Grandpa Dave."

"Let's call them that. It somehow seems a little *kinder*," Khalil said.

Dave beamed when he saw the pickup roll up the drive. He opened the passenger-side door and took Amr from his daughter's arms. He was tickled that the baby reached out his arms toward him.

Emily sat in her rocking chair. She was pleased to see her daughter and her daughter's children but didn't quite know how to show it. It had been *seventeen* years after all.

"There's coffee in the pot and milk in the fridge," she said as she shifted in her chair.

"Yasmeen and I will get it, Mom. You just sit and relax," Sarah said as she opened the screen door and stepped into the hall she hadn't stepped into in seventeen years.

Mansur and Khalil sat on the porch steps and leaned their backs against the railing. Amr sat for a little while in Dave's lap and then began to squirm.

"He's probably getting tired," Mansur said, "I'll take him."

Dave put Amr down and watched him run the short distance across the porch and fall into Mansur's arms with a giggle. Mansur raised him high in the air and rubbed his head into Amr's belly. *"Ish'ta'till'luck, habeebee,"* he said.

"What did you say to him?" Emily asked with more asperity than she had intended.

"He told him that he has *missed him,*" Khalil said. "I suppose it seems funny to you that we speak Arabic with Amr. I think it is partly because Arabic is just a *loving* language."

"And, he doesn't criticize our pronunciation," Mansur laughed.

"Well, he is surely lucky to have two older brothers like you," Dave said.

"We're the lucky ones," Khalil smiled tickling Amr under his chin. *"Muzboot, habeebee?* (Isn't that right, my love?)"

The screen door opened and Yasmeen and Sarah came out with trays of coffee, milk, and plates of coffeecake.

"I see you are all getting acquainted," Sarah smiled.

"Here, give me Amr," Yasmeen said. "I'll hold him while you two eat." She took Amr from Mansur and sat down on a lower step, resting her back against the banister.

They were making small talk when they noticed another pickup driving down the lane towards the house.

"I wonder who that can be?" Dave asked.

"Why, I suspect it might be Sam. I was on the phone with his mother today and happened to mention that Sarah was coming over this evening," Emily said, trying to sound innocent.

"*You what?!*" Both Sarah and her dad exploded.

"Well, they were childhood friends after all, and neighbors. What's wrong with him dropping by?"

"*Yallah, ya'awlad ihna rye'heen,*" (Come on kids, we are leaving) Sarah said to the children in Arabic.

Emily's mouth dropped open to hear Sarah speaking Arabic to her children.

The children were puzzled that Sarah was *speaking Arabic* to them. She *never* did unless she was really upset. They were quick to obey.

Without a word, they headed toward the pickup.

"I can't believe you did this," Sarah said to her mother. "After what Sam tried to do to me! How could you be so thoughtless? Things were going so well, and then you do something like this!"

Dave walked her to the pickup. "I'm so sorry, Sarah. I had no idea."

"I know, Dad. I know," Sarah said as Yasmeen passed her Amr. "We need to be going. If you want to see us before we go, we are leaving tomorrow just after lunch. Why don't you stop by Uncle Ken's to say good-bye?" She then turned to Khalil. "*Yallah, habeebee,* let's go."

They pulled out just as an overweight, balding man was getting out of his green pickup. Sarah looked straight ahead fighting the bile that rose in her throat. *I'm never going to speak to my mother again. How could she invite him over?* she thought. When they were half way down the lane she asked Khalil to pull over.

"I'm going to be sick," she mumbled, passing Amr to Khalil. She just got the door open before vomiting. Some of the bile splashed onto her skirt. "Wouldn't you know, I don't even have a hanky," she tried to smile through her tears, wiping at the snot that bubbled out of her nose.

Khalil reached into his back pocket and pulled out a not-too-clean handkerchief. "It's not too clean, Mama," he said concern in his voice. "Yasmeen, come and take Amr. Mama's been sick."

Yasmeen went over to the driver's side and took Amr from Khalil. "Are you okay, Mama?"

"I'm fine. It must have been something I ate," Sarah lied.

Yasmeen passed Amr over the side of the pickup to Mansur. She then climbed in and took Amr from him.

"It wasn't something she ate," Mansur said. "It has something to do with that man. I wonder what he did to Mama. I have never seen her so upset before. I'm going to ask Grandma and Grandpa."

"Just don't ask them in front of Mama," Yasmeen warned.

"You're back early," Mohammad said going to the pickup. "Come here, little guy," he said taking Amr from Yasmeen. "How come you're riding in back?" He looked at the sober faces of Yasmeen and Mansur. "What happened?"

"Some man came and Mama got really upset. She ordered us in *Arabic* to go and then she got sick and threw up."

Mohammad passed Amr back to Yasmeen and opened Sarah's side of the pickup. "What happened, *habeeptee?*" he said helping Sarah out of the truck.

"It's nothing really. Must have been something I ate," she lied.

"*You* are also not a very good liar," Mohammad said putting his arm around her. "Come on upstairs, change your clothes and tell me what happened."

Sarah gave a half-smile as she passed Aunt Martha and Uncle Ken.

"I'm going to take Amr up and get him bathed and ready for bed," Yasmeen said.

'We'll come with you," Khalil and Mansur chorused.

"Oh, no you don't. You two are telling us what happened," said Aunt Martha steering them into the kitchen.

"We don't know exactly," Mansur said.

"We were just having cake and milk when a pickup turned in the drive. Mom's dad asked who it was, and her mom said it was probably a man named *Sam* – I think that was the name. She said she had talked to his mother that afternoon and had told her that Mom would be there."

Aunt Martha dropped the cup and saucer she was holding and it shattered on the floor. "Are you sure she said *Sam!?*"

"That was the name," Khalil said. "Both Mom and Grandpa Dave got really upset, and then Mom told us in Arabic that we had to leave immediately."

"She *rarely* speaks Arabic with us; only when she is *really, really upset,*" Mansur added.

"Anyway, this guy gets out of his pickup. Mom tells me to floor it, and half-way down the lane tells me to pull over as she was going to be sick," Khalil said.

Aunt Martha got a broom and dustpan and began sweeping up the shards of broken cup and saucer.

"Would you like to throw your cup and saucer on the floor?" she asked Uncle Ken.

"I'd like to, but I won't," he grimly smiled. He pushed his chair away from the table.

"Where are you going?" Aunt Martha asked to his back.

"I'm going to hide the tire iron."

"What does he mean?" Mansur asked.

"Oh, years ago, you two weren't even born yet, there was a story involving that man. I took a tire iron and went on a rampage. He is just making sure I won't do it again," Aunt Martha said trying to smile. "You don't want to arm an angry fat lady with a tire iron."

Chapter 6

After seventeen years, Sarah finally told Mohammad what had happened between her and Sam. "I didn't want to tell you," she said. "I made Aunt Martha promise she would never tell you or Uncle Ken."

"Aunt Martha knew?" Mohammad asked through clenched teeth.

"She saw him through the kitchen window and came running down to help me waving a tire iron. I think she wanted to brain him."

"She should have," Mohammad grimly said.

"She *did* go and tell Mom and Dad, and his parents," Sarah whispered.

"And they *did nothing?!*" Mohammad asked in disbelief.

"I think Sam's dad punished him. Aunt Martha said his folks were really angry at him."

"But *your folks* did nothing?" Mohammad persisted.

Sarah only shook her head.

"It was a long time ago; I feel funny having this violent reaction after all these years. I still can't believe that Mom invited him over."

"It is *unforgivable* that your mother did what she did. You have men to protect you. You should have told me when it happened," Mohammad gently scolded, pulling Sarah tightly against him.

"I handled it," Sarah said wearily. "Plus Sam wasn't worth the trouble."

"Try and get some sleep," Mohammad said kissing the top of her head.

Sarah *did* finally doze off safe in Mohammad's arms.

Mohammad did not sleep at all. He couldn't wait for morning to do what he had to do.

Sarah didn't go down for breakfast the next morning.

"Sarah is getting a few extra winks," Mohammad said carrying a smiling Amr to the breakfast table. He placed Amr in his highchair and ran a hand over his sandy curls.

"When we're done with breakfast," he said to Yasmeen, "take Amr upstairs, change his diaper and get him dressed for the day. The boys and I have an errand to run."

Khalil and Mansur looked questioningly at their father.

"I need directions to Sam's parents' farm," Mohammad said to Uncle Ken.

Uncle Ken stared at Mohammad before answering. "I don't think you should go there, son."

"I have some unfinished business with him, and I think the boys should go along," Mohammad said.

"Then I'm coming with you," Uncle Ken said.

"Thanks, Pop, but this is something the boys and I need to do. You live in the neighborhood, and I understand from Sarah that you went to school with Sam's parents."

"Does Sarah know you are going?" Aunt Martha asked.

"No, I will tell her when we are back." Mohammad paused. "I wish you had told me seventeen years ago what happened."

"I *wanted* to, but Sarah made me promise not to tell you or Ken," Aunt Martha said. "I only told Ken a couple of years back."

"I understand that you are pretty good with a tire iron," Mohammad said trying to smile.

"I *would* have killed him," she simply said. "But Sarah took care of it."

"I know," Mohammad said.

The children listened in shocked silence. It didn't need to be spelled out to them what had probably transpired.

Mohammad looked over and saw his sons' hands were clenched into fists.

"I'm driving, *habeebee*. Give me the keys," Mohammad said to Khalil.

Mohammad and his sons piled into the front seat of the pickup.

"I wish you'd let me go too," Uncle Ken said leaning in the truck window.

"I know you do, Pop," Mohammad said briefly covering Uncle Ken's hand with his. "This is something I need to do; something the boys need to see."

"You boys are to do *nothing* but watch," Mohammad said. "Is that clear?"

"Yes, *Baba,*" they both answered.

Mohammad pulled the pickup into the drive and parked in front of the garage. He and the boys got out, and as they were approaching the breezeway door an older man came out.

"Good morning," Mohammad said. "You must be *Sam's* father?"

"Yes," he replied. "Who are you?"

"Sarah Goldman is my wife. These are our two older sons. I would like to speak with Sam."

"I see," he said looking knowingly at Mohammad. "Sam," he called, "there is someone here to see you."

If Mohammad hadn't known who it was, he would not have recognized Sam. The man before him was overweight, balding, and looked older than his forty years. He *immediately* recognized Mohammad. Except for a little gray hair at the temples, Mohammad looked much like he had at twenty-four. And there was no mistaking that those two teenage boys were his sons.

"I see you remember me," Mohammad said. "These are Sarah's and my oldest sons," he said nodding toward Khalil and Mansur.

"Sarah told me what you attempted to do seventeen years ago. She kept that secret all these years because she knew what I would do," Mohammad calmly continued. "Then when she saw you at her parents', that memory spilled over into her present." Mohammad paused.

"We, Arabs, take the honor of our women very seriously. Seventeen years may have elapsed, but the fact that you tried to dishonor my wife remains. I am here to settle a score. My sons are here to bear witness, and to learn that Arab men protect the honor of their mothers, their sisters, and their wives."

"What are you going to do, *kill me?*" Sam said with more bravado than he felt.

"No, I'm not going to kill you. I'm here to teach a lesson," Mohammad said as he tackled him and threw him to the ground.

Sam had been surprised by the attack. They wrestled in the gravel of the drive. Sam *did* get in a few lucky punches, but he was no match for Mohammad. Finally, he lay exhausted – almost senseless – in the drive. Mohammad stood over him; chest heaving and fists clenched. His shirt and trousers were torn. "*If* you ever come within sight of Sarah again, *I will kill you* and the *devil be damned,*" Mohammad panted. "Come on boys, get in the truck," he said to Khalil and Mansur.

"I'm sorry," Mohammad said to Sam's father. "I know it has nothing to do with you, but no man should have to stand by and see his son beaten."

His dad only nodded. His arms were folded across his chest as he looked down at his son.

"You drive," Mohammad said fishing the keys out of his pocket and handing them to Mansur. "I'm too sore to turn the key in the ignition," he smiled.

"You were *awesome,* Baba," Khalil said with admiration in his voice.

"We want to grow up to be just like you, Baba," Mansur said backing out of the drive and turning the pickup toward home.

"I want you to swing by your mother's parents'," Mohammad said. "There is one more thing I need to do."

It was an angry, resolute Mohammad who got out of the truck in front of the newly-painted white picket fence. "You boys stay in the truck; I won't be long," he said to Mansur and Khalil.

He rang the wrought iron bell and waited.

A surprised Emily opened the door.

"What are you doing here?" she asked surveying Mohammad's disheveled look.

"I've just come from beating the hell out of Sam," Mohammad said. "Something that I should have done seventeen years ago, but I didn't know. I *know* what you think of me, and it *really doesn't matter.* I had wanted

Sarah to have a different relationship with you than she has had these past seventeen years, but that is ultimately up to her. But as far as *I am concerned,* and as far as my children are concerned, this is the last time you will ever see *me,* and you will never see *them* again*!"*

Mohammad turned away from an opened-mouth Emily. Dave was just coming into the hall.

"Did you hear what he said to me?" Emily asked as she turned to Dave.

"Yes, I heard. You have gotten only what you deserve," he said as he walked past her, went down the porch steps and headed for the barn.

"Did you kill him?" Aunt Martha asked Mohammad as he limped into the hall.

"Almost," Mansur beamed. "You should have seen Baba. It was *awesome!"*

"It was like watching *Monday Night Wrestling,* only *better!"* Khalil said.

"Now, you see why I took the boys along," Mohammad smiled. "I needed someone to sing my praises."

Sarah was just coming down the stairs. She took in the sight of the disheveled Mohammad; she noticed the bruise under his eye and the purple swelling of his cheek.

"So, did you defend my honor?" she said. "He sure did," the twins said in chorus. "You should have seen him!"

Sarah went down the steps and put her arms around Mohammad. She kissed his cheek and laid her head against his chest. "Thank you," was all she said.

Aunt Martha wiped the tears from her eyes, "You boys go and help your Grandpa stack the wood you cut yesterday. I have things to do in the kitchen. We can't be standing around all day goggling at these two lovebirds," she affectionately said nodding in the direction of Mohammad and Sarah. "Off with you!"

They had just put the last suitcase in the trunk when Dave drove up.

"I'm glad I caught you in time," he said. "I would have felt bad if I had missed you."

"I'll let you talk to Sarah," Mohammad said moving toward the house.

"No, I want to talk to you first," Dave said. "I heard what you said to Emily, and I drove over to see Sam's parents." Dave hesitated as he searched for the right words. "I want to thank you for beating the *shit,* excuse my French, out of that piece of crap. I should have done it seventeen years ago. I'm *proud* of you son. You've taken good care of my Sarah. I can see that now. You have raised remarkable kids. It is easy to see what a good father you have been. Kids don't just *turn out that way.*"

Dave offered his hand, and for a fleeting moment, he thought that Mohammad wasn't going to shake it.

Mohammad *didn't* shake it. He grabbed Dave in a bear hug and held on. Mohammad's eyes were bright with tears as he whispered into his father-in-law's ear, "You have done a good job in raising Sarah. She is partly who she is because of *you.* Don't you ever forget that!"

He gave Dave one more powerful hug, and unexpectedly kissed him on the cheek. "I think there is one more bag to get from upstairs," he said making an excuse to leave.

"Your dad is waiting for you outside," Mohammad said as he passed Sarah and went into the little lavatory under the stairs.

"What did you say to Mohammad?" Sarah asked kissing her dad.

"I was just telling him what a good husband and father he is," Dave said. "I'm sorry that it took me seventeen years to see it. I can see how good he has been for you. I am glad that you two are together."

"Oh, Dad, I am so glad to hear you say that," Sarah said hugging him. "I so want you to like him."

"You have a good man there, Sarah. Anyway," he said putting his arm around her, "now that we have found each other again; now that I have met my grandchildren, I am going to be driving down to see you. I'm going to be calling. We're not going to lose contact again. And *that's a promise!*"

The grandchildren dutifully hugged the grandfather they didn't know. Amr easily went to him and even planted a sloppy kiss on his cheek.

"Have a safe trip back. Call when you get home," Aunt Martha instructed as she waved at the departing car and truck.

"They are a wonderful family, aren't they?" Dave said. It was more an observation than a question.

"Yes, they are," Ken said. "There is no family quite like theirs. Come in and have a cup of coffee."

"I think I will," Dave said. "It's been much too long."

On the farm a mile away, Emily sat and rocked. The tears gently flowed as she wondered why she was the way she was.

Chapter 7

Nijmeh, swishing the hot soapy water over the courtyard tiles, hummed as she worked. She enjoyed the warmth of the stone tiles under her bare feet. One, to glance at her would think she was perhaps a woman in her forties, not a woman who had passed her *seventieth* birthday. *Imagine, seventy years,* she thought. *I may be seventy on the outside, but inside I am still fifteen,* she chuckled to herself.

It wasn't the thirty-six grandchildren or the thirty-six great-grandchildren that reminded Nijmeh that she was seventy; it wasn't the white that threaded her braids and peppered Omar's impressive mustache; it was her *toes!*

"Why are your toes like that, *Sitteh?*" her great-granddaughter, Warda, asked. Five-year-old Warda was *helping* her great-grandmother swish the clean water over the tiles. "It looks like your big toe is riding piggyback," she laughed.

"It's *not* riding piggy back, *Sitteh.* The second toe is *playing hide-and-go-seek* with you," Nijmeh smiled. The truth was that years of plastic sandals and ill-fitting shoes had twisted her feet in such a way that the big toes *did* ride bareback on the second toes, and *all* the toes wore callous crowns.

She sometimes had to remind herself that *six* of the ten children she had borne were *grandparents!* Her five daughters were all grandmothers, and last year Mansur had had his first grandson, named after him, *Mansur*. *Tradition,* she thought, *the first born son of a first born son was always named after his paternal grandfather.*

"The tea is ready, *Mart Am'me,*" Yasmeen said. "Let Jamileh and Lily finish the sweeping with Warda," she smiled. "It is time you and I sat in the sun and had tea."

Nijmeh relinquished the broom to fourteen-year-old Jamileh and went to sit in the sun with Yasmeen.

"In three weeks, Mohammad and Sarah and the children will be here," Yasmeen said. "I can hardly wait to see them! It is hard to believe that it has been *seventeen* years. We have pictures, and we *know* what they look like, but it isn't the same as being able to hug them and hear them; to *have them in the same room.*"

"Except for Hasna's children and your children, may Allah preserve you, most of my grandchildren I *only* know through *pictures.* I can count on one hand the number of times I have seen some of my grandchildren, and Mohammad's children I have *never* seen," Nijmeh said as she took a sip of the hot tea.

"That will soon be over, *Mart Am'me.* In three weeks' time, they will be here. I'm disappointed that they won't be staying with us until their flat is ready but Sarah wrote that the UN made reservations for them in a hotel for the first night or two."

"It will be more convenient for them, *binti,*" Nijmeh said. They will have *beds* to sleep on," she laughed, "not pallets spread on the sitting room floor. Sarah and the children would probably think it quite strange for all six of them to be sleeping on the floor in one room!"

"I don't think Sarah and the children would mind, *Mart Am'me*. Sarah is an *American fellaha*. She is a *peasant* just like us – but an *American* peasant," Yasmeen laughed.

"Of course we will have a big feast when they come and invite all the family. We'll have to borrow tables and chairs from Hasna, Im Najib, and your mother. The men can eat in the sitting room and the women and girls here in the courtyard. There will be over fifty of us." Nijmeh said. "And of course, we will want to invite Hasna's in-laws, and your grandmother, parents, and siblings. That makes it closer to sixty," Nijmeh said moving her fingers as she mentally tallied the number.

Omar opened the door and stepped into the courtyard.

"Salam aleikum," he greeted them.

"Aleikum salam," Nijmeh and Yasmeen replied.

Omar was followed into the courtyard by his grandson, Saji. At twenty-eight, the shy, withdrawn child who had been brutalized by soldiers and settlers years ago was gone. In his stead stood a tall, handsome, confident man who bubbled with talk. He was engaged to Yasmeen's youngest sister, Nadia. Though the years had altered his appearance, the bond that existed between him and his *Sidi* Omar remained.

"Did you finish rebuilding the stone fence, *Sitteh?*" Nijmeh asked.

"It should be finished in one more day," Saji smiled. "No one can build a stone wall like *Sidi* Omar. He is a true craftsman," Saji said placing a hand on his grandfather's shoulder.

"I am surprised that a new lawyer like you still finds time to go out into the hillside and work with his grandfather repairing stone walls," Omar warmly joked.

"I may be a lawyer on the outside, but on the inside, I am still *fellah!*" Saji grinned. "I like working with my hands, and I *love* working beside you, *Sidi.*"

"We are planning the welcome feast for Mohammad and Sarah," Nijmeh said excitedly. "Perhaps instead of tables, you could borrow long boards and sawhorses from your father?"

"What a good idea, *Sitteh,*" Saji said. "I am sure that my father would be glad to bring some over and set them up for you. It will be much more practical. Leave it to me; I'll take care of the tables."

Sixty miles away in Amman, Khalil and Amr were having morning coffee with Mansur and Zaleena. They, too, were anxiously anticipating Mohammad and Sarah's move to the West Bank.

"I wish they could have come here first," Mansur said. "But I understand that they have to enter through Ben Gurion airport. It will still be weeks before we actually *see* them."

"Mohammad wrote that they will come for a visit *the first chance* they get," Khalil said as he smilingly took a cup of black coffee from Zaleena. "I wish it were easier for us to cross the bridge and visit them," he sighed. "I would love to be able to meet them at the airport. I can almost *see* the look of surprise on their faces when they spotted us in the crowd!"

"We will take them to Petra when they come," Amr said. "The boys will like riding horses down into the valley. We will also take them to Aqaba for snorkeling and windsurfing. The boys are just the right age for windsurfing."

"Don't forget, they have to have their picture taken on a camel," Mansur laughingly added.

"I am so glad that Sarah and her father are finally reconciled," Zaleena said more seriously. "It is unfortunate that her mother is being so stubborn."

"I feel sorry for her mother," Amr said. "It must be heartbreaking for her to be estranged from her only child."

Khalil looked meaningfully at Amr. He knew that Amr was thinking of his own mother. They had never been close and Amr, looking back, was aware of how that estrangement must have affected her, and the knowledge made him sad.

"Only *three weeks*," Yasmeen sighed. "Only *three weeks* and we will be leaving all we know to go and live in a place we have never seen. I can't *believe* that Mama and Baba are forcing us to do this!" she said to her brothers.

"We feel the same way you do," Khalil said. "I'm tired of hearing: *it will be hard at first, yes, but it is a wonderful opportunity. Look at it as an adventure. And, you will be coming back in the summer.* I guess there is nothing we can do about it."

"Have you finished with those boxes?" Mansur asked. "Baba wants everything packed today so we can load up the pickup and drive up to the farm. He wants to store our personal things in the attic there."

The college was going to sublet the house to a visiting professor and his family from Pakistan. The family had to remove all their personal items and put them in storage. Some of the things were already in boxes in the attic, but the really personal stuff: photo albums, family heirlooms, Sarah's wedding *thob* – that kind of thing they were going to store at the farm.

"Do you think Baba will allow me to attend the going-away party that your friends are throwing?" Yasmeen asked.

"Maybe, because it is such a special occasion, he will allow you to go for a little while since *we* will be there." You can ask," Khalil said, "but you know how he is about *mixed* parties.

"Are you kids almost finished?" Mohammad said coming into the room. "We want to get an early start tomorrow. We want to load the pickup tonight. We'll move it into the garage, and park the car out front."

"Baba," Yasmeen asked. "Would it be alright if I, just this once, attended the going-away party that Khalil and Mansur's friends are throwing? Some of my classmates will be there too. I'd *really, really* like to go," Yasmeen asked hopefully.

"You know how I feel about mixed parties, Baba," Mohammad said noticing the hopefulness in Yasmeen's eyes. "However, since this is such a *special* occasion, and since your older brothers will also be present to look out for you, and *if* you promise *not* to dance, you can go."

"Oh, Baba! *Thank you! Thank you!*" Yasmeen squealed throwing herself into Mohammad's arms.

Mohammad drove up to the farm in the SUV with Sarah, Yasmeen, and Amr. Mansur and Khalil followed in the pickup with a happy *Kalb* riding in the back. *Kalb,* along with the pickup, was to remain at the farm.

Uncle Ken, Aunt Martha, and Dave planned on driving down to see them off the day before their departure. Dave would drive their SUV back to the farm where it would be housed in the barn. "I'll take it for a spin every whip stitch," Uncle Ken had said "just to keep it in running order. The same with the pickup," he smiled at the boys. "So, when you come back next summer, it will be *good-to-go.*"

On the night they arrived at Uncle Ken's and Aunt Martha's, Sarah's dad joined them for supper. They were all sitting around the table finishing dessert when there was a knock at the door.

"I'll see who it is, Aunt Martha," Sarah said as she pushed back her chair and went to the door. On the other side of the screen door, her features blurred a bit by the mesh of the screen was *Emily!"*

"Mom! What are you doing here?" Sarah asked in a stunned voice, not moving to open the door.

"I heard you were leaving and I wanted to come and see you," Emily said, trying to keep her voice from cracking. "May I come in?"

Sarah pushed the screen door open to allow her mother to enter. Emily followed Sarah into the kitchen.

Eight sets of eyes looked at Emily and Sarah. The silence was deafening. One could have heard a *pin* thunder against the floor.

It was Yasmeen who moved first. She pushed back her chair, picked up Amr from his highchair and silently left the room. She was followed by Khalil and Mansur who walked by Emily with their eyes straight ahead, their fists clenched. Mohammad also rose and giving an apologetic look at Sarah, followed his children out of the room.

Emily felt her lips quivering and unshed tears threatening to fall.

"Have a seat," Martha said pulling out the vacant chair next to her. "Let me get you a cup of coffee."

Emily sat down and looked at the faces of her sister, brother-in-law, and husband. She thought she saw just a shred of sympathy in their eyes.

Sarah went and sat across the table from her mother. She waited, not saying anything.

Finally Emily broke the silence. "I have been wrong," she said trying to get the words past the lump in her throat. "I know I have been stubborn, and pigheaded, and hard to get along with. I have been giving this a lot of thought. I just *couldn't* bear you going away and leaving things the way they are." She looked around the table, and then looked directly at Sarah, *waiting* for Sarah to say something.

Sarah didn't.

"I pray that you can find it in your heart to forgive me," Emily said hopefully. "I'd like for us to begin a new page. I hope that is possible."

Sarah just looked at her mother. She felt nothing. It was as though she was looking at a stranger and a stranger whom she didn't really *like* or want to get to know.

Again Emily looked around at the faces around her. "Someone *say* something!" she said with just a touch of her old asperity.

Aunt Martha, Uncle Ken, and Dave all looked at Sarah.

Sarah cleared her throat. "I really don't know what to say. I can appreciate you coming here. I realize that that took courage. But in some ways, this feels like *closing the barn door after the horse has been stolen.* There is no point in rehashing the past, not even talking about the last incident with Sam." Sarah paused and moistened her lips.

"As far as starting a clean page, I suppose that is possible, but I am not sure you really *want* that. I guess, what I am really saying is, *I don't know if I want that.*"

Emily was stunned by Sarah's words.

"You and I have a history, and I suppose because of that, I should be willing to make the effort and at least keep some kind of *contact* with you. As far as Mohammad and the children are concerned, that is another story. You saw their reaction. They have no fond memories of a past with you. They have only known you to be judgmental; disliking them because they are Arab – or *half-Arab* in the case of the children. The irony is that they could have loved you if you had let them. *You* were the one who closed that door. And the loss is yours, not theirs."

"So there is no hope?" Emily said choking on her tears.

"There is *always* hope, but it's going to take time, Mom," Sarah quietly said. "I am willing to keep in touch with you. I can occasionally write and send pictures of the children if you like. Beyond that, well, we will just have to play it by ear. I am making no promises."

"I suppose that will have to be enough," Emily sighed pushing back her chair. "Enough for now," she added. "I probably should go."

"I'll walk you to the car," Sarah said. Martha, Ken, and Dave said nothing.

"Can I give you a hug before I leave?" Emily asked through quivering lips.

Sarah allowed herself to be hugged, but she kept her own arms at her side. She watched as her mother backed up and drove down the dirt lane. The tail lights bounced when hitting one of the many ruts in the road. Sarah stared into the blackness long after the lights had disappeared.

Chapter 8

The flight to Tel Aviv, though long, was uneventful. They each took turns walking the aisles with Amr. He seemed to delight in the attention and thankfully slept when the lights were dimmed. Khalil, Mansur, and Yasmeen watched movie, after movie, after movie. The earphones became part of their anatomy, or so it seemed. Sarah managed to doze a bit with her head against Mohammad's shoulder.

Security at Ben Gurion was another matter entirely. As soon as the customs officer saw the name *Mohammad Omar Mansur* little red flags started waving. She looked at Mohammad and then looked at the computer screen. She opened the door to her cubicle, called to someone in Hebrew, and then passed over their passports and tickets.

"Please, come with me," a young woman in a blue blazer said. "Go and get your bags and bring them back to this room," she said motioning to a room with the word *Security* printed in white letters over the open door.

It took some time to locate twelve large suitcases. They finally pulled all twelve off the rolling belt and loaded them onto five aluminum trolleys.

"What is the purpose of your visit to *Is'ra'el?*" she said in heavily-accented English.

"You can see from our papers that we will be working for the UN," Mohammad said.

She glanced at the official letter from the UN.

"You are Palestinian, are you not?" she asked. "Why do you not have an ID card?"

"I lost it many years ago when I was studying in the States," Mohammad answered.

"Do you have relatives in *Is'ra'el?*" she asked.

"Yes, my parents and two of my siblings and their families live in the West Bank," Mohammad answered.

The woman turned to Sarah. "You are Jewish. How is it that you are married to a Palestinian?"

"I was raised a Christian," Sarah calmly answered, though the butterflies in her stomach were doing flip-flops. "My husband and I met in college."

"Do you realize that you and your children have the right to enter *Is'ra'el* under the law of *the right to return?*"

"I did not realize that," Sarah said.

Their suitcases were placed on the tables in the room. "Please open your bags."

The twelve bags were opened and meticulously every item was taken out. The hems of collars and cuffs were felt.

"Who packed these bags?" They were asked.

"We did." They answered.

"Were you given anything to carry for someone else? Are you carrying any weapons?"

Some of the questions were absurd. The inspection of the bags was clearly harassment.

The interrogation went on for close to two hours. First Yasmeen, and then Khalil would juggle Amr; then Mansur would take a turn walking with him. He was tired and the usual contented little guy got fussy.

Finally, the inspectors shoved the things back into the bags and told them to put them back on the trolleys.

The woman in the blue blazer with the heavily-accented English finally said, "You are free to go. Enjoy your visit to *Is'ra'el*," as she handed Mohammad their passports and tickets.

"We were treated like criminals," Mansur whispered to Khalil. "We're American-born and they treated us like criminals!"

There was a mob beyond the fence at the arrival gate. The late summer breeze was stifling. They scanned the faces and finally saw a heavy-set man raising a placard above his head that read: *Mohammad Omar/UN*.

"I'm Mohammad Omar," Mohammad said, "And this is my family."

"I am Aref," the man smiled. "I was sent to meet you. The van is parked just over here. Follow me. Here, let me push that," he said to Sarah taking the handle of the trolley from her.

It took them an hour and a half to reach Jerusalem.

"You have been booked into the *American Colony Hotel,*" Aref said. "I will come back in the morning and drive you to Ramallah."

"It's almost like coming home," Sarah smiled. "This is where my husband and I spent our honeymoon."

Two rooms had been booked for them; one for the children and the second one for Sarah and Mohammad.

"Well, we're here," Khalil said to his siblings. "I don't know about you, but I'm ready to turn around and go home."

"Me, too," Mansur and Yasmeen said in chorus.

As exhausted as they were, none of them slept well that night.

Aref arrived promptly at 10. "I hope you slept well," he said to them in Arabic.

"I think we are all suffering from jet lag," Mohammad said. "Once we are really rested things will look different."

They piled into the van and were driven the nine miles to Ramallah.

Aref pulled up in front of a rather new-looking apartment building. "This is where you will be living," he said.

He helped them unload their suitcases. It took several elevator trips for them and their luggage to be carried to the second-floor apartment.

The apartment was quite large. There were three spacious bedrooms and two and a half baths. It was furnished with the basics and looked a bit like a generic hotel suite or a furniture ad in a magazine.

"It will be better," Mohammad said. "Once we get our bags unpacked and put our own personal touch on it. You'll see, it will look like home in no time," he said more optimistically than he felt.

The kids knew that would *never* be true.

They had just started unpacking their bags when the doorbell rang!

"Who could possibly know we are here?" Sarah asked.

"I'll get it, Mama," Mansur said.

He opened the door and there stood an old man in a striped *umbaz,* a white *kuffiyeh* on his head with a very bushy salt-and-pepper mustache that hid his lips, and beside him stood a handsome man in his late thirties with curly auburn hair.

"*Sidi! Ammie* Issa!" Though he had never met them he instantly knew who they were from the pictures he had seen, plus they looked remarkably like Mohammad.

"*Illhumdillah ala'salameh, Sidi,* (Praise the Lord for your safe arrival)" Omar said as Mansur grabbed his hand, kissed it and touched it to his forehead.

"*Illhumdillah ala'salameh,*" Issa said, grinning as Mansur also kissed his hand and touched it to his forehead.

"*Yaba!*" Mohammad shouted as he grabbed his father in a bear hug. There were tears of joy in his eyes as he kissed his father's hand and touched it to his head. "*Habeebee, Yaba, habeebee!*" Mohammad kept repeating as he patted his father's shoulder. It had been seventeen years since they had seen one another.

Mohammad grabbed his brother Issa and kissed him on both cheeks. "You've aged!" he laughed.

"Look who's talking," Issa grinned.

Sarah and Yasmeen stood back as the men hugged and kissed.

Omar turned to Sarah and opened his arms wide. Sarah went up to him and kissed his hand, before kissing him on both cheeks.

"*Illhumdillah ala'salameh, binti,*" Omar said. "And this must be Yasmeen and Amr. Come, *Sidi*, come," he said opening his arms to them.

Yasmeen like her brothers and parents also kissed his hand and raised it to her forehead.

Amr made them all laugh when he walked over to the old man he had never seen before and put his arms up.

Omar immediately lifted him, tickling his cheek with a whiskery kiss. Amr looked at him, ran tentative fingers through the bristly mustache, before giving Omar a sloppy kiss on the cheek. "Ah, he knows his *Sidi*," Omar smiled.

"We have come to pick you up," Issa said. "*Yumma* has been cooking since dawn. She has invited all the family for a lunch in your honor. She can't wait to see you. We brought two taxis to take you to the camp."

Khalil's, Mansur's and Yasmeen's first impression of the camp was much like their mother's first view of it seventeen years before. They were silently appalled at the squalor; the closeness of the houses; the narrowness of the streets; the refuse in the alleys.

Nijmeh was standing at the metal door when the taxis drove up and parked. As soon as she saw Mohammad and Sarah and the children she raised her hand to her mouth and trilled in joy. Yasmeen, Hasna, and Im Najib also rushed to the door and raising their hands to the side of their mouths began to trill.

"*Illhumdillah ala'salameh. Illhumdillah ala'salameh*," their joyous greetings punctuated the air.

"*Yumma habeeptee*," Mohammad cried as he kissed and hugged his mother. "How I have missed you!"

"*Marhaba* (hello) *Mart Ammie*," Sarah smiled as she kissed and hugged her mother-in-law.

"*Ahlan, ahlan, binti*. (welcome my daughter). We have missed you."

"Marhaba *Sitteh,*" Mansur and Khalil said in chorus as they stepped forward.

Nijmeh looked at these two identical grandsons she had never seen. "Looking at you is like looking at your father when he was a boy, *Sitteh,*" Nijmeh said as she kissed them loudly. "Where are Yasmeen and Amr?"

Yasmeen, carrying Amr on her hip, made her way to her grandmother and kissed her.

"You look just like your mother, *Sitteh.* You are a beauty, *ma'shallah.* And this little one," she said putting her arms out to Amr, "must be Amr. Come, *Sitteh,* come."

Like Amr had done with his grandfather, he went to his *Sitteh* without hesitation. He put his head down on her shoulder and let his well-worked thumb slip into his mouth.

"*Habeebee, Sitteh. Habeebee,*" Nijmeh said and she patted his back. Tears of joy fell unhindered down her cheeks.

It seemed to Mohammad, Sarah and the children that all they were doing was kissing and hugging. There must have been sixty people crammed into the courtyard and sitting room.

The children knew that they were related to all these people, but weren't sure what the relationships were. There were cousins about their ages, they weren't sure of the names and they had difficulty understanding them as they spoke Arabic so fast. All these people were family, and yet they were *strangers.* They could never remember feeling *so* out of place.

When the men were ushered into the sitting room to eat, Mansur and Khalil were pulled in with them. Yasmeen stood alone holding Amr in her arms. The women and girls were all busy carrying plates of food to the men, busy between kitchen and sitting room. Even Sarah seemed to be busy in the kitchen chatting with her mother-in-law, Nijmeh, and sister-in-law, Hasna.

Yasmeen felt close to tears. She was surprised to feel an arm around her shoulder.

"This must all seem very strange to you, *habeeptee,*" the woman with a very kind face said to her in English. "Too many people; too many names to remember; everyone speaking Arabic *so fast,*" she smiled. "I am also *Yasmeen*; in fact, your mother and father named you after me," she smiled. "I am your aunt; your Ammo Issa's wife. Your mother is like my sister. I have a daughter, Jamileh, just your age. Tomorrow, when there is less confusion, Jamileh and I will come to visit you, *Amti.*"

"Thank you for talking to me," Yasmeen said unable to keep her lips from quivering. "It all *is* a bit overwhelming."

"*Habeeptee, roh'el'be,* (spirit of my heart)" her aunt said giving her a hug and kissing her on top of the head. "Jamileh, *Yumma,*" Yasmeen called to her daughter. "Come here," she said in Arabic.

She introduced the two girls. *"Yum'ma,* I want you to take care of Yasmeen. She speaks Arabic, but it is also a good opportunity for *you* to practice your English, *Yumma."*

The two girls looked at each other shyly. "I wish I had a *little* brother," Jamileh said in classroom English. "My youngest brother is ten, and he *thinks* he can tell me what to do.

"I also have an older brother, Jamil, who is sixteen, who doesn't *just think* he is my boss, but *knows* he is!" Jamileh laughed.

"I have *two* older brothers who are sixteen," Yasmeen volunteered. "And they may think they are my boss, but I keep reminding them that they *aren't,* though sometimes I do humor them."

"What does *'humor them'* mean?" Jamileh asked.

"It means I *let them think* they are superior," Yasmeen said.

"Oh, we do that *all* the time," Jamileh laughed. "It is a trick we learn from our mothers!"

Sarah and Yasmeen looked over at the two girls. "I think our daughters are going to be good friends; *sisters* just like we are," Yasmeen said.

"If Jamileh is anything like you, there is *no doubt* that they will be best friends," Sarah said giving Yasmeen a hug.

Chapter 9

Sneakers! That had been the gift of choice for all the cousins sixteen and under. Issa's wife, Yasmeen, had sent a list of cousins (both first and second), their ages, and shoe sizes. Sarah and her daughter Yasmeen had taken the list and bought dozens – or so it seemed – *Reebok* and *Nike* sneakers at *Dick's Sporting Goods*. They had filled one of the large suitcases.

"Are you opening your own store?" the clerk at the cash register had asked.

"No," Sarah laughed. "These are all gifts for my husband's nephews, nieces and grandnephews, and grandnieces. "

"He must come from a very large family," the girl said as she rang up each pair of shoes. And you are buying gifts for all these people?"

Sarah smiled. "It is a cultural thing. It is customary when one is traveling from the States to take presents to the family. The kids like to be able to say *this is from America,*" she laughed.

Of course, another two suitcases had been filled with all kinds of gifts for the adults in the family: Omar and Nijmeh; Issa and Yasmeen; Hasna, Imad and their seven sons and their wives. Sarah had also bought things for Im Najib and Yasmeen's parents and siblings. She had purchased *extra* gifts just in case she had forgotten someone. It would have been insulting to go empty-handed.

"I think I have gifts for everyone," Sarah had said to Mohammad looking at her list and the checks beside each name.

The morning of their third day in Ramallah, Mohammad and Sarah, with their children in tow, went to the Friends School to check on the kids' enrollment.

The office secretaries were very nice and they had the opportunity to meet the principal. Everything seemed to be in order. Khalil and Mansur would enter the eleventh grade in the two-year International Baccalaureate program. Everything would be in English except for special Arabic classes. Yasmeen, on examination of her school records, had been placed in the tenth-grade class, rather than the ninth.

"We feel that ninth grade would just be a repetition of what Yasmeen had in eighth grade in the States. We don't want her to get bored. More of the classes are taught in English in the tenth grade. We will try her out in tenth if that is alright with you?" the principal had said.

Yasmeen was pleased. *It means I only have to spend three years here instead of four. My sentence has been reduced,* she thought to herself.

Sarah bought two sets of the school uniform for each of the children: gray pants with a striped shirt bearing the school name in red Arabic calligraphy on the shirt pocket. There was also a maroon tie and blue v-neck sweaters for cooler weather.

"I can't believe we have to wear uniforms," Mansur said to Khalil.

"Are there required shoes?" Sarah asked the secretary.

"No, most of the students wear sneakers."

"Are there other English-speaking students?" Mohammad asked.

"Yes, there are usually a few in each class," the secretary smiled. "There will be other kids who have transferred here from the States."

"At least we won't be in this boat alone," Khalil said under his breath to Mansur.

"Did you happen to catch the *name* of this boat?" Yasmeen whispered as she juggled Amr on her hip. "It wasn't by chance the *Titanic?*"

"Remember that film we watched about World War I?" Mansur whispered back. "I think the name of this boat may be the *Lusitania.*"

"I think you are going to like being in school here," Mohammad said optimistically as they walked through the well-tended garden. "The IB program is outstanding. The principal was telling me that many of the students who do well on the IB exam are exempt from their first year of university in the States."

Khalil, Mansur, and Yasmeen just looked at each other.

As they walked down the crowded street to catch a taxi to take them back to the apartment, they wished they were back in Iowa, not here in the Middle East.

"Why aren't we going to school with Ammo Issa's children?" Yasmeen asked.

"They go to government schools where everything is in Arabic except for English as a foreign language," Mohammad had said. "Your spoken Arabic is fine, but you don't read and write Arabic well enough to take all your classes in Arabic. The Friends is a good place for you as it will prepare you for university in the States."

"What about the *Or'dun'nee'ya* school, *Baba?*" Mansur asked. "Jamil was telling us that most of the English-Speaking, like us, go there."

"I asked about the Jordanian English-Speaking school. Everyone I asked was saying that the Friends School is the best because of the IB program."

"I feel funny going to a school like the Friends when all of our cousins go to government schools," Khalil said. "It seems to set us apart even more. They live in the camp; we live in this fancy apartment; we are going to a posh, *elitist* prep-school, and they attend camp schools."

"I *want* you to remember your roots," Mohammad said seriously. 'But the reality is that you can't attend a camp school. Your Arabic isn't good enough, and you don't have an ID card. I also want you to have every advantage that I can provide. Look, I'm a product of the camp, and I *never* forget that. I also never forget that my mother and father pushed all of us to get educated.

Your uncles and aunts and I all graduated from the camp schools, and your uncles and I were pushed to go on to university to *better* ourselves by developing the potential we have been given."

"*Bettering themselves* doesn't mean thinking they are better than anyone else. Your Baba and your Uncles know where they come from and who they are," Sarah added. "Though they may look sophisticated, they are peasants deep down inside, and proud of it!"

"Probably the one who will be the *most fellah (peasant)* among you, is this little guy," Mohammad smiled tickling Amr under his chin. "He will be spending every day in the camp when we are working and you are in school. *Sitteh* Nijmeh is insisting she wants to look after Amr during the day. She is looking forward to having him around to spoil."

"He'll think he is a little prince," Sarah smiled taking his hand and kissing it.

"He *already* knows he's a prince," Yasmeen laughed. "Now he will begin to think that he's a *king.*"

"Especially after you kiss his hand," Mansur smiled.

"Just don't touch it to your head," Khalil laughed, "then he will be convinced he is our respected *elder* and royalty!"

"Royalty in *diapers,*" Yasmeen added.

Mohammad's sister, Hasna, had organized their main meals for the next ten days. Six of her sons were married (Saji was the only one still at home) and they would each have them for a meal one day; Nijmeh and Yasmeen would have them for another three meals, and she would have them for the remaining two. It was customary for the family to invite them for a meal, and Mohammad had a *large family.* They would fix breakfasts and light suppers at home, but the big meal of the day would be cooked by someone else.

"That will give you time to get situated and a chance to get to know everyone better," she had said to Sarah. "Of course, *Yumma* will want you every Friday for lunch, and I will want you every Sunday."

Sarah started to protest but Hasna would not have it. "We have s*eventeen* years of Fridays and Sundays to make up for," she laughed.

Sarah was anxious to establish her own routine and feared the constant visiting would be a bit draining, but she understood that it was *expected* and part of the *custom.* Once they started their new jobs, they would not be free to accept dinner invitations.

The second week of their move saw two very important events: the arrival of a flat-screen TV with a DVD player, and a UN car.

The TV was installed in the family room so the kids could retreat there and watch TV undisturbed if there were guests around. UNRWA had given Mohammad and

Sarah a car to use as they traveled around the West Bank. There was only one problem; it was a tight fit for six and there was no room for a car seat.

"There are no laws in the West Bank that require a car seat. We can hold Amr on our laps," Mohammad had said. "Eventually, we will buy a second-hand car big enough for all of us *and* a car seat. In the meantime, we will make do."

The kids were slowly, reluctantly adjusting. They couldn't change the inevitable, so they were determined to make the best of it. Thankfully, they each had their own laptops and access to email so they could be in constant contact with their friends in the States.

"It is their lifeline," Sarah commented to Mohammad. "They would find this transition much harder if they didn't have this daily contact with their friends at *home.*"

"Even Aunt Martha and Uncle Ken bought a computer and are learning how to use it so they can email the kids," Mohammad laughed. "This move has taken them, feet-dragging, into the twenty-first century. They're both typing with one finger, but they're typing!"

"Aunt Martha emailed Yasmeen and told her Dad was thinking about coming over a couple times a week to email the kids," Sarah said. "It is ironic, isn't it? We will probably have more daily contact with them than we did in the States."

Out of the three older kids, Mohammad and Sarah were most concerned about Yasmeen. They had sat down with her and given her a few *rules* that they wanted her to follow regarding certain cultural norms for young women.

"We don't want you going anywhere alone. When you are walking in the street, keep your eyes either straight ahead or look down. Do not make eye-contact with anyone. Some *shabab* (boys) in the street may cat call or make comments about you, *ignore* them. If you have to ride in a taxi make sure that you sit either between Mansur and Khalil, or sit next to the window. If there is ever an occasion when you are traveling alone, never get in a shared taxi with only men in it," Mohammad said.

"Maybe I should just cover my head, not go to school, and go with Amr to stay with *Sitteh* Nijmeh and Amti Yasmeen," Yasmeen said trying to keep the sarcasm out of her voice.

"I know it's hard," Sarah said sympathetically. "But these are the same rules we would give you if we lived in a big city in the States. Girls *have* to be cautious. It is *not* just because we are here."

It was two days later that their warnings were put to the test.

Chapter 10

Not all the residents of the camp were like the family of Omar and Nijmeh. There were *shabab* (young men) like Abed. At seventeen he was six feet tall, muscular from lifting weights, and thought himself the perfection of masculinity. He even had a missing part of a finger on his left hand to *show* his unique toughness. He had been in and out of jail a number of times having been arrested for petty theft. He thought this only added to his image as a *badass,* a phrase he had picked up from watching American action films with Arabic subtitles.

The past week he had seen the blonde *American'nee'ya* girl going back and forth in the camp when she was with her family visiting her grandparents. She was *different.* She had caught his eye. He *knew* about American girls from the films he had seen; *they were easy.*

Abed began to talk about her to the other boys he hung out with; he would brag about *how he was going to 'have'* her. "Her dad is going to let me marry her," he boasted. "You know these Arab-American girls; they'll drop their panties for anyone."

Boasting among boys is sometimes like dandelion down blown in the wind. One boy tells another boy; that boy tells another, and so on. By the time the rumor reached the ears of Imad, Hasna's eighteen-year-old grandson, *there was a beautiful, blonde American'nee'ya who was 'giving it away' to anyone who asked. In fact, Abed had had her several times and she was insatiable.*

"Do you know the girl's name?" Imad asked. "No, but her mother is American; she's only half-Arab. Her mother is probably a *sharmoota* (whore) too," the boy laughed not realizing to whom he was speaking.

"Have some respect and watch your tongue" Imad warned. "You are speaking of someone's mother. Who is this guy, Abed?"

"You know Abed; he's the guy who has been in and out of jail. He has part of a finger missing."

Imad knew whom he meant.

Yasmeen had gotten out of the taxi at the entrance to the camp. It was just a short walk from the entrance to her grandparents' house. She thought she knew the way. She didn't.

Mohammad had wanted her to take a taxi on her own to get the experience. It was broad daylight; he had phoned to tell his mother that Yasmeen was coming so that they would be on the look-out for her.

When she should have turned left, she turned right. *I know the house is right down this alley,* she said to herself. Unfortunately, all the houses looked the same to her; the same plain metal door leading into the courtyard; the same shuttered windows facing the street; the same flowering vines creeping over the concrete walls. She was shy to knock on a door and ask directions. There was no one in the street.

She had decided that she should turn around and go back to the entrance of the camp when she saw him. He was leaning against a concrete wall; one hand was looped in his belt just above his crotch, from the other a cigarette dangled.

Remembering her father's instructions, she kept her eyes down and walked swiftly on the other side of the alley. Just as she was passing he said something to her. *"Wain rye'ha ya hilweh?"* (Hey, beautiful girl, where are you going?) She ignored him and walked on.

He stepped in front of her, blocking her path. *"Entee bit'jen'nini!"* (You are crazy beautiful) She could almost hear her heart beat! She was terrified but knew she had to appear calm.

When he reached out and touched her arm, *she attacked him!* *"Tim'sick'neesh, ya kalb!"* (Don't touch me, you dog!) She shouted at him hitting him hard in the chest with her finger.

Abed was caught off guard. This wasn't how it had gone in the films he had seen. *"Mean bit'fek'er halak, ya jahish!"*(Who to you think you are, you jackass?) she shouted continuing to hammer his chest with her finger.

He was surprised at her grasp of Arabic.

He laughed and grabbed her arms, but she kneed him in the groin. He let go and had bent over cursing her when he felt a strong hand grab his shoulder.

He was spun around and pushed against a concrete wall. Imad's arm was braced against his throat, cutting off his ability to breath.

"I'll kill you right here," Imad sneered in Arabic. "You won't just be missing part of a finger, you'll be missing these," he hissed grabbing a hold of Abed's balls and squeezing hard. "You ever come near this girl again and your body will never be found; my brothers, cousins, uncles, and I will *see* to that! If I hear *one word* spoken about this girl, *we'll* come looking for you and *we'll* kill you. And you *know* I mean what I say. Now, get out of here!"

It is hard to swagger away when your balls are throbbing and you are having difficulty breathing, but Abed tried.

"Are you okay?" Imad asked. "You handled yourself very well back there."

"I am fine. Thank you." Yasmeen replied. "I was going to my grandparents' and took a wrong turn. I had a self-defense course in high school," she laughed shakily. "The teacher felt strongly that girls should be able to defend themselves. Her mantra was: *be calm; take the offensive!*"

"It certainly surprised that guy. I'll walk you to your grandparents' house," Imad said.

"Do I know you?" Yasmeen asked. "You look familiar. Are we related?" Yasmeen said trying to laugh.

"Your *Amti* Hasna is my grandmother," Imad said. "We met the first day you arrived. It is not surprising you don't remember me; there were so many people there. Your father and my grandmother are brother and sister."

"No wonder you look familiar," Yasmeen smiled.

"You really shouldn't be walking in the camp alone," Imad said a bit sternly. "Some of the *shabab* see a pretty girl who looks American, and well..." he stammered, "they think that she is like the Western girls they see on the TV. Really, you had no business walking alone in the camp," Imad scolded. "If you were my sister I would never have allowed it."

"*Allowed it?*" Yasmeen said tilting her head and looking directly into his dark eyes. "If you hadn't noticed, *I did* deal with the situation. There are punks like him everywhere. It *is* broad daylight; all I would have to do was scream and fifty people would be in the street."

"Anyway, maybe you should consider covering your hair," Imad said.

"You are *not* my father, or uncle, or brother, or *boss,*" Yasmeen said not trying to keep the anger out of her voice.

"No, but *I am* your cousin," Imad said with finality in his voice, as though that should be sufficient reason for his words.

Within minutes they were in front of her grandparents' gate. Imad rapped on the metal door and waited. Neither he nor Yasmeen said anything more to each other.

When Jamileh opened the door she knew immediately that something was wrong.

"What happened?"

"Oh nothing much," Imad sarcastically said. "It seems our young, American cousin thought she would take a stroll through the camp on her own and got propositioned. *Illhumdillah* I just happened to be there."

Yasmeen just looked at him. "Why don't you tell her *exactly* what happened?" she said. "I am glad he came along when he did, but *I did* have the situation under control."

Imad's lips twitched into a smile. "Okay, I will admit that she *was* handling the situation, but I have warned her that she shouldn't be walking alone in the camp, and certainly not with her hair uncovered."

"Won't you come in?" Jamileh said to Imad, "Jamil is inside and so is my father."

"Another time perhaps; I just wanted to make sure that Yasmeen got here safely. Tell Jamil that I will be over later with my brothers and some of our cousins. There is some business we need to discuss. *Salam aleikum,*" Imad said giving a slight bow to Yasmeen. "Until next time, *bint Khali* (uncle's daughter)."

How arrogant he is, Yasmeen thought unable to completely ignore his good looks and dark eyes.

When Mohammad heard what happened he blamed himself. "I should have had someone meet you at the entrance to the camp."

"I can take care of myself, Baba," Yasmeen said defensively, "I did what we were taught to do in school: *don't show fear and take the offensive.*"

"You handled yourself very well," Sarah said approvingly. "You were lost, within shouting distance of your grandparents', and you kept your head. You have shown that you are someone with whom to reckon. I am proud of the way you handled yourself."

Mohammad, though clearly upset, had to smile. "You have a lot of your mother in you," he said looking meaningfully at Sarah. "And it is *reassuring* to know that not only do you have a father and brothers who will look out for you, but you also have *cousins* who will be watching out for you. You are probably safer here than you would be in almost any place else in the world."

That night three people did not sleep very well. There was Abed, who had been beaten to within an inch of his life by Imad, Jamil, and several of their cousins. He would *never* go within sight of the American girl, and he would never say anything about her. He *knew* that if he did, he was a dead man.

Then there was Imad, though normally a sound sleeper who seldom dreamt, he was having disturbing dreams about a beautiful American second cousin with blonde hair, blue eyes, and a temper.

And last, but not least, there was Yasmeen who lay awake thinking of a tall, handsome second cousin with curly black hair, jet black eyes that sparkled when he was angry, and who irritatingly thought he was her boss.

Chapter 11

The first day of school went surprisingly well, though Khalil, Mansur, and Yasmeen discovered that out of 400 students only *three* were wearing ties – *them!* They quickly unknotted them, pulled them from around their necks and stuffed them into their backpacks.

The students lined up outside according to grade. Even though it was a co-educational school, the boys lined up together in front, and the girls lined up together in the back. *Typical,* Yasmeen thought. In the classrooms, the boys sat on one side and the girls on the other. *So, this is co-education in Palestine,* Khalil and Mansur said to each other.

There was a smattering of Arab-Americans like themselves; kids who had been uprooted and brought back, or *sent* back to the *Old County* to be removed from Western temptations. They soon discovered that they were in the minority of having *both* parents with them. Many of the Arab-Americans had only their mothers living with them, a few lived with their grandparents.

"I guess we are lucky," Khalil said to Mansur, "to have both Mama and Baba here."

"I was talking to this kid, Bashar, and he is living with his mother. His dad is working in the States and comes once a year to visit," Mansur added. "He was saying the main reason he is here is because he has three sisters; his folks don't want them raised in the States."

Yasmeen caught up with her brothers during the lunch break.

"There are three Arab-American girls in my class," she said. "And they *all* wear *hijab* – they have their heads covered! When I asked them why, they said it was *less hassle*, that being *American* they kind of had to *prove* themselves, and if they wore the scarf they didn't get hassled as much in the street and even their relatives were more accepting."

"You better watch out," Khalil teased. "Baba will want you to cover your hair as well."

"Especially after that incident at the camp the other day," Mansur joked.

"I'll wear *hijab* when Mama does. And that will never happen!" Yasmeen replied.

The first day was an abbreviated day: there was an assembly program where everything was said in Arabic, even though it was supposedly an IB-school where English was the primary language of instruction; they met their teachers and got their textbooks. They had *one* American teacher and the rest were Palestinian.

"It's a good thing that we *understand* Arabic," Khalil whispered to Mansur.

"I feel sorry for those kids who don't," Mansur whispered back.

The kids were friendly enough, but it is rarely easy adapting to a new school.

Mohammad picked them up at noon.

"How was the first day?" he asked.

"It was okay, I guess," Khalil responded.

"There are a couple more kids like us in the class," Mansur said. "One of the guys is from Detroit and another from San Francisco."

"How was your day, Yasmeen?" Mohammad asked.

"Okay, Baba. There are three English-speaking girls in my class and all three wear the *hijab*. They said they weren't *forced*, but they were strongly *advised* to wear the head scarf so they wouldn't get hassled in the street. They said they kind of had to *prove* themselves to their relatives here that they hadn't been *contaminated* by the West," Yasmeen said.

"Did they use the word *'contaminated'*?" Mohammad asked surprised.

"That's the word they used. Though they were *laughing* when they said it," Yasmeen added.

"It's kind of funny when you think about it, Baba," Khalil said. "All of them, and not just the English-Speaking, were talking about studying in the States when they go to college. A lot of them were talking about spending their holiday in the States this summer. Yet, they were saying they didn't want to be *westernized.*"

"The English-Speaking girls were saying that their parents brought them back here because they didn't want them dating in the States and picking up

American habits; that in spite of all the political unrest, *this* was a better environment for them than America. At least, that is the line their parents are feeding them," Yasmeen said.

"So, when are you going to *suggest* that Yasmeen should wear the *hijab?*" Mansur asked playfully poking Yasmeen in the ribs.

"You really should, Baba," Khalil said playfully poking her other side. "She should be *made* to cover up that blonde hair!"

"Yasmeen doesn't have to wear the *hijab,*" Mohammad smiled into the rearview mirror catching Yasmeen's eye, *"unless* she really wants to!"

Yasmeen, smiling back, said, "I'll wear it when Mama does! And *that's a deal,*" she laughed. She *knew* she was on safe ground.

Mohammad and Sarah's work for UNRWA (United Nations Relief Work Agency) was going well. They were involved in irrigation planning, the use of water resources, and crop rotation. Mohammad had *longed* to be able to put some of his training into practice in the West Bank. It had taken seventeen years, but now he was finally *home.*

Out of all of them, the one who was adjusting best was *Amr.* The mornings they worked, Mohammad and Sarah would drop him off at his grandparents' house in the camp. Nijmeh would be waiting on the stone step when the car pulled up in front of the house. Amr no sooner saw her and his whole body began to quiver in excitement.

"Look at him," Sarah said to Mohammad. "He is wiggling to get out of my arms and start his day!"

Amr would reach out his arms and almost fling himself towards his grandmother.

"Habeebee, Sitteh," Nijmeh would say hugging him as his arms encircled her neck and squeezed. "We're going to have a wonderful day, aren't we, *Sitteh?"*

Now that he was two, unbeknownst to Sarah, Nijmeh was determined to *train* him.

"You shouldn't still be in diapers," Nijmeh would smile. "You're a smart little man, aren't you, *habeebee?"* she would say to Amr as she removed his diaper. She took him every hour on the hour and stood him in front of the toilet. Whenever he was successful in making *pee-pee,* she would applaud and praise. After lunch, she would set him on a little enamel potty and tell him stories. Again, if he was successful in *pooping* in the potty, she applauded and praised.

It didn't take long for Amr to get the idea. When he stayed with his *Sitteh,* he never wore a diaper. If the weather was warm enough, she would let him run around the house without his shorts on. Within a matter of days, she had him trained.

One afternoon Mohammad and Sarah were having tea with Nijmeh and Yasmeen after work. Amr ran up to Sarah and crawled into her lap. He was all smiles.

Sarah patted his bottom as he sat with his knees in her lap. "Amr, *habeebee,* where's your diaper?"

"*Bah!*" Amr said spreading his hands in the air, using the Arabic baby term for *gone/vanished.*

"*Bah, habeebee?*" Sarah questioned. Sarah looked at Nijmeh, surprisingly a little irritated that she had taken it upon herself to train Amr.

"Amr has trained himself," Nijmeh smiled. "At least during the day," she added. "He still may need to wear a diaper at night."

"So, you're a big boy now," Sarah smiled blowing bubbles in his neck, pleased with him, yet somehow not pleased that her mother-in-law and sister-in-law, whom she loved dearly, had done this.

"*Zay, Baba,*" Amr said.

"So, you are *like Baba,* are you?" Mohammad laughed taking Amr from Sarah's lap and settling him on his own.

"It is so easy to train the smart ones," Nijmeh laughed. "And Amr is very, very smart, *ma'shallah.*"

On the way out the door, Nijmeh took Sarah aside. "I just realized I may have over-stepped. I lived with *Sitteh* Hasna all my married life. The women in a family do so much work, that it is natural for us to help each other out with the children. Amr seemed ready and I wanted to *surprise* you. I keep *forgetting* that you are not used to this," she smiled, "and might see it as a reflection on you. *It certainly is not, habeeptee.*"

Sarah hugged Nijmeh. "I *was* a little irritated," she smiled. "I don't even know why. I want so much for you to think I am a good mother."

"*Of course,* we all think you are a *good mother!*" Nijmeh smiled hugging her back.

The thing that surprised Khalil, Mansur, and Yasmeen the most about school was the *noise!* It really depended on the teacher. In some classes, the kids were attentive and *seemed* to be absorbed in what the teacher was saying. However, in other classes, it was a constant *battle.* It seemed that if the teacher had little or no control, he or she would have to shout above the students to be heard. The teacher would scold and for a moment there would be silence, but as soon as the teacher's back was turned, the talking continued.

"I can't believe this is a private school," Khalil said to his siblings during the break.

"In some classes, they act as though the teacher is their *servant,*" Mansur said.

"It's really a popularity contest," Yasmeen added. "If they *like* and *respect* the teacher, they are good. If they don't particularly *like* or *respect* the teacher, they are constantly *testing* him. They *know* which buttons to push."

It was interesting to watch the dynamics at play. In some classes, the students dutifully took out their notebooks and pens, while in others they had to be *invited* to take out these tools. In some classes the students always had their textbooks; in other classes it was common to hear: *I forgot it at home; I don't have a pen;* and *can I borrow a sheet of paper?*

Even though it was forbidden to have cell phones at school, *everyone* had one. They would secretly *text* each other when the teacher's back was turned. During the breaks, they would hide behind a tree on the grounds and make personal calls.

Occasionally someone was caught and the cell phone was confiscated. It was turned into the school office and locked away in a drawer until the student came to beg for its return, or a parent called to promise *it will never happen again.* The parents would rationalize that *due* to the volatile and unpredictable political situation, their son or daughter really *needed* to have his/her cell phone at school.

Gradually, the administration turned a blind eye to the presence of cell phones in student backpacks and pockets, the only compromise being that the phones be put in *silence mode.* They could still *vibrate* in a student's pocket, but they were not to ring. If the phone *did* ring, it was taken by the teacher and returned to the student at the end of the day.

Khalil, Mansur, and Yasmeen began to campaign that *they, too, needed a cell phone.*

"Everyone has one, Baba. You don't want us to be different," they each, in turn, said to Mohammad.

"We are really *safer*," Yasmeen said. "If I had had a cell phone on me when I had that run-in with that guy, I could have called for help immediately."

Mohammad was finally convinced and bought cell phones for the three.

"The West Bank has certainly changed," Mohammad commented to Sarah. "It is really *too* much like the States, especially at the Friends."

Chapter 12

Khalil and Mansur stood at side-by-side urinals. As the urine splashed against the stained porcelain Khalil said to Mansur, "What are we doing here? I wish we could go back to America. It stinks here, and I don't mean *this*," he said gesturing with his free hand.

"Did you see the basketball court?" Mansur commented. "It's patched concrete. There are no nets on the baskets, the backboards are in need of painting, and the hoops are bent by guys who imagine themselves Michael Jordan."

They shook and zipped up, washing their hands in the one sink. There was no hot water. The bathroom was dimly lit and smelled of urine and feces. There was no mirror and the paper towel dispenser was empty.

Khalil and Mansur patted their hands dry on their gray uniform pants.

"And this is supposed to be the best school in the country," Mansur sighed.

As they walked up the narrow stairs to the second floor, they mumbled to each other. "These stairs are too narrow. Two people can barely walk abreast; no one wants to move aside so someone can get *up* the stairs when they want to get *down* the stairs."

"It really makes me miss the *stairs* and *halls* at home," Mansur grimly smiled. "Imagine; I'm missing the *stairs!* How fucked-up is that!"

Khalil and Mansur entered their history class and took two seats at the back. They dutifully took out notebooks and pens and waited expectantly. Except for two other students, they were the only ones who had notebooks out.

The history teacher was an inexperienced, young, foreign woman.

"Good morning class," she said. "Please take out your notebooks." She waited, a few students complied with her request; the majority ignored her.

One boy raised his hand. "Aren't you going to give us printed notes?"

"No, I will expect you to take notes from what we discuss in class. This will be preparation for you for when you go to university," she added. "In university, your professors will not be giving you handouts."

Another boy raised his hand. "Will this be on the test?"

"Of course, anything we discuss may help you in answering test questions. The IB is designed to give you information that you can use to support general questions. It will not be specifically asking you for certain facts, but will be measuring how well you can *support your opinion.*"

For some of the students, this concept was baffling. They had been used to memorizing information and regurgitating it.

Khalil glanced at the boy next to him. The boy was doodling on his paper. The figure he was drawing looked unmistakably like the teacher: prominent boobs, narrow waist, ample hips.

Mansur and Khalil tried to concentrate on what the teacher was saying, but every time she turned her back to write something on the white board with a marker, the class broke out into pandemonium. As soon as the teacher turned and faced the class, there was silence. It was as though an invisible string was attached to their mouths and her back. She'd turn her back and the mouths would open; she'd face the class and the mouths would snap shut.

If Khalil and Mansur hadn't been so frustrated, it would have been humorous.

Yasmeen was not faring much better in her classes.

The English teacher she had was a young man. He also, like Khalil's and Mansur's history teacher, was inexperienced. It was obvious he was bright, but his way of dealing with the rowdiness was by putting the kids down.

"You are *animals*," he said. "You should be in a zoo, not in a classroom."

The boy next to Yasmeen whispered to the girl on the other side of him. "He's only teaching because he can't get a *real* job. This is the third school he has been in."

"What happened in the other schools?" the girl whispered back.

"The students and their parents ran him off," the boy chuckled. "He won't last very long here," he smugly said.

They were reading *Wuthering Heights.* "Open to page twelve and read for us, please. How about you, Faisal," he said looking down at the list of names in front of him.

Faisal began to read; he stumbled over some of the archaic words.

"What does the passage mean?" the teacher asked hopefully looking into the blank faces.

Yasmeen raised her hand. "It means that the children see the arrival of the orphan as an intrusion. They can't understand why their father brought this gypsy boy home. They would rather have had the promised fiddle and toys. Even his wife is perplexed over what he has done."

"Right!" the teacher beamed. It seemed at that moment that the only student he had in the class was Yasmeen.

"Brown-noser," one of the English-speaking girls said to her under her breath.

When the teacher asked the next question, Yasmeen kept her hand in her lap.

Math class was a bit better. All the students had their notebooks out, their pens and pencils handy, and were furiously copying down whatever the teacher wrote on the board. There was no talking; it was obvious to Yasmeen that *math was considered important and English was not.*

"Who can give me an answer to the equation?" the teacher asked.

Twenty-five hands were waving in the breeze. Some students even *snapped* their fingers to get the teacher's attention.

It hardly seemed that the class had begun when the bell was ringing for them to change classes.

Fatima, one of the other English-speaking girls in the class said, "It all depends on who the teacher is and what he is teaching. If the teacher is teaching math or one of the sciences, the class tends to be orderly and attentive. Most of the kids here see high scores in math and science opening the doors to university in the States for them. Some of the students with high scores in math and science get into MIT and Yale. If the teacher is young, inexperienced, and teaching English or history, there is often little control."

"But it shouldn't be that way," Yasmeen said as they headed for their next class.

"That's just the way it is," Fatima said hesitating a bit. "By the way, you don't want to look *too* smart. You can be smart on paper, but don't volunteer too much in English class or history class. The kids will think you are stuck-up, and you don't want to appear smarter than the boys."

Yasmeen didn't say anything. *This is not the way school should be*, she thought. *I'm going to be me. I wish we were back in America. I don't like it here.*

Sarah was enjoying her work, but she was worried about the kids.

"They are making the best of it," she said to Mohammad. "But they are not really happy. The boys miss all the activities they had at home: football, basketball, wrestling, swimming, and of course, the freedom of having the truck. And Yasmeen was telling me today that one of the other girls advised her not to *appear too smart*, that it was okay to be *smart on paper, but not in class!*"

"I know; it will just take a little more time to get used to things. Of course, they will initially be unhappy about being here and think about all the things they are missing, but gradually they will come to appreciate all the opportunities that are possible here," Mohammad said trying to reassure himself as much as Sarah.

"Perhaps we should have come only for a vacation," Sarah said. "Maybe it's asking too much of the kids to force them to be here."

"Let's give it a little more time," Mohammad said rubbing her shoulders. "If we find at the end of six months that the kids are really miserable we'll see about making some changes."

"I'm surprised at myself, too," Sarah said. "I'm so used to having no one tell me how to raise my kids. Now I am in the midst of a caring, loving family and I am seeing their help as *interference!* It sounds absurd, even to me! But Aunt Martha never commented about how I raised the kids as she never had kids herself. And Mom wasn't speaking to me, so I was really on my own.

"I understand how you feel," Mohammad smiled taking her hand. My mother always lived with her mother-in-law. There were so many of us, that it was natural – even *welcomed* – that *Sitteh* Hasna would be involved in the childrearing. Yasmeen has always lived with *her* mother-in-law. They both love you and would be distressed to think they had upset you in any way."

"Your mother did apologize," Sarah said. "Maybe *apologize* is not the right word. She said that it had dawned on her that I might see what she had done as an intrusion. I am touched by her sensitivity. I am really *upset* with myself for feeling this way. I'm not upset with her or Yasmeen."

"This is a novelty for us; living so close to family. We saw Uncle Ken and Aunt Martha several times a year, but it was nothing like these weekly Fridays with my parents and Sundays with Hasna. It *does* take some adjusting. I'll suggest to my mother and Hasna that we go to one of their homes one week and the other the next week. Instead of twice a week, we'll cut it down to once a week. How does that sound?" Mohammad said.

"No, let's leave it the way it is for the moment," Sarah replied. "I love seeing your family. For seventeen years we didn't see them at all. It's also nice not having to cook on those days," she laughed. "I am spoiled."

"You would be proud of me," Mohammad boasted. "I convinced Yasmeen and my mother *not* to send Jamileh and Lily over on Fridays to clean; that this was something you and Yasmeen wanted to do!"

"What?! They wanted the girls to come and clean for us?"

"It was no reflection on your housekeeping. My mother said that you worked too hard and that you shouldn't have to clean house on Fridays when she had granddaughters who would happily do it. She did add that the girls could *help* teach our Yasmeen to clean as one day she would have her own house to take care of."

"When I told her that our Yasmeen would be going on to college, she just smiled and said that high school was enough for a girl; that even though Yasmeen was only fourteen she was thinking of possible husbands for her." Mohammad laughed at Sarah's shocked expression.

"She was just teasing. She *knew* I would tell you, and she *knew* you would see that she was joking. What she really said was: *Yasmeen must go to college like her mother and find a handsome, smart, educated husband like you.*"

"You *added* that last part," Sarah said lovingly striking Mohammad on the shoulder. "Your mother didn't say that at all!"

"*Said'ee'nee,* (believe me)" Mohammad said raising his hand to heaven. "Those were her exact words. She realizes your *good fortune* and wants the same for our daughter!"

Sarah rolled her eyes. "Yes, *my good fortune* indeed."

"Think who you could have married," Mohammad teased. "In comparison, I must look pretty darn good."

"You look more than *pretty darn good*," Sarah said kissing him. "You look *almost* perfect."

"What's with the *'almost'*?"

"I want you to think that there is always a margin for improvement."

Chapter 13

Wednesday, the third week of school, when Mohammad and Sarah went to pick up the kids only Yasmeen was waiting on the curb.

"Where are your brothers?" Mohammad asked.

"They went home early," Yasmeen answered. She avoided looking at her parents.

"Were they sick?" Sarah asked.

"No," was all Yasmeen said.

"Did they have a free class this afternoon?"

"No," Yasmeen replied.

"Well, then what happened?" Mohammad asked, not liking the fact he had to pump Yasmeen for information.

Yasmeen was silent.

Mohammad turned off the engine. "We're going to sit here until you tell me what happened."

Yasmeen looked out the window and watched the pedestrians dodge between the cars. A driver of a van honked his horn and the woman walking in the street continued to talk on her cell phone and ignore him. Three young men walked almost in the center of the road forcing traffic to weave around them. She counted ten cars parked on the *sidewalk!*

"Well?" Mohammad asked again, growing more and more irritated.

"They were suspended from school," she said turning to her parents. "They were suspended from school for fighting."

"Suspended?" Sarah gasped. *"Suspended for fighting?* I don't believe it."

"Who were they fighting with?" Mohammad asked trying to remain calm.

"Some of the Arabic-speaking boys," Yasmeen answered in a dead voice. "The English-speaking boys and the Arabic-speaking boys don't really get along."

"Do you know *what* they were fighting about?" Mohammad further questioned.

There were tears of defiance in Yasmeen's eyes. "Yes, they were fighting about me!"

"About you?" Sarah asked looking into Yasmeen's eyes. *"What* does it have to do with you?"

"Some of the Arabic-speaking boys were making comments about me," Yasmeen said. "They didn't know that Khalil and Mansur were my brothers." Yasmeen paused. "You know the kind of comments some guys make about girls," she said looking at her parents.

"Anyway, Khalil and Mansur stopped to ask them who they were talking about. One word led to another. When Khalil and Mansur realized they were talking about *me*, they began to shove the boys."

"Soon the Arabic-speaking boys had them surrounded. Khalil and Mansur laid into them with their fists and wrestled them to the ground. Two of the teachers on yard duty separated them and hauled four boys into the principal's office. I don't know what happened there, but the Arabic-speaking boys came back outside, and Khalil and Mansur were suspended."

Mohammad turned on the engine and pulled into traffic.

"You shouldn't have brought us here," Yasmeen said under her breath softly so that her parents couldn't hear.

Both Mohammad and Sarah heard.

The door to Khalil's and Mansur's bedroom was closed when Mohammad, Sarah, and Yasmeen got home. There was an envelope addressed to *Mohammad Omar Mansur* on the kitchen counter.

"It's a letter from the principal," Mohammad said to Sarah as he skimmed down through the short note. "It says that they have been suspended for three days for fighting and that they will not be allowed back in school until he has met with us. We are to call and make an appointment."

"The boys have *never* been in trouble at school," Sarah said. "They have only been in school here *three* weeks and they get *suspended!* Something is definitely wrong."

"Yasmeen, go call your brothers," Mohammad said.

Yasmeen went and rapped on the door. "Baba wants to see you in the family room," Yasmeen called through the door.

She got no answer. She knocked again. Still, there was no response.

Finally, she opened the door and looked in. The twin beds were neatly made-up. The boys were *not* there!

"They're not in their room, Baba," Yasmeen worriedly said.

"*Not* in their room?" Mohammad said raising his voice. "Where could they have gone?"

He picked up the phone to call his mother. He waited. The phone rang ten times but no one picked up. He was just about to hang up with he heard his mother's voice on the line.

"*Salam aleikum. Mean?* (Peace be on you, who is it?)"

"*Aleikum salam, Yumma,*" Mohammad responded. "Are Khalil and Mansur there?"

"Yes, *Yumma. Habeebatee* (the dears), they came and had lunch with us and are just about to leave with Amr."

"Tell them to wait, *Yumma,*" Mohammad said. "I'll be over to pick them up."

"Did Baba sound mad?" Khalil asked his *Sitteh.*

"He's is going to be really angry that we got suspended," Mansur said.

"Those *other boys* should have gotten suspended," *Sidi* Omar replied. "You did *right* to fight with them over saying things about your sister. *Abou'kum* (your father) will not be angry. He will be *proud."*

"He'll be mad," Khalil sighed. "We've never gotten in trouble in school before.

"He'll be mad that we didn't leave a note telling him where we were," Mansur added.

Mohammad *was* angry.

As soon as he came in the metal gate and saw Khalil and Mansur he said, "Into the sitting room, *now!"*

He saw his father and mother *also* going into the sitting room; he started to stop them when he saw the look in their eyes. He stepped aside to let them ahead. Sarah and Yasmeen, under protest, had stayed back in the apartment.

"This is something between the boys and me," Mohammad had stated as he went out the door. "You can deal with them when we get back."

Sarah looked at the closed door and she was fuming mad- *at Mohammad!*

Khalil and Mansur sat side-by-side on two straight chairs. Mohammad and his parents sat opposite them on the daybed under the collage of family photos.

"First," Mohammad said raising his finger and shaking it in the boys' direction, "don't you ever leave the house

without telling me where you are going, or asking *permission* to go; you have cell phones, at least at the moment you have cell phones, *call* me or your mother!"

"*Second,* when you are in trouble – any kind of trouble – you call me, or your mother, or your grandparents, or your Uncle Issa or your Aunt Yasmeen. You call someone to come and be with you; all of us are here for you. I don't want you ever to think that you are on your own. Is that clear?"

Khalil and Mansur dutifully, gratefully, nodded their heads.

Mohammad began to calm down. "Now, tell me what happened at school."

Khalil looked at Nijmeh and swallowed. "Some of the Arabic-speaking boys were talking about this girl. Mansur and I were walking by them and we heard them talk about this girl's..." Khalil paused and again looked embarrassedly at his grandmother, "breasts and how well her pants showed her behind."

"They then were commenting about her blonde hair and blue eyes and the fact that she was an *American'knee'ya,*" Mansur interjected. "We knew they were talking about Yasmeen."

"So we went up to them and said they should shut their mouths about the *American'knee'ya,*" Khalil continued.

"One of them kind of sneered and asked if the *American'knee'ya* was our girlfriend," Mansur added.

"We told them 'no, she is our sister,' then *we* shoved them," Khalil explained.

"Their friends seemed to materialize out of nowhere. We were surrounded; so we started punching and pushing. We wrestled them to the ground," Mansur said.

"Two teachers came over and pulled us apart and dragged four of us to the office," Mansur continued.

"The principal listened to the story and decided that we started it since we had struck the first blow. He scolded the two Arabic-speaking boys and he suspended us," Khalil said. "We can't go back to school until you and Mama meet with him."

"We're sorry we got in trouble," Mansur said. "But we are *not* sorry that we fought those boys. No one will say anything about Yasmeen again knowing that they will get the crap beat out of them."

Mohammad and Omar tried to hide their smiles and look stern.

Nijmeh was the first to act. She walked over to both boys and kissed them. "You did the right thing, *Sitteh,* in defending your sister's honor. And I am proud of you." Then she took off her plastic *babooj* and hit them twice, symbolically, on each shoulder. "But, *Sitteh,* you were wrong not to tell your father where you were. You were wrong not to call someone to be with you. You do that again and *Sidi* Omar will take a strap to you," she said winking at both boys so neither Mohammad nor Omar could see. "Now, I am going to make tea for all of us."

"Your three days of suspension from school will be spent helping your *Sidi*," Mohammad said. "There will be no sleeping in, or lying about the house watching DVDs or playing on the laptops. You will come in the mornings when we bring Amr and spend the day working with *Sidi.*"

The boys nodded.

"As far as *not* telling us where you were," Mohammad continued, "for those three days you will not be allowed to use your laptops for emailing."

"Khalil and Mansur started to groan in protest.

"Maybe you should give them a choice?" Omar said to Mohammad, "You can prevent them using their laptops, or they can be strapped."

There was a twinkle in Mohammad's eye as he asked which they would prefer.

Without hesitation, both Khalil and Mansur said, "*Strapped!*"

Omar left the sitting room for a moment to get the razor strap he used to sharpen his razor.

Silently he handed it to Mohammad.

"Bend over," he told his sixteen-year-old sons.

They bent and Mohammad gently grazed their backsides with the worn leather strap that had occasionally been used on him.

When he was done, the boys kissed his hand and placed it against their foreheads.

That night in bed he told Sarah about the discussion with the boys. She listened in silence as she lay rigidly at his side.

"What's wrong, *habeeptee?*" Mohammad asked genuinely puzzled.

"*What's wrong?*" Sarah angrily whispered. "You tell me that this is between *you and your sons* and *order*ed me to stay at home. *That's what's wrong.* They are *our* sons, not just *your* sons! Don't you ever even *think* that you can do something like this again," she said grabbing a handful of Mohammad's chest hair and pulling.

"Ouch," Mohammad said, "that hurts!"

"*I'll hurt you!*" Sarah continued, "If you ever forget that these are *our* children. Is that clear?"

"Crystal," Mohammad said rubbing his chest where Sarah had yanked on the hair.

"Now that is out of the way, did I *really* hurt you?" Sarah said acting concerned.

"I think you should kiss it and make it all better," Mohammad smiled. "I promise I will never do something like that again."

"See that you don't," Sarah smiled kissing him on the chest before laying her head down in its usual place.

Chapter 14

Sarah *was* getting concerned about the subtle changes in Mohammad. *He's becoming more Arab,* she thought. In the seventeen years they had lived in the States, except for occasional visits from his brothers Khalil and Mansur and Amr, or visits to his sisters Mona and Manal, their association with other Arabs had been quite limited.

They had always done things as a *couple;* gender segregation had never been part of the dynamic. Now, on most visits to his family and former friends, men sat in one room and women in another. Initially, it had been alright with Sarah, now she was finding the change irritating – no not really irritating, but *alarming.*

"I don't like what is happening to us," Sarah finally said to Mohammad.

"What do you mean by *what is happening to us?"* Mohammad asked perplexed.

"It's little things. We go to visit your sister, Hasna, for example, and you sit with your brother-in-law and grown nephews in one room; I sit with Hasna and her daughters-in-law in another. We go to dinners at her sons' homes and you and the men eat first and then the women eat."

"That's just the way things are done in the camp," Mohammad said, somewhat disregarding her concern.

"Then there is that incident with the boys; you just *assumed* that I would stay back while you *handled* it. That was unlike you," Sarah asserted. "We always did everything as a couple. I feel like you are seeing me as your *wife....*"

"You *are* my wife," Mohammad interrupted smiling and taking her in his arms. "And *I'm very happy* you are my wife," he said nuzzling her neck.

Sarah raised her head and stepped back, yet still in his arms. "I'm not *just* your wife, Mohammad," she said seriously looking him in the eyes. "I'm your partner; your friend; your *equal."* She paused, "sometimes you make me feel my place is just a step or two *behind* you, not *beside* you."

Mohammad was shocked by the seriousness of her tone and the sentiments she was revealing.

"Sarah, *habeeptee, of course,* you are my friend, my companion, my partner. You will always be *beside* me. I do realize, more than you know, that we are *not equal.* You *are* and *always have been* superior to me. I knew that when we first met seventeen years ago; and I know it today. If I haven't made that clear then I am truly sorry," Mohammad said drawing Sarah tightly into his arms, kissing the top of her head.

"You shouldn't have to remind me," Mohammad said thoughtfully, "but I can see now where I have slipped back into some of the more traditional, gender-biased attitudes of our society. If I thought that *here* was changing *us,* we would be on the next plane to America tomorrow."

"You're serious, aren't you?" Sarah said once again lifting her head to look into his eyes.

"Nothing, *nothing* is more important than you and the kids," Mohammad said trying to blink the tears from his eyes.

Sarah sighed and tightened her arms around him. "I guess I needed to be reassured," she said. "I feel so much better now. Thank you."

"You must *always* tell me what is on your mind. Shake me and say, *Mohammad, I want you to be my friend right now. Forget you are my husband. I will listen as a friend, and if need be, I will call that husband of yours a no good so-and-so,*" he laughed.

Sarah laughed. "I love you so much that the thought that you might be slipping away – even a little bit – scared me. I would fight tooth-and-nail for us!"

"I'm *not* slipping away," Mohammad said. And he meant it.

The meeting with the school principal did not go as the principal had assumed it would go.

"I am so glad that you could come in," he said shaking both Mohammad's and Sarah's hands.

"Please sit down," he said gesturing to the two arm chairs in front of his desk.

"As you know, we cannot have fighting on school property. And as Khalil and Mansur *started* the fight, by their *own admission* I might add, it seemed the only recourse was to suspend them for three days."

"You *are* aware of what prompted the fight?" Mohammad asked.

"Some disagreement about a female student," the principal said. "None of the boys would elaborate."

"It seems that the other boys said *suggestive* things about our daughter; Khalil and Mansur's sister," Sarah said. "Though not completely *condoning* their fighting on school property, I completely understand and *applaud* their actions."

"Surely, Mrs. Omar, you cannot *applaud* their actions!" the principal responded.

"Though I am American," Sarah continued, "we have raised our children as Palestinian – though defense of one's sister is hardly *just* a Palestinian value. In Iowa, we also hold defense of our sisters and daughters as a sacred trust. Our sons have been raised to look out for Yasmeen," Sarah said turning to give Mohammad a smile.

"It seems *unjust* to me that only Khalil and Mansur were suspended. The other boys should have been suspended as well."

"As my wife has so succinctly said," Mohammad began, "we do not think that you were wrong in suspending Khalil and Mansur. However, we think you were unfair. They broke the rules; they needed to be punished. I also punished them," Mohammad added, (trying not to smile as he remembered Nijmeh striking them with her plastic *babooj* and his gently grazing their backsides with Omar's razor strap).

The principal was at a loss for words.

"I hope you weren't too hard on the boys," he finally said. "I can see now how they may have been justified in what they did."

"There is no *'may have been'* about it," Sarah said. "If we truly felt that they had been wrong, we would have no argument with you and they would have been severely punished at home. The discipline to which my husband refers was *not* because of the suspension, but because they *failed* to inform us immediately so someone from the family could have come to support them, *and* because they went to their grandparents without telling us."

"I can see how I misjudged the situation," the principal said a smile tugging at his lips. "I certainly misjudged you. I had thought, and please excuse me," he said facing Sarah, "that you would perhaps be a bit *lax* with your children. I wrongly assumed that the boys, *being American* would not be *disciplined*."

Sarah did not smile. "The children *are* American, but they are *also* Palestinian. My husband is strict with the children. He was raised in a refugee camp. His parents are of peasant stock but so am I," Sarah proudly asserted. "We believe in loving the children but we also believe in discipline. When they are wrong, they must bear the responsibility."

"The boys are outside waiting to apologize," Mohammad said. "They are not to apologize for defending their sister's reputation. They are to apologize for fighting on school grounds."

"That won't be necessary," the principal said.

"Yes, *it is necessary,*" Mohammad replied. "I'll call the boys."

Mohammad went to the door and motioned for Khalil and Mansur to come in.

"We are sorry for fighting on campus," they both said shaking the principal's hand. "*Inshallah* it won't happen again," Khalil added.

"*Inshallah,* it won't happen again?" the principal questioned.

"If anything is ever said about our sister again, we will take the fight off campus," Mansur said, "if we can."

The principal, Mohammad, and Sarah each had a hard time not smiling.

That evening at supper, Khalil and Mansur were talking about their three days of working with Omar.

"The great thing about the suspension," Mansur said, "was that we got to work with *Sidi.*"

"The man is an *artist* when it comes to building a stone wall," Khalil said with admiration. "And the *stories* he knows. He told us great stories about his mother, *Sitteh* Hasna.

"He also told us about one time taking the razor strap to you, Baba," Mansur smiled.

"You sure it was me, and not one of your uncles?"

"It was *definitely* you. Something about eating *too many figs,*" Khalil said trying to jog his father's memory. "*Sidi* said that there was a dish of figs on the table and when he came back into the room the bowl was empty. You were sitting there and he asked you if you had eaten all the figs. You couldn't speak as your mouth was full of figs, so you just shook your head no. He asked you again, and again you shook your head."

"Ah, yes, I *do* remember now. He got the razor strap and hit me, *not* for eating all the figs but for *lying* to him," Mohammad laughed.

"I remember him strapping your Ammo Khalil and Mansur for fighting with each other, and then *Im'me* taking her plastic *babooj* to them and beating them saying '*if anyone is going to give you a bloody nose or black eye it is going to be me.*' Mohammad started to laugh. "I was just a little tyke, but I can remember *Sitteh* Hasna telling the story. She would always add a part saying, '*I would have beaten them too, but I was barefoot.*'"

The three children and Mohammad and Sarah were laughing so hard that the tears were literally flowing. Even Amr, sitting in his highchair, was all smiles.

Chapter 15

It is surprising how a bloody nose, a black eye, and applauded suspension can alter one's attitude: the classes became more interesting; some of the teachers were quite inspiring, and there was something to be said about playing basketball under the sun on a concrete court; the ball swishing through a bent, net-less hoop was still exhilarating.

Khalil and Mansur were now friends with the other English-Speaking students and had a nodding acquaintance with some of the Arabic-speaking boys. They had also developed a cordial relationship with the Arabic-speaking girls. The fight had bought them a certain amount of respect and acceptance.

"Sometimes using your fists is the only way to make a point," Khalil joked with Mansur.

"A lot in life requires a little *muscle-flexing,*" Mansur replied. "Feel that baby," he said to his brother as he curled his arm and a bicep swelled.

"The point is never to back down from a fight and to get nose-to-nose with your opponent," he continued. "Close enough that he can feel the spray from your words on his face."

"As Baba says, *imagine a line between you and your opponent and once his toe crosses that line – hit him hard!"* Khalil said. "Take the offensive, don't just defend."

Through Fridays with Hasna's grandsons, Khalil and Mansur were learning the fundamentals of soccer. The *shabab* (youth) from the mosque in the camp held a soccer match every Friday after prayers. It had become a routine for Khalil and Mansur to attend Friday prayers and then to play soccer. Surprisingly, they had felt more accepted by the boys from the camp than the boys at school.

"I suppose it is because we are *related* to half the team," Mansur joked.

"It is also because *Sitteh* and *Sidi,* and *Ammo Issa* and *Amto Hasna* all live in the camp. We are seen as an extension of them," Khalil observed. "We have over *sixty* family members living in the camp!"

"At school, we are seen as *Amer'i'can;* in the camp, we are seen as *family."*

There was no one among the student population who had grandparents or uncles and aunts living in a refugee camp. Oh, there were kids at school whose parents or grandparents had been refugees from 1948, but their grandparents had never lived in a camp.

"At least, we get along really well with Mahmoud, the guard; Abed the maintenance man, and Im Mohammad the woman who makes coffee," Yasmeen stated. They were the only folks on staff who still lived in a camp. The three siblings felt that their own connection to a camp further separated them from the student population.

"Don't forget the physics teacher," Mansur added. "He is also somewhat like us. He has two brothers living in the States and one of them is married to an American, but he lives in a camp."

"I have always felt *different*, even when we lived in the States," Yasmeen said. "I was the only girl in my class who couldn't go to mixed parties, who couldn't go to sleepovers or wear shorts or sleeveless blouses, and who was never allowed to go swimming in a public pool. Now we are here and I am *still* different. I speak an accented Arabic; I am blonde and blue-eyed where the majority of the girls are dark-haired and brown-eyed; our relatives live in a camp, and I don't cover my hair." Yasmeen sighed. "It seems wherever I am, I am different. Sometimes I wish I could just *blend in*."

"It is easier for us," Mansur admitted, "because we are boys. Oh, we still stick out. As soon as we open our mouths to say something in Arabic everyone knows we are foreign. We walk down the street and anyone glancing at us immediately knows: *English-speaking.* They just need to look at our sneakers!" Mansur laughed.

"It is fortunate that we *look* Arab," Khalil smiled. "We don't look as *American* as you do," he teased Yasmeen.

"And you two get away with a lot of things that I could never get away with because I am a *girl*," Yasmeen said. "Baba and Mama keep a pretty tight rein on me. My life seems to revolve around home and school with occasional excursions into the camp to see *Sitteh* and *Sidi*. It really *isn't* fair!"

"Your life isn't any worse than Jamileh's. She goes to school; she comes home; she doesn't even need excursions to see *Sitteh* and *Sidi* as she lives with them!" Khalil laughed.

Yasmeen rolled her eyes. "Well, in the States I wasn't gawked at because I have blonde hair and blue eyes. People didn't look at me and just *assume* that I was *easy.*" Yasmeen continued. "I wish we hadn't come here," she sighed.

"We'll be going back in the summer," Mansur said feeling a bit of sympathy for his sister.

A week later, when Yasmeen was spending a Sunday afternoon at her grandparents', the subject of the *hijab* came up.

She was sitting and chatting with Jamileh as they both worked on the breast panel for a *thob* (a native embroidered dress). *Sitteh* Nijmeh had decided that they should work on some cross-stitch every Sunday afternoon. She had given them a sample breast plate from an old *thob* to copy.

The girls had sewn the white *marka* (stiff canvas with tiny squares) onto red velvet, and with multicolor embroidery threads were sewing different colored flowers blossoming from a green, cross-stitched vine. As they worked, they talked. Jamileh practiced her English and Yasmeen practiced her Arabic.

"You're much better at this than I am," Yasmeen commented in frustration, trying to get the knot out of the thread she was using.

"I have had a lot more practice," Jamileh said. "You really are doing remarkably well considering that you've only been doing traditional embroidery for a short while. *Sitteh* is well-known in the camp for her fine embroidery. In no time you will be even *better* at doing this than I am," Jamileh said generously. "I suspect you will one day be just as good as *Sitteh*."

"You're only saying that to make me feel better," Yasmeen smiled. "I *know* how bad I am. The backside of your work looks as good as the front. The backside of my work is a jumble of knots and broken threads and doesn't look neat at all."

"You'll get the hang of it," Jamileh said returning Yasmeen's smile. She paused as she bit off the end of a length of thread. "There *is* something I wanted to talk to you about.

"I know you have been hassled because of your blonde hair. Boys can't help but stare at you in the street. You are so *beautiful*," her cousin said. "And with your blonde hair, you *do stand out*. I wonder if you have ever considered wearing *hijab*. A lot of girls our age, or even younger, cover their heads with a scarf when in the street. They don't wear the scarf at home, only in the street or at school," Jamileh added. "It seems to stop the boys from staring and *talking*. It might be something you'd wish to think about."

Yasmeen stopped drawing the needle through the red velvet and white *marka*. She just stared at her cousin. "Do *you* think I should wear a scarf?"

"I think you don't want people staring at you, or making comments about you. I think you really want to blend in, and I know that is hard to do because of how *beautiful you are* – beautiful in a foreign *way.*" Jamileh saw the hurt look on Yasmeen's face, and knew she hadn't completely understood what she had meant.

"I don't mean *foreign* in a bad way – I mean it as *exotic – unusual.* It's not your fault that boys stare at you. For them it is like seeing a *living* film star," Jamileh said.

Yasmeen had to smile. "Yeah, I'm a film star alright."

"I do want to blend in, but I also want to be true to who I am. If I was religiously convinced that this was the right thing to do, I would do it. But just to wear it in order to stop some silly boys from gawking and commenting doesn't seem like a good enough reason," Yasmeen asserted.

"Think about it; maybe talk it over with your mother and *Sitteh* Nijmeh," Jamileh said. "I think you will find that things will be better for you at school and you won't feel quite as *foreign* when you are walking in the street."

The next day when Yasmeen and Sarah were shopping, they passed a shop where hundreds of multicolored scarves fluttered in the afternoon breeze. Some of them hung so low that they brushed against the tops of their heads.

"What would you think if I started wearing a scarf?" Yasmeen asked. "Jamileh seems to think that it would help me fit in...that it would solve the problem of me being stared at in the street and gawked at by some of the boys at school."

Sarah turned and looked at Yasmeen. Yasmeen and Sarah were almost the same height. *When did Yasmeen grow so tall?* Sarah thought. "Are you seriously considering wearing *hijab?*" She asked in astonishment.

"I *do* want to blend in. I am so tired of being stared at, of sometimes having boys say things about me. It may be the answer," Yasmeen said. "I *know* I should be religiously convinced that this is the right thing to do. But maybe it is okay to do it socially. I think Baba would be pleased," Yasmeen added as an afterthought.

"Baba would want you to do what you were *convinced* was right for you. I don't think he would want you to do something that you were *not* thoroughly *sure of,*" Sarah said. "You need to give this *careful, careful* thought," she said trying to keep the concern out of her voice.

There are too many changes happening, she thought to herself. *Three months ago – even last week – Yasmeen would have laughed at the idea of wearing hijab. And today she is giving it serious consideration!*

Sarah was shocked at Mohammad's reaction to Yasmeen's suggestion.

"It might not be such a bad idea," he said. "It would certainly stop some of the *talk,* and it would help her blend in more. She might be more comfortable."

Sarah was irritated. "Would you like *me* to wear *hijab,* too? Are you embarrassed by your *foreign-looking* wife and daughter?" she said.

"Of course, I am *not embarrassed.* I am proud of both of you!" Mohammad said grabbing Sarah's hand. "Wearing the *hijab* is a personal and serious decision. But Yasmeen seems so uncomfortable some days and I would like the talk to stop. I want her to be happy." He let go of Sarah's hand and rubbed his forehead. "I don't know the answer. The Quran says 'there is no compulsion in religion'- and I truly believe that. I only want you both to do what you *want* to do, what you feel is right for you."

"Some days I think you would have been happier with a Palestinian wife," Sarah sighed. She pushed back the kitchen chair and got up. "I need to get supper ready," she said in a dead tone picking Amr up out of his highchair and calling to Yasmeen to come and take him.

That night, for the first time in seventeen years, they lay apart in the big bed. "Good-night," Sarah said turning on her side with her back toward Mohammad.

Mohammad switched off the bedside lamp and lay on his back in the darkness. He could hear muffled sobs.

Turning on his side he drew the huddled form of Sarah into his arms. "Don't cry, *habeeptee, ya ro'he* (my love, my soul)," he said, his own voice breaking. "I don't *want* a Palestinian wife. I *want you!* You are the only wife I have *ever* wanted," he said kissing the top of her curls. "I feel horrible that I have made you feel this way. I don't want to *change* you or Yasmeen – not one little bit.

Forgive me for how I have made you feel. *You* and *the kids* are the most important things in my life! Don't you ever forget that! If you weren't in my life, I might as well be dead."

Sarah grabbed the hand that was tight around her waist and drew it to her lips. She kissed the broad fingers and wet the hairs on the back of Mohammad's hand with her tears.

Mohammad moved closer to her so his body was molded against hers. He kissed the top of her head. He hadn't anticipated these subtle changes that were taking place.

Chapter 16

A shop for meat, a shop for chicken and eggs, a shop for fish, an open-air market for fruits and vegetables, peasant women sitting on the sidewalk selling garden-grown vegetables and fruit; then there was a grocery store for everything else. Shopping, to say the least, was an adventure. *It isn't anything like shopping in the States,* Sarah thought as she trudged from shop to shop. The meat was not packaged on Styrofoam trays and wrapped in plastic-wrap. One walked into a butcher's shop and told the butcher how many *kilos*-not pounds- of meat one wanted; whether or not one wanted lamb or beef (there was no pork), whether one wanted it ground or cut into the size of *birds' heads;* and whether or not one wanted the fat trimmed off or left on. Nijmeh had told her *a little fat makes the food taste better.* Sarah was not convinced.

Once the cut was selected, the butcher cut it into the desired size on a blood-seasoned tree trunk, or ground it in an electric grinder, pushing the meat into the hole with a wooden pestle. *It's certainly different,* Sarah mused as she went on to the chicken shop to buy a tray of thirty eggs wrapped in newspaper and tied with a string,

"I would also like two kilos of chicken breasts *without the skin please,"* Sarah said in her broken Arabic. *Sometimes I feel like I just stepped off the boat,* she thought to herself, *or maybe that should be slid off the back of a camel,* she sighed.

There were days when she enjoyed the novelty of a different culture; there were days when she didn't. It was hard on her at times; harder on her older boys, hardest on Yasmeen. The only one who seemed to take it all in stride was Amr. She thought that it was probably even hard on Mohammad as his family was not adjusting as he had expected.

"If you aren't really into politics; if you weren't here during the *intifada* (the uprising), you don't really count for anything," Khalil commented to Mansur on their way home from school.

"It doesn't help that we also speak fractured Arabic," Mansur observed. "Oh, we can communicate alright, but whatever we say is first seen as comical because of the *way* we say it."

"Remember when we were walking down that side street in Ramallah, and there was only a blind man in the street? Remember how he asked me what time it was in Arabic, and when I told him the time -in Arabic- he asked *where I was from in the States!?*" Khalil said. "He didn't even have to *see* me! He just had to *hear* me and he knew right away that I wasn't from here!"

"It *is* kind of discouraging to have a *blind* man know you aren't local," Mansur agreed trying to laugh, "But we were still different, even in the States," he observed.

"Yeah, but it was a *good* different. Here, no matter what we do, or what we say, or how we look, we are always *ajanib* – foreigners. We are always *English-Speaking* even though our names are Khalil and Mansur; even though we are Moslem; even though our grandparents and cousins live in a camp; we are seen as *outsiders*." Khalil added.

"This class-ism gets to me at times. We have English-Speaking and Arabic-speaking; we have *mid'da'knee* (city folks) and *fellaheen* (peasants); there is *min hone* (locals) and *laje'een* (refugees), Mansur continued.

"And don't forget *kubar* (upper class) and *busata* (simple folks);" Khalil said. "Oh, there are different classes of people in the States, but where we lived it wasn't as obvious as it seems to be here."

Yasmeen had walked along beside her brothers making no comment. It was unusual for her not to take part in the discussion. "I *think* Baba wants me to wear *hijab*," Yasmeen said looking at Khalil. "I know he doesn't want the boys to talk about me, and that he wants it to be my decision, but I also believe it would please him to think he had raised me right. Sometimes I think that he wants to *prove* that even though we were raised in the States, we are as good, as or even *better*, at being Palestinian than the kids here."

"I heard one of the men he went to school with when they were boys ask him when he was going to marry a *Palestinian wife!*" Mansur said soberly.

"What did he say?" both Yasmeen and Khalil questioned.

"Oh, he put the guy in his place and said he never again wanted to hear anyone asking him when he was taking a Palestinian wife; that he would never find a wife like Mama." Mansur paused, "But the very fact that some people *asked* shows that some folks don't accept or like the idea that Mama is American."

"Who cares? We *know* our relatives love Mama – especially *Sitteh*, *Sidi*, and *Mart Ammie* Yasmeen. She is like Mama's sister," Yasmeen asserted.

"Well, no matter how hard it is for us," Khalil said, "it must be doubly hard for Mama. We are at least half-Arab; she's *all-American!*"

"Not only American but *half Jewish*," Yasmeen whispered. "Imagine what some of the kids at school would do if they *knew* that Grandpa Ken and Mama's dad are Jewish!"

"Shhhh," Mansur whispered back angrily. "The only thing Jewish about them is their *name!*"

"You don't need to convince us," Khalil said putting a hand on his brother's shoulder. "Besides, don't Jews trace their *being* Jews through their *mothers* and not their *fathers?* If we look at it legally, Mama isn't Jewish at all because her mother is Christian – a *Methodist* no less!"

"Aren't we Arabs – Palestinian – because our father is Palestinian?" Yasmeen added. "It doesn't *legally* matter that Mama is American. In the eyes of the society, we are Arabs because Baba is an Arab."

"It also means that we *belong* to Baba and not to Mama," Mansur said. "There is no question here that Baba would have the legal right to us and Mama would not. If they got divorced we would automatically go with Baba and *he* would decide if Mama could even see us or not."

"That's *never* going to happen," Yasmeen stated. "Mama and Baba are always going to be together. I don't know why you even brought it up!" she said close to tears and angry with Mansur.

"I was just being hypothetical," Mansur said trying to soothe Yasmeen. "*Of course,* Mama and Baba would never divorce. I was just pointing out how *different* things are here. "

"I wish we were back in the States," Khalil, Mansur, and Yasmeen each said under his/her breath.

As they neared their apartment building they noticed a young man leaning against the stone wall.

"Isn't that Imad?" Khalil said. "I wonder what he's doing here."

"*Salam aleikum,*" all three said.

"*Aleikum salam,*" Imad smiled in response. "I was in the neighborhood and thought I would drop by to see you."

"Come in," Mansur smiled back. "We're just getting home from school and you are just in time for lunch."

"I think Mama is making fried chicken and *hashwa* (stuffing)," Khalil said slapping Imad on the back. "She will be glad that you dropped in."

Yasmeen said nothing.

The boys joked as they took the elevator to the second floor. The elevator was a bit crowded with four people in it and Yasmeen was forced to stand very close to Imad.

They rang the bell and waited for Sarah to open the door.

"Imad!" she said in surprise. "How glad I am to see you! You are just in time for lunch. *Ha'mat'tuck bit'hib'buck,"* (your mother-in-law loves you- a common Arabic saying when a guest stops in at meal-time) she said jokingly. "You boys wash up. Your father is already here. Yasmeen, lay an extra place for Imad."

"Imad! I am happy to see you, *Khali,"* Mohammad said as he placed Amr in his highchair. "Your timing is perfect. You must have been able to smell Im Khalil's fried chicken all the way from the camp," he joked. "No one can make fried chicken quite like Im Khalil can," he said smiling at Sarah and winking.

There was much chatter and laughing over lunch. Every once in a while Imad would steal a look at Yasmeen. Yasmeen did not look back, though she *did* feel the flutter of butterfly wings in the pit of her stomach.

Both Sarah and Mohammad noticed Imad's furtive glances at Yasmeen.

She's only fifteen, they both thought. *Imad is close to twenty. He shouldn't be looking at her that way.*

Imad *knew* he shouldn't have made an excuse to *just drop in.* He *knew* that Yasmeen was only fifteen, but he couldn't get her out of his mind. He thought she was the most beautiful girl he had ever known. He *knew* she was too young to get married, but she was not too young for there to be an *understanding* between his parents and hers. He was willing to wait until she was eighteen. He would be content to wait, *as long as there was an understanding.*

Chapter 17

Kareem, at sixteen, was not as tall as he would have wished to be. Oh, if he jumped high enough he could still touch the rim of the basketball hoop when he swished the ball through the net-less ring but still... He envied his younger brother, Hakam, who at fifteen was already taller than he was. Somehow being older, yet *shorter* didn't seem quite right. There was a bench press in the garage of his home in the village, and he lifted weights every afternoon when he got home from school. He was muscular and an undefeated wrestler – at least undefeated considering the competition he had at school.

Kareem had been at the Friends School for three years. He was popular. He liked the fact that the Friends school was co-ed. He liked the fact that he had girls in his classes and that he could get to know girls as *friends.* There was one particular girl who had attracted his attention. She was blonde, blue-eyed and had a smattering of freckles across her nose. He had never actually *spoken* to her but he was going to remedy that situation.

It was one of those winter days when it was warmer outside than it was in. It seemed as though spring was flirting with winter. The sun warmed the old stone wall where some of the students sat. The blonde-haired girl was sitting alone on the concrete bench that overlooked the basketball court. She was watching as some of the boys played a pick-up game. Kareem knew that two of the boys were the girl's brothers; they were in some of his classes.

"Your brothers play pretty well," Kareem said. "Were they on the basketball team in the States?"

Yasmeen looked up at the boy who was speaking to her and smiled. "Yes, they would have been on the varsity team if we had stayed in the States. I don't believe I know you?"

"I'm Kareem. I'm in some of the classes with your brothers. We have Theory of Knowledge and College Prep together."

"I'm Yasmeen."

"Yes, I know," Kareem smiled. "You're in class with my brother, Hakam." Kareem paused as he noticed her puzzled expression. "We don't look anything alike. To see us together you wouldn't think we were brothers."

"To see me, and my little brother, Amr, with Mansur and Khalil," Yasmeen said nodding to her two brothers playing basketball, "you wouldn't think we were siblings. Mansur and Khalil look like my father and my little brother Amr and I look like our mother. Though Mama says that Baba's grandmother had red hair, blue eyes and freckles," she laughed.

"Would you like to walk around the courtyard?" Kareem asked.

"I better not," Yasmeen said looking at her brothers. "But thanks for asking."

Kareem also glanced at Mansur and Khalil. "I'll catch you later. It was nice talking to you."

"It was nice talking to you, too."

Khalil and Mansur bounded up the stone bleachers and plopped down beside Yasmeen.

"Who was that you were talking to?" Mansur asked wiping some of the sweat from his brow.

"That was Kareem. He said he is in two of your classes. *Theory of Knowledge* and *College Prep* I think he said."

Khalil glanced over his shoulder and watched Kareem mingle with some of the guys from his class. "Ya, he *is* in a couple of our classes, though I have never really spoken to him."

"What did you talk about?" Khalil questioned.

"He was commenting about how well you two played basketball and asked if you were on the team in the States. He thought you played quite well," Yasmeen added.

"Is that all he said?" Mansur asked.

"He asked if I would like to walk around the courtyard with him. I told him that I shouldn't."

"Good. You know what Baba would think," Mansur said. "If you walked around the courtyard together people would think that you were boyfriend and girlfriend and *that* gossip would get back to Baba. You need to be careful," Khalil warned.

"Yes, I know," Yasmeen sighed. Inside she wished it were different. It would be nice to have a friend – a male friend – with whom to talk.

Kareem lay awake for a long time. Images of Yasmeen kept dancing in his mind; he played over and over again what *he had said* and *what she had said;* he remembered her smile, the tone of her voice, and the way the breeze gently brushed her curls. He remembered the smattering of freckles across her nose. She was English-Speaking like him, and *that* mattered as he thought she would better understand what he was feeling – or *so he hoped.*

The next week, Kareem saw Yasmeen at school, and she saw him, but always from a *distance.* They were never in close enough proximity to actually speak. When she sat out in the sun she was always with a group of other English-Speaking girls. If she did stroll around the school yard, it was always in the company of other girls. He wanted to be able to speak to her alone, but he wasn't quite sure how that was to come about.

One lunch break she was not outside sitting on the wall; he looked around, she was not walking in the sun with the other girls. He went into the cafeteria and did not see her. He climbed the stone steps to the second floor and looked through the plate-glass door of the library. There she was sitting alone, and the library was practically empty.

"Why aren't you out in the sun?" he whispered as he pulled out the chair opposite to her. "It's warmer outside than it is in."

Yasmeen looked up from the book she was not really reading and smiled. "I felt like sitting inside today." Yasmeen paused. "What brings you inside?"

"I was looking for you," he boldly said. "I looked for you outside, looked in the cafeteria, and thought just maybe you might be here."

Yasmeen smiled. "Well, you've found me."

Kareem wasn't quite sure what to say. "What book are you reading?"

"Oh, it's a book on Palestinian costume. My *Sitteh* Nijmeh wants to make a *thob* for me – or rather she wants to help me make a *thob* for myself. I am just looking at different designs. If I find one I like, I will Xerox the picture and show it to my *Sitteh.*"

"You should come with your *Sitteh* and mother to visit our village. My *Sitteh* also wears a *thob,* and my mother and aunts wear traditional dresses for weddings and such."

"That would probably be a bit awkward," Yasmeen smiled. "It would be awkward for me to explain to my mother and grandmother why I had been invited to a village to look at dresses, and who had invited me."

"I see what you mean," Kareem laughed. "I can almost hear you trying to explain how a boy from your brothers' class had been sitting with you in the library and had invited you to come to his village to meet his grandmother, mother, and aunts."

"Even in the States," Yasmeen said more seriously, "my father would not approve of me sitting alone with a boy. I look at some of the other girls here and how some of them are free to walk in the courtyard with boys. I would never be allowed such freedom. It is almost ironic that though I was raised in the States and my mother is an American my father is very conservative. It might be because he is from a camp."

"You should see how conservative my father and uncles are with my sisters and female cousins. We boys are allowed a remarkable amount of freedom. We can come and go as we please; we can stay out after dark; we can walk in the street together. My sisters are not permitted to do any of this. It is as though we are socially fifty years behind."

"It sounds like your village is like the camp, Yasmeen added.

"I know it isn't quite *proper*," Kareem said. "But do you think it would be alright if we emailed, or occasionally talked on the phone?"

"I don't know," Yasmeen hesitated. Her mind was telling her one thing; her emotions were prodding her into doing something else. She wrote down her email address on a slip of notepaper and passed it across the scarred library table to Kareem.

Kareem took it, folded it, and slipped it into his wallet. He reached over and pulled Yasmeen's notebook toward him. "Here, this is my email address and my cell phone number," he whispered. "What's your phone number?"

Yasmeen reluctantly gave him her cell phone number and he programmed it into his phone.

"I'll email you," he said as the bell rang and he pushed his chair in.

On the way up the stairs to class, Yasmeen ran into Khalil and Mansur. "Where were you?" Mansur asked. "We looked for you outside and didn't see you."

"I was in the library looking at a book on Palestinian costume. *Sitteh* Nijmeh wants to help me make a *thob,*" Yasmeen said.

"Did you find what you were looking for?" Khalil asked nudging her in the back.

"Yes, I think so," Yasmeen replied thinking of Kareem.

Chapter 18

There is something exciting about a secret, especially when that secret involves rebelling against something forbidden. Yasmeen's English class had been reading Shakespeare's *Romeo and Juliet.* In her adolescent daydreams, she could see herself as *Juliet* and Kareem as *Romeo.* Not that Kareem was the member of a feuding clan. He wasn't. Not that her parents were pressing her into an unwanted marriage. They weren't. Her parents, if they knew, would have nothing against Kareem. Kareem was Moslem; he was from a good family; Kareem was a nice kid. The only problem with Kareem was he was a boy, and she was not permitted to date.

What they were doing could hardly be defined as *dating.* They had slowly fallen into the routine of emailing every day; and had arranged a discreet time when Kareem could call her on her cell: *10:30 at night.* Her parents would be in bed; her brothers would be in their room; Amr, with whom she shared a room, would have been asleep for hours. She would hide the cell phone under her pillow and have it on *vibrate.* At 10:30 every night, Kareem called and they talked – *in whispers. It was so romantic,* Yasmeen thought.

They occasionally sat together in the library; they *never* walked together in the courtyard. They had to be discreet. After all, what they were doing was taboo.

Yasmeen emailed her friend, Molly and told her about Kareem; about the emailing; about the 10:30-phone calls. She was shocked by Molly's response.

Molly had written: *So, are you ever alone with him so you can kiss him? Do you ever make-out? I can't imagine any boys in the States being content with just emailing a girl, or talking to her on the phone. You're going to lose him if you aren't careful.*

Yasmeen typed the words: *What are you suggesting?*

Molly replied instantly. *Arrange some time to see him alone. See what develops. After all, you are almost sixteen. You are not a baby!*

If my brothers or father found out that we were emailing and that Kareem was calling, they would have a fit. What we are doing, in their eyes, is trouble, Yasmeen typed.

You've got to be kidding! It's not like you are having sex!

Yasmeen read the words on the screen and hit the delete key. She went back to the emails she had sent Molly and deleted all those in which Kareem had been mentioned.

When Kareem called that night, she turned off the phone.

The next day in school, Kareem sought her out. He found her in the library.

He pulled out the chair opposite her and sat.

"What's wrong? How come you didn't answer last night?"

Yasmeen looked up, but she didn't meet his eyes. "I don't think we should email anymore or talk on the phone. It's too risky. If my brothers or father found out I would be in big trouble, and so would you."

"We're just talking," Kareem said.

"You *know* it would be exaggerated if people found out," Yasmeen answered for a moment looking directly into his dark eyes. "We can't really talk together at school. We certainly can't walk together in the courtyard, or sit in the sun together. The very fact that we're keeping this to ourselves tells you it is wrong –according to my parents, my siblings, my cousins, and my grandparents, a girl should not spend time with a boy unless there is an understanding they will marry!"

"I understand, but you are half-American," Kareem argued.

"I may be half-American by birth," Yasmeen responded, "but I am *all* camp-Palestinian in the way I was raised. My father may have spent almost eighteen years in the States, but he is camp-Palestinian at heart. Part of the reason he brought us here was so we would not be tempted to date in the States. He didn't want us forming romantic relationships with Americans."

"I have an American passport," Kareem said, "but *I* am *village*-Palestinian. I can understand where your father and brothers are coming from, but I don't think what we are doing is wrong! This is the twenty-first century, things are changing – even here in Palestine. Talking with you is the best part of my day..."

The bell rang. "We haven't finished our conversation," Kareem whispered as he gathered up his books. "Please email me this evening, and let's talk on the phone tonight. *Please!*" He said looking searchingly at Yasmeen.

Yasmeen avoided his eyes but nodded her head.

That same morning, Hasna went to have coffee with her mother.

"*Sabah el kheir* (good morning), *Yum'ma,*" Hasna said as she kissed Nijmeh on both cheeks.

"I finished my work early and wanted to come and have coffee with you. Where is *Mart Issa?*" she asked about her sister-in-law, Yasmeen.

"No school today but she had some errands to run and was going to stop and see her grandmother," Nijmeh answered. "Your father is also out, as is Issa, so we have some time to ourselves."

"Perfect," Hasna smiled as she went into the kitchen to make coffee. "There is something I wanted to talk to you about."

Hasna let the coffee come to a foamy head three times before turning off the flame. She covered the pot with a saucer, and set it – along with two handless cups - on a brass tray.

"Let's sit out here in the sun," Nijmeh said as she moved two stools against the concrete wall of the courtyard. She slipped off her plastic sandals so the sun could warm her crooked toes. "Ah, that's better," she signed.

Hasna poured the steamy coffee into the little cups and passed a cup to her mother.

"What is it you wanted to talk to me about, *binti?*" Nijmeh asked sipping the sugarless coffee.

"It is about my grandson, Imad," she said.

"What about Imad, *habeebee?*" Nijmeh questioned.

"Well, Imad is thinking of getting married," Hasna smiled. "And it is about time too, but there is a problem," she sighed.

Nijmeh looked at her questioningly.

"The problem is that he has made up his mind to ask for the hand of Mohammad's daughter, Yasmeen."

Nijmeh set her coffee cup down on the tray. She smoothed an imagined wrinkle from her embroidered skirt.

"Mohammad will never agree," she finally said. "First, his daughter is just fifteen – much too young to even consider marriage. I know, I know," she said as she saw Hasna about to protest. "You were only seventeen and I was a little over fourteen when I was married. But those were different times. Second, he would never agree because Imad is a cousin. He has been in the States most of his adult life. He thinks marrying cousins is not right. And," she added, "Sarah would *never* agree to such a suggestion. She would want, as does Mohammad I think, for their daughter to go on to college and to choose the man that she marries. You must tell Imad that it is impossible."

"I *have* told him. In fact, I have used some of the same arguments that you have used. He realizes all these things but he counters with the fact that he doesn't want to get married *now;* he is willing to wait until she is eighteen. He is even willing to let her go on to college *after* they are married if that is what she wants. He argues that they are cousins, but not *first* cousins and that the fact her mother is American and not even Arab should count for a better mix for the *bloodline* – I think those were the words he used."

"So, what *does* he want?" Nijmeh asked, not really convinced.

"He wants an *understanding.* By that, he means he wants Mohammad to agree that Yasmeen will be saved for him and that he can occasionally see her and spend time with her as there would be this *understanding.* He wanted me to talk to you and to ask you if *you* would broach the subject with Mohammad."

"Let me think about it," Nijmeh finally answered. "I want to talk to your father about it as well. I wish Mansur or Khalil were around; they would be able to advise me as to what I should do," she said as an afterthought.

"Please don't say anything to Issa or my sister-in-law Yasmeen," Hasna cautioned.

"Of course not, *binti,*" Nijmeh said resting her hand briefly on Hasna's knee. "This is just between the two of us for the moment."

On the way to the village bus, Kareem passed several shops. There were cartons of red, plush teddy bears with white lettering: *Be my Valentine* written on them. It was almost February 14th – Valentine's Day in the States – a custom that was becoming somewhat popular in the city, especially among Friends' School students. He would have loved to have bought one for Yasmeen, but he didn't dare.

Imad also passed the shops with the cartons of red, plush teddy bears. "I bet Yasmeen would like one of these," he thought as he stopped to look at the heap of teddy bears. There were also piles of cheap, red, plush pillows made in China with the words: *I love you* scrawled across the top. He was tempted. But he didn't dare.

"How was your day at school?" Sarah asked as Yasmeen opened the door.

"Aren't you feeling well?" she concernedly asked as she noticed her daughter's pale, drawn face. "You're not coming down with something are you?" she questioned kissing Yasmeen's forehead. "You aren't feverish."

"I guess it was just a long day," Yasmeen smiled hugging her mother. "I'm okay, *really* I am."

"And how is this little guy?" she said as she stooped and picked up Amr. "Did you miss me?" she asked him in Arabic.

When he smiled and nodded his head, she asked him, "How much?"

"This much," he said to her in Arabic as he stretched his arms out. "I love you, this much!"

"And I love you *this* much and *more*," she laughed.

"Where are Khalil and Mansur?" Sarah asked.

"There was a game after school," Yasmeen said. "They told me to tell you that they would be a little late."

Yasmeen turned on the TV and sat Amr down in front of it to watch *Sesame Street* in Arabic.

"I'm going to change my clothes," Yasmeen called to her mother. "Then I will come and set the table for lunch."

As she slipped out of her school uniform and hung it in the closet, she switched on the computer. She had mail. She opened the inbox to find she had an email from Molly, one from Grandma Martha, and one from Kareem.

She was tempted to read it right away but switched off the computer. She would read it tonight when everyone was asleep.

Chapter 19

Amr was finally sleeping; his thumb was loose in his mouth, yet his lips moved slightly in memory as though making sure his thumb was still there. The bedroom was dark except for the light from the computer screen. Yasmeen read, and reread the short note from Kareem before pressing *delete.* She did not respond to his email.

She straightened the blanket covering Amr before slipping into bed. Her cell phone was under her pillow but turned off. Her sleep was restless; she was burdened with dreams of Kareem; in the morning she saw that she had five missed calls – all from Kareem.

It was an unusual February. The almond trees were already in bud and blossom; the rains had been tardy and people were compelled to water their gardens. Mohammad had commented at dinner that the *Imam's* message at that Friday's service had centered on the fact that rain was needed and implored the people to pray for rain.

"He did make reference to *Sura* 30: *He sends down water from the skies and He revives the earth thereby after it is barren. Surely in that are Signs for people who understand,"* Mohammad quoted dipping a piece of pita bread into the *hummus.*

"You certainly *were* listening," Sarah smiled, "weren't you? I'm impressed. You even remembered the *Sura.*"

"I always pay attention," Mohammad grinned.

Sarah just rolled her eyes. "Of course you do *habeebee.*"

"How are you feeling this morning, Yasmeen?" Sarah asked as she filled Yasmeen's cup with sweetened mint tea.

"I'm fine. I think it was just a hard day at school yesterday. I'm okay today."

"Did you see all the Valentine things for sale?" Mansur said.

"You wouldn't think that Valentine's Day would be such a big deal here," Khalil added. "Almost every place you look there are red, plush Teddy bears– all bearing the banner: *Be my Valentine* or *I love you.* There were even Valentine *bunnies* – now how weird is that? Whoever heard of a Valentine *bunny?!*"

"They are all made in China. I even saw a red plush pillow with the phrase, '*I love you*' written on it in Arabic. I think that's the one I'm getting for my girlfriend," Mansur joked.

"What do you mean *your girlfriend?*" Mohammad asked taking the bait.

"I was just checking to be sure you were *paying attention, Baba*" Mansur laughed. "I think that Khalil and I should buy a rose for each of the girls in our class. Just to keep them guessing."

"Buying roses for the girls? Is that something that happens at the Friends?" Sarah inquired.

"Apparently," Khalil added. "The Student Council sells individual roses wrapped in cellophane on Valentine's Day as a fundraiser."

"One of the guys was saying that some girls – the popular girls – get bouquets of flowers."

"I wonder how many bouquets Yasmeen will get," Khalil teased.

"Don't worry, I won't get any," Yasmeen said as she pushed her chair in and lifted Amr from his highchair.

"The only boyfriend I have," she smiled tickling Amr under his arm, "is this little guy."

"And that's the way I want it," Mohammad said as he smiled at his youngest two children. "You still have lots of time before you begin to even *think* of boys. When that time comes, I will pick out just the right boy for you!" he teased.

Yasmeen hugged Amr as she carried him to the bathroom to wash his face. Her attention was not totally on Amr; images of Kareem kept intruding into her thoughts.

"We want to walk to school today," Mansur informed Mohammad.

"Yasmeen, do you want to walk with us?" Khalil asked.

"I think I'd rather have a ride this morning, if that's okay with you, Baba?"

On the way to school, Mansur and Khalil bought a red plastic bucket. It seemed that on every street corner there were vendors selling red roses and red carnations.

"How many girls are in our class?" Mansur asked Khalil.

"Well, there is Ruba, Zeina, Mona, Manal, Ikhlas, Mira, Kareemeh," Khalil said counting them off on his fingers as he named them.

"Don't forget: Hiba, Kholood, Nida and Reem," Mansur said.

"That makes eleven. Plus we should get a flower for each of our female teachers and the librarian," Khalil added.

"We should also get a flower for the two secretaries and for the cleaning lady, Im Mohammad. That brings the number to eighteen. Let's get twenty, just to be on the safe side," Mansur added.

They purchased the flowers from the street vendor on the corner next to the Arab Bank and placed them in the red bucket."

Yasmeen saw Kareem when they lined up outside. He glanced in her direction, and then glanced away.

I've hurt him, Yasmeen thought. It saddened her to think she had hurt him, but *what else could I do?* She thought feeling defensive.

Yasmeen climbed the stairs to the third floor and her homeroom. She was one of the last ones to enter. Some of her classmates were giggling as they looked at her.

"Look what you got," Sawsan said as she pointed to a package on Yasmeen's desk.

Yasmeen looked in the plastic bag and there was a red, plush teddy bear mutely stating: *Be My Valentine.* There was no note, but Yasmeen knew who it was from.

"Who is it from?" Sawsan asked. "You must have a secret admirer!" she giggled.

"How do I know who it's from?" Yasmeen laughed. "Someone is probably just playing a joke on me. I wouldn't put it past my brothers," she said unconvincingly.

The girls in Mansur's and Khalil's class were thrilled to receive a red rose from them. Even the unpopular girls had been remembered. "It was really thoughtful of them to include everyone," Hiba said. "The one thing I really hate about this day is that some girls get lots of flowers, and some girls get none."

As Yasmeen was going out the school gate that afternoon, Mahmoud the guard stopped her. He was from the same camp as her grandparents. "This was dropped off for you this morning," Mahmoud said as he handed Yasmeen a box.

"Thanks, Ammo," Yasmeen said. "Do you know who dropped it off?"

"No, it was a kid that said he had been given five shekels to deliver the box to the school guard -to me," he grinned, "to give to you."

Mohammad was waiting for the kids when school let out.

"How was Valentine's Day?" he joked.

"Khalil and I got flowers for all the girls in our class, all our female teachers, the school secretaries, the librarian, even for Im Mohammad the woman who makes the coffee," Mansur said. "We even have two left over to give to Mama."

"And did you get lots of flowers?" Mohammad asked twisting around so he could look at Yasmeen.

"No, not even one flower," she said. "There are no guys in our class like Khalil and Mansur who thought to bring flowers for all the girls," she smiled nudging Khalil with her shoulder.

"She *did* get a red, plush Teddy bear," Mansur teased. "I wonder who from?"

"You *know* who it is from," she tried to laugh. "It is from you and Khalil."

"It isn't from us. Yasmeen has a secret admirer. That's my guess," Mansur said poking Yasmeen in the arm.

"It's just someone playing a joke. That's all," Yasmeen countered.

"What's in the box?" Mansur asked.

"I don't know. Ammo Mahmoud, the guard, gave it to me just now. He said a boy delivered it to him this morning."

"Open it! Let's see what you got," Khalil said excitedly.

Yasmeen reluctantly broke the string around the box and opened the flaps of the carton. Inside there was another red, plush teddy bear mutely glaring at her with button eyes and asking her to be his *Valentine*.

"It seems you have another secret admirer," Mohammad grimly said.

Yasmeen closed the flaps on the carton and stared out the car window. *Who could have sent the second bear?* She wondered.

Mohammad was *not* amused that Yasmeen had *secret admirers. I should have sent her to an all-girl school* he thought to himself. *She is beautiful. I'm not surprised that she has admirers, but still...I don't like it.*

Sarah could read his thoughts. "I know you aren't happy about those Valentine bears. It is an adolescent gesture. It is natural that boys will like Yasmeen. There *is* no dating here, and you can trust our daughter." Sarah said as Mohammad brushed his teeth in preparation for bed. "I remember being fifteen. It seemed at that age that *all* I thought about was boys. Yasmeen probably thinks about going to dances, holding hands with a boy, *and dating,* but she knows that isn't allowed. Yasmeen is a good kid."

"I know," he said having gargled and rinsed the spit down the drain. "Still, it is hard for me to realize that we have a daughter who is attracting the attention of boys. And when you were fifteen," he paused as he screwed the cap onto the toothpaste tube and placed the tube in the vanity, "that guy you went to dances with, held hands with and dated was *Sam!*"

"Yes, unfortunately, it was," Sarah said soberly. "Sam at sixteen was not the Sam he was at twenty-four. There are jerks everywhere," Sarah sighed.

Sarah pulled back the bedspread and folded it neatly at the foot of the bed. "Your own mother was married by the time she was Yasmeen's age and pregnant with your brother, Mansur."

"Those were different times," Mohammad said switching off the bathroom light. "Yasmeen is still a child!"

"Your mother and grandmother were also just *children*," Sarah said kissing his shoulder but people looked at them as being ready for marriage. People don't look at Yasmeen in the same way. She will finish high school, go on to college, *inshallah* (God willing)– perhaps even graduate school before she even *thinks* about marriage."

"From your mouth to Allah's ears," Mohammad joked kissing her behind the ear and pointing a finger toward heaven. "That reminds me, I *do* have something for you this Valentine's Day!"

He opened the closet door and took a heart-shaped box from off the shelf. "Belgium chocolate," he smiled, "for MY Valentine!"

"Sarah smiled and kissed him on the lips. "Under all that gruffness there is a born romantic. You are just a boy at heart," she laughed.

"I may be a boy at heart, but I am a *man* where it counts," he laughed.

Chapter 20

Nijmeh *did* talk to Omar about their great grandson Imad's desire to have an *understanding* about Yasmeen.

Her head rested in its familiar place on Omar's chest. The bristles of his impressive white mustache grazed the top of her white hair; his breath gently moved the strands.

"Hasna came to see me a few days ago," Nijmeh said against his chest. "Her grandson, Imad, wants us to talk to Mohammad about Yasmeen."

"What do you mean *about Yasmeen?*" Omar questioned as he peered down into her upturned face.

"He is interested in eventually having Yasmeen as his wife," Nijmeh continued. "He knows she is too young at the moment and he is willing to wait until she is eighteen. However, he wants to have an *understanding* from now – so that Yasmeen will be *saved* for him."

"Mohammad and Sarah will never agree to such a thing," Omar said as he rubbed Nijmeh's shoulder. "Times are not like they were. Many girls want to finish school, go on to college, and choose their own husbands. They certainly won't agree to an *understanding* when they are only fifteen. Mohammad didn't marry the girl you had picked out for him, nor did Mansur. Imad forgets that Yasmeen's mother is

American. She would never agree. He is foolish to think that she would."

"Hasna says he is adamant. He says he will allow her to go on to college if that is what she wants, but he *wants* an *understanding* now."

Omar paused and licked the tips of his mustache. "He is saying this now, but once they were married he would expect her to act like one of the girls who were raised in the camp. He has never been to America. Yasmeen spent the first fifteen years of her life in America. His English is not good. He would not understand her, and she would not understand him."

"I agree. Both Mohammad and Mansur met their wives while living abroad. Both Zaleena and Sarah were in their twenties – not fifteen. Both Mansur and Mohammad had experience in their future wife's world. It would be different for Imad and Yasmeen." Nijmeh paused, absently stroking Omar's chest. "Imad is ready for marriage, but he should choose a girl from among us – a girl from the camp. Issa and Yasmeen's daughter, Jamileh, would be more suitable."

"He may be like me," Omar chuckled as he hugged Nijmeh to him, "once he has seen the girl he wants to marry, no other will do. You were not even fifteen when I first saw you at the well," Omar said as he gently kissed her.

Yasmeen lay awake for a long time. Her room was illuminated by the soft golden glow of light from a street lamp. She could make out the shapes of the two plush teddy bears as they sat sentinel – one in each corner of Amr's crib. *I wonder who gave me the second one,* she thought. *Surely Kareem didn't buy two bears!*

Kareem, too, lay awake. His brother, Hakam, was snoring; their brother Shareef was curled into a ball, though one leg dangled over the side of the bed. *I wish she would send me a message,* he thought. *She had to know that the Valentine teddy-bear was from me.* He punched her number into his cell phone and before it could ring, he hit the cancel key. *I need to give her some time. I **know** she feels the same about me that I do about her.*

Imad also lay awake. He tossed; he turned; he punched his pillow; first he lay on his side, then on his stomach, finally on his back. He stared at the naked light bulb that swung – ever so slightly – just above his head on its frayed cord. *She won't know that the Valentine bear is from me. I should have left a note. How will I let her know how I feel?*

"I will talk to Mohammad," Omar said as he slurped his morning coffee. "I will only sound him out," he quickly added seeing the look of protest in Nijmeh's eyes. "I will only tell him that there have been inquiries about Yasmeen. I won't mention Imad."

172

Nijmeh drew up a stool next to Omar. "Perhaps you are right. Once you have spoken with him, I will relay what he says to Hasna."

When Mohammad and Sarah dropped Amr off for the day, Omar was waiting for him. "*Yaba,* there is something I wish to discuss with you," Omar said. "I will be working all day in Abu Jamil's olive grove repairing the *sin'slee* (stone wall). You remember where Abu Jamil's olive grove is? I will be there at lunch time. You get an hour for lunch, why don't you come and have lunch with me? I will have your mother pack some of the *ma'toot'ta* she made yesterday."

"Alright, *Yaba.* It sounds serious," Mohammad said looking keenly into his father's eyes.

"It's nothing serious, *Yaba.* I just want your opinion," Omar smiled patting Mohammad's head as Mohammad bent to kiss his hand.

"What did your father want?" Sarah asked when Mohammad got back in the car.

"There's something he wants to talk to me about. So, we have a lunch date," Mohammad smiled.

"He has even tempted me with some of *Im'me's ma'toot'ta* –those delicious loaves of bread she makes seasoned with olive oil and *yansoon.* That's *anise,*" he said to Sarah's unasked question.

At 12:10 Mohammad was winding his way up the hillside to where he could see Omar repairing the stone wall.

"It's a perfect day, *Yaba,* for this kind of work. It is still cold inside, but here the sun is warm," he said sitting down on the low stone wall.

Omar unwrapped the loaves of *ma'toot'ta* that Nijmeh had wrapped in a piece of old muslin sheeting. He poured fragrant Arabic coffee from a thermos into two handle-less cups handing one to Mohammad.

Mohammad carefully balanced the cup on the stone wall and tore off a hunk of the *yansoon* seasoned bread. "What did you want to talk to me about, *Yaba?*"

"There have been inquiries about Yasmeen," Omar said as he plopped a piece of bread into his mouth.

"What kind of inquiries," Mohammad said. "Surely *not* inquires about *marriage?!* She's only fifteen!"

"Fifteen *is* young," Omar said sipping his coffee. "When your mother and grandmother were fifteen, they were already married, but that was another time. Girls were expected to marry young and take up the responsibilities of caring for a husband, children and a mother-in-law. Fifteen today is much too young. I realize that."

"I bet it is someone who wants an Arab girl who has an American passport," Mohammad said. "A ticket to the US," Mohammad muttered.

"No, nothing was mentioned about her passport. The boy saw her and thinks she would make a suitable wife."

"Yasmeen is still in high school. And then there is college and probably graduate school," Mohammad said. "I won't even consider offers of marriage until she is finished with college."

"Do you want her to marry an Arab?" Omar asked tearing off another piece of bread.

"Of course I want her to marry an Arab. That is part of the reason that Sarah and I brought the children here. I don't want Yasmeen, or her brothers for that matter, marrying a foreigner."

"Yet, *you* married a foreigner. Your brother Mansur married a foreigner. Why would you object to your children marrying foreigners?"

"That's different. Both Mansur and I were lucky. Zaleena and Sarah are exceptions. Even in the States, Sarah was in agreement with the restrictions I placed on the children. She wanted to bring the children here as much as I did. She would *want* the children to marry someone from here – but not at *fifteen!* To that, she would never agree."

"So, when Yasmeen is finished with college, you would still expect to *pick out* a suitable husband?" Omar asked brushing some of the bread crumbs from his mustache.

"*Wanting* and *doing* are two different things," Mohammad smiled. "I would *want* to choose a suitable husband, but Yasmeen, like Sarah, has a mind of her own. Once she is finished with college, I am not sure I will have much to say about whom she marries – even though I might want to."

Omar poured more coffee from the thermos into Mohammad's cup. "How would you feel about her marrying a distant cousin?"

Mohammad looked at his father. "*Has* a *cousin* asked about Yasmeen?"

"I am just asking *what if?*" Omar replied. "None of the immediate family has married cousins. Oh, I suppose it could be stretched a bit to say that Issa's wife, Yasmeen, is a distant relative as she is from the same clan, but she is not a first, second, or even a third cousin. Your sisters did not marry cousins, your mother and I are only distantly related; your *Sitteh* Hasna did not marry a cousin, and *her* mother and father were not even from the same village. But lots of people *do* marry first cousins. The Quran approves of such marriages."

"I would never agree for Yasmeen to marry a cousin. I think if the question ever arose that Sarah would be adamantly opposed. In this day and age, it is frowned upon as being genetically inadvisable."

Mohammad glanced at his watch. "I need to get back to work."

As Mohammad wound his way back to the road and his car he *knew* that a cousin had asked about Yasmeen. *And I think I know who it is,* he thought to himself.

Chapter 21

If Yasmeen had had even a *hint* that her Aunt Hasna had talked to her *Sitteh* Nijmeh, that her *Sitteh* Nijmeh and talked to her *Sidi* Omar, that her *Sidi* Omar had talked to her father, she would have been enraged and had campaigned to be sent back to live with her Grandma Martha and Grandpa Ken immediately! Fortunately, she knew nothing about the conversations.

Mohammad *did* tell Sarah about the talk he had had with his father. She listened intently before commenting.

"It *does* sound like someone from the family has made inquiries about Yasmeen. It does sound, from what you have said, that everyone is on the same page: Yasmeen is too young; Yasmeen is going to go to college, God willing; and that times have changed and early marriages – even marriages when the girl is eighteen – are frowned upon; definitely marriages between cousins!"

Sarah paused and smiled at Mohammad. "You gave all the appropriate answers, *habeebee*. I think you were quite candid with your father."

"I knew that people would find Yasmeen attractive, but I am still a little shocked that someone would think that we would sanction an *understanding* of this sort when she is only fifteen."

"I am glad you said *'we'*," Sarah said taking his hand. "I know you would like Yasmeen to marry an Arab, and frankly – I'm a bit surprised with myself – so would I. But it is still a long time away, and ultimately, whoever she marries is up to her. The final decision is hers. *Isn't it?*" She challenged Mohammad.

"Of course, the final decision is hers *habeeptee*. After all, she is *your* daughter," Mohammad said choosing to keep his eyes on the road.

"Who do you think has asked about Yasmeen?"

"I suspect it is Hasna's grandson, Imad. He is twenty, no longer in high school. He graduated from the trade school in Deir Debwan and is working with his father and grandfather. He is at the right age to think of marriage. Yasmeen did have that encounter with him when he rescued her from that boy in the camp who was hassling her; he has turned up here at mealtime a couple of times. He's a nice kid, but I don't want him to think that there could be an *understanding* between us and him about Yasmeen."

"Are you going to talk to him about it?" Sarah asked.

"Not directly. I don't want it to be an issue. He will get the word. My father will tell my mother; *Im'me* will inform Hasna, and Hasna will tell him. What we can do when he is over is have Yasmeen busy herself with Amr, or homework, or helping you in the kitchen so that she has very limited contact with him."

"I suspect that second Valentine teddy-bear that Yasmeen received through the guard at the gate is probably from him," Sarah added. "I *do* wonder though who gave her the first bear. She must have a special friend at school. I don't want to pry, but I think I will have a talk with her."

Mohammad drew Sarah into his arms and adjusted the blanket. "You know, it was so much simpler in the old days. The groom never saw the bride; the bride never saw the groom until he lifted her veils with his sword."

"What do you mean *with his sword?*" Sarah asked incredulously lifting her head from its place on Mohammad's chest.

"You know the stories my mother told about *her* wedding night and that of *Sitteh* Hasna. She used to joke that the only part of my father she had seen before the wedding were his toes! And when he lifted her veil with the traditional wedding sword, she really saw him for the first time. And as for *Sitteh* Hasna – she had never even seen my grandfather, or he her, until the wedding night when he lifted her veils with a sword. All he had requested of his mother was a *blue-eyed girl with red hair!* It was really *so much simpler"* Mohammad joked. *"*There was that element of *surprise – gee, who did I get?"*

"I'm surprised that *you* didn't opt for that too, my fine Arab *sheik,"* Sarah teased tickling him under his arms.

"Alas, when I first saw you I was a goner," Mohammad sighed. "I couldn't imagine being married to anyone else. I *suppose that possibility* was the reason my parents were hesitant about me studying in the States," he teased back. "They had seen what happened to Mansur and didn't want the same *fate* for me."

"*Fate,* was it?" Sarah said in mock seriousness.

"Yes, my *hourieh,* you were written into my life and I was consequently *fated* to be with you. Such is my life," Mohammad tried to convincingly sigh. "What could I *do* but marry you?"

"You poor boy you," Sarah smiled. "You certainly got a *raw* deal, didn't you?"

Mohammad smiled. "I must have racked up some pretty good points to be blessed with a wife like you."

The next morning at the office, when Sarah was taking a coffee break, Sarah sent her Aunt Martha an email. She reiterated the conversation between Mohammad and his father only adding two personal comments.

*Despite the drama, I am somewhat relieved that we have removed Yasmeen and the boys from American high school environment. (I have just typed that, and it does seem strange to me that **I** have typed this! Who would have thought that I would ever feel this way!)*

I look at teenagers in the States dealing with peer pressure; drugs, pre-marital sex, teenage pregnancies, sexually transmitted diseases and I must admit that it scares me. At the moment – here seems safer!

Sarah checked her email just before she left work. There was an email, as she had expected, from her Aunt Martha.

"Dear Sarah,

I am still somewhat in shock. I can't believe that in this day-and-age a twenty-year-old cousin would be asking about Yasmeen! You know I haven't completely agreed with you and Mohammad about not allowing the children to date, but what you have written is hard for me to get my mind around. It seems so <u>natural</u> for young folks to go to parties together, to pair off, and to date! You did it. I did it. It is all part of growing up and getting experience before choosing a partner.

It seems so foreign to me that Mansur, Khalil, and Yasmeen would not be allowed to date – considering the ages they are. Of course, you would not want them experimenting with sex, but one can date and not have sex! What's wrong with holding hands or a good-night kiss?

I do agree with you that things can be too 'casual'. But then, I think they probably always have been somewhat 'casual.' Your grandmother used to joke that 'there were just as many babies made in the back of a buggy as there were in the back of a Packard.' Not that I am advocating this! But it seems to me that there should be some middle ground. You don't want to be too conservative with the children. After all, they are adolescents and half-American. This is the time they are supposed to have experience with the opposite sex so they can best judge the kind of person they wish to marry. They are good kids. I think you could expect them to make good choices.

Your Uncle Ken is just coming in from the barn, so I best get lunch on the table.

Give my love to Mohammad and the kids.

Love ya, Aunt Martha

PS. You know that if Yasmeen ever wanted to run away and come here, we'd help her! (I'm smiling here, love.)

Sarah logged off, pushed in her chair, picked up her purse and joined Mohammad who was waiting in the car.

"I just read an email from Aunt Martha," Sarah said sliding into the passenger seat. "She sends her love. She also said that if Yasmeen ever wants to run off to the States that she'll send the ticket!"

"I gather you wrote her about the talk with my father," Mohammad said as he backed out of the parking space.

"Yes, she wrote she was having *a hard time getting her brain around the idea* of someone being interested in Yasmeen. She disagrees with our policy of not allowing the children to date but does understand where we are coming from. She thinks that there must be a *middle ground* between the *casual* dating of the States and our strict *conservative* stance."

"Do you agree with her?"

"I have to give it more thought. But at the moment I tend to believe that it is better to be *safe* than *sorry*. We have really great kids, and they have good heads on their shoulders. I think they are fine the way they are at the moment. I don't want them getting caught up in serious relationships at this age," Sarah said glancing over at Mohammad. "I *am* becoming very conservative! I *never* thought *I* would be this way!" Sarah said in disbelief.

"You're the mother of teenagers, *habeeptee*," Mohammad smiled reaching over and squeezing her hand. "It was so much easier when they were Amr's age," he chuckled.

Chapter 22

It was amazing how the thoughtfulness of Khalil and Mansur in passing out red Valentine roses to all the girls in class, all their female teachers, the school secretaries, the librarian and the cleaning lady affected their popularity! They could easily have tied for president if there had been a Student council election, and been voted by their class the *Most Popular, Most Likely to Succeed, Best Dressed,* and *Handsomest* in the Yearbook page designated for Juniors, *if* it had been up to the female students.

The male students were not so impressed (though they did respect the twins' skills on the basketball court and the soccer field.)

All in all, the twins were feeling pretty good about themselves at the moment

"Who would have thought a bucketful of roses would have this effect?" Mansur said.

"Don't forget our *innate* charm and good looks," Khalil joked.

Yasmeen came up to her brothers as they walked in the courtyard and inserted herself between them. She slipped a hand into the crook of Khalil's and Mansur's arms. "I thought I would walk with the two most popular boys in school," she laughed.

"And absorb some of our popularity by association?" Mansur smiled.

"You are pretty popular yourself, *habeeptee*," Khalil said pressing Yasmeen's hand that rested in the crook of his arm. "I don't recall seeing any of the girls – even the most popular girls - with *two* red plush teddy bears."

"You're *sure* you don't know who they are from?" Mansur teased.

"Both anonymous," Yasmeen lightly replied.

"You're sure one wasn't from Kareem?" Mansur pointedly asked.

"Kareem is in *your* class, not mine," Yasmeen answered. "Why would he be giving me a Valentine bear?"

"I think he likes you," Khalil said. "I've noticed the way he sometimes looks in your direction when he thinks no one is watching. I've seen him sitting with you a couple of times in the library," he warned.

"Look, I can't help if he sits at the same library table," Yasmeen said feeling defensive. "I've done nothing wrong. I need to get ready for class," she said disengaging her hands from her brothers' arms. "See you after school."

"Maybe we should have a *talk* with Kareem," Mansur said. "We don't want him bothering Yasmeen. She seemed upset. She's probably worried about getting a reputation. You remember what Khaldoon said about his older sister, how she was caught in an empty classroom *talking* to a boy. All innocent stuff – but when the rumor got back to their village – the family that had asked for her hand withdrew their request. No one wanted her. It was that old *where there's smoke there's fire* bunk. Khaldoon says she is now working in the States in her father's clothing store and that no one is ever going to ask for her."

"I guess a girl can't be too careful," Khalil soberly said. "Especially an English-speaking girl with an American mother," he added. "People are more likely to judge her behavior. I sometimes think that the Arabic-speaking girls have it a bit easier. Customs have changed here. But, kids like us who were raised in the States are brought up old fashioned- the way it was here in Palestine forty years ago. Jeez, Baba has always been stricter with us *because* we were raised in the States. It is almost like he is trying to prove something."

"Yasmeen is lucky that she has the two of us to look out for her," Mansur said. "We better keep a closer eye on Kareem. I would bet my last quarter he gave her the teddy bear."

"And I'd bet the second bear came from our cousin, Imad," Khalil said perceptively. "You saw the way he kept looking at her when he *just happened* to come by at lunch time."

"But Imad is *twenty!* Why would he be interested in Yasmeen?" Mansur asked in astonishment.

"Well, she's pretty and smart. She has a lot going for her."

Mansur looked over and caught sight of Yasmeen's back as she walked through the lower-level door. "You're right; we *do need* to protect her."

Later that afternoon, just before they were ready to sit down to a late lunch at home, the doorbell rang. Khalil went to open it and there stood Imad.

"*Ahlan wa sahlan* Imad, you're just in time for lunch. Mama has made *mu'sa'khen.*" (Grilled chicken served on a bed of onions and bread)

"My father asked me to deliver the side table you ordered," Imad said nodding toward the table he held in his hands.

"Come in, come in. You must stay for lunch," Mohammad said coming to the door and putting his hand on Imad's shoulder. "That is a fine piece of work," he commented running his hand over the polished surface of the table. "Put it down over there, right next to the sofa. Perfect. I'll stop in tomorrow and pay your father."

"Please, *Khali.* Let it be our housewarming gift," Imad said.

"No, that is most kind of you, but I insist. I will stop and see your father tomorrow. You must stay for lunch."

"I've already set a place for you," Sarah said.

"Thank you, *Mart Khali,*" Imad smiled pulling out a chair.

Sarah and Yasmeen placed plates of *mu'sa'khen* before Mohammad, Imad, Khalil, and Mansur.

"Aren't you going to join us, *Mart Khali?*" Imad asked.

"This is such a messy dish that Yasmeen and I are going to feed Amr in the kitchen," Sarah smiled. *Mu'sa'khen* must be eaten with your hands, and Amr makes such a mess that we don't want to feed him here in the dining room. Enjoy your meal."

Imad was disappointed that Yasmeen wouldn't be eating with them. In his own home, especially when there were guests, it was normal for the men to eat first and the women did not sit with them. But this was the first time that it had happened in his uncle's house.

When the empty plates were taken way and the fruit brought in, it was Sarah who cleared the table and brought in the fruit.

"Let's have coffee in the sitting room," Mohammad smiled getting up and pushing his chair away from the table. "We can admire this lovely new table," he joked.

It was Sarah who brought in the tray of coffee.

This is the way it would be at home, Imad thought. *My sisters would not bring in the coffee if there was a young male relative visiting. I thought with Khali Mohammad it would be different.*

When Imad left, Yasmeen asked Sarah why they had eaten in the kitchen and why she hadn't served the coffee as she would normally have done.

"I'm trying to be more considerate of the customs," Sarah smiled at her daughter. "I was noticing that when Khalil and Mansur are visiting your *Sitteh* and *Sidi*, your *Amto* Yasmeen doesn't allow Jamileh to serve the coffee or sit with your brothers. I don't want your cousin, Imad to get the wrong impression."

"You think it was Imad who sent me the Valentine teddy bear, don't you?" Yasmeen challenged.

"I don't know that he did, but I do think that he is intrigued by you. Why wouldn't he be?" Sarah said impulsively hugging Yasmeen. "But he is *twenty* and you are fifteen. We don't want to give him false hope. He *may* assume that because you were raised in the States and are new to the culture here, that we are less – *concerned* – perhaps that's the word I am looking for. I think in the future," Sarah said rinsing off the dishes in the sink, "whenever Imad is here – and we *do* want him to come and visit – that it is best if you take Amr to your room to play, or do your homework, or busy yourself here in the kitchen."

"I understand," Yasmeen said as she filled the sink with hot soapy water and began to wash the dishes. *Imad. I can't believe it,* she thought to herself. *What would my family do if they knew about Kareem? I must be careful!*

When Yasmeen had finished her homework, she turned on the computer to check her email. She had five new messages: there was one from Molly, one from Grandpa Ken, one from Grandma Martha, even one from Grandpa Dave, and one from Kareem.

She opened the one from Kareem, read through it several times then deleted it.

She didn't respond. *I will see him, but only briefly, tomorrow in school. What I have to say to him is better said in person.*

That night she shut her cell phone off and put it in the drawer of her desk. Her sleep was troubled. She kept dreaming of Kareem, then of Imad, then of Kareem again. In one dream she saw her parents and brothers pointing accusing fingers at her.

Finally, she got up and switched on the lamp beside the bed. She picked up the novel by Hawthorne that she was reading for an oral book report. She moved the scrap of notebook paper that she had been using as a bookmark. She read the passage where Hester sewed the scarlet letter to her bodice. *Oh brother,* she thought, *I can't believe this! Even seventeenth-century literature is warning me!*

Chapter 23

The next morning, after Mohammad and Sarah had dropped off the older kids at school, Khalil and Mansur slipped out of the lower gate. There was no guard there. They walked toward the bus station near the school to wait for Kareem. They had asked around and knew which bus he took.

They didn't have long to wait. Kareem was the third person to step off the bus.

"We've been waiting for you," Mansur said as he smiled and put his hand on Kareem's shoulder as though they were friends.

"We need to have a little *talk* before school starts," Khalil said putting his hand on Kareem's other shoulder and guiding him towards the alley.

"What's this all about?" Kareem asked as he pulled away from their hands.

""We don't want to talk about it right here," Mansur said. "Come with us."

Kareem reluctantly followed them. The alley adjacent to the bus station was deserted and the stores were still shuttered. It was too early for anyone to be there.

"We want you to stay away from our sister," Mansur warned as he got in Kareem's face and pushed him up against a stone wall.

"What do you mean *stay away* from your sister? I don't hang around your sister," Kareem stated as he pushed back against Mansur. "Stand back," he warned as his hands became fists.

"We've seen you sitting with her in the library and we've seen the way you look at her," Khalil replied leaning his shoulder against Kareem's.

"What about the *bear?*" Mansur said. "We *know* it was you who gave her the stuffed bear."

"I *said* BACK OFF*!*" Kareem shouted pushing both boys away.

Mansur grabbed the front of Kareem's shirt and twisted it. Kareem raised his fist and punched him square in the eye. "Two against one is it!?" Kareem shouted as he turned toward Khalil.

Khalil and Mansur both rushed him and started hitting him in the stomach with their fists. What they had wanted to be just *words* turned into shirt ripping, blood dripping, and fists pumping.

Kareem was strong. He was a wrestler. He had been in a lot of fights. (A village boy had to prove early on that he could stand up for himself.) Kareem *could* stand up for himself.

In no time, all three of the boys were on the ground. Taxi drivers at the taxi stand across from the shops saw the fight and rushed over to break it up.

The boys were pulled apart. Their shirts were torn; their eyes were blackened; their lips were split. They panted as they glared at one another.

"You boys shake hands," an elderly taxi driver said.

The boys refused. Mansur even spat on the ground. "I'll not shake hands with the likes of him."

"Remember what we told you," Khalil said as he licked the blood from his lip already feeling guilty.

Two men had to hold Kareem back as he tried to lunge at the twins again.

Khalil and Mansur slipped into school through the lower gate; Kareem entered through the front.

"What happened to you?" the guard asked.

"A little *difference of opinion,*" Kareem said wiping at the blood that spattered his shirt. "It's nothing to worry about."

"You should go to the office and have the secretary look at that eye," Mahmoud said.

"I'm fine. I'll go to the washroom and clean up a bit." Kareem said as he tucked his torn shirt into his school trousers.

The three boys were in the same homeroom. Ms. Rahman took one look at them and promptly sent them to the school office.

There they sat: Mansur, Khalil, and Kareem waiting for the principal. They didn't look at each other.

The secretary looked up from her desk, replaced the phone's receiver, and said. "The principal will see you now."

The three stood before the principal's desk, their hands behind their backs, and stared at the pattern on the stone tiles.

"Look at me," the principal said. "It is obvious that the three of you have been in a fight. I am assuming *with each other.*" He paused, waiting for the boys to say something.

"That's true, isn't it? You three were fighting with each other?"

Khalil, Mansur, and Kareem only nodded.

"Would you care to tell me *what* the fight was about?"

Silence.

Finally, Kareem spoke. "It was just a misunderstanding – at best a *difference of opinion.*"

"A *difference of opinion?*" the principal repeated making an arch with his fingertips.

"We had a point to make, and we made it," Mansur said glaring at Kareem.

"We weren't fighting on school grounds," Khalil added.

"I should suspend you three for fighting, but, as you said, *the fight did not occur on school grounds.* But let me caution you, I will be calling your parents, and if this happens again – even off school property – I *will* suspend you."

As the boys turned to leave his office, the principal added, "It isn't exactly *fair* two against one, is it?"

"They knew it would take *two* of them," Kareem muttered under his breath. "I gave better than I got."

"One-on-one *can* be arranged," both Mansur and Khalil whispered back, though their consciences pricked them; two against one *wasn't* fair. They didn't like themselves at that moment. What they had intended to be just a *talk* – a warning at best - had turned into a display of teenage macho-ism.

Yasmeen passed Kareem on the way to her first class. She was shocked by the way he looked. "What happened to you?" she said stopping Kareem in the hall.

"Ask your brothers," was all Kareem said as he moved around her.

All during first, second, and third periods, Yasmeen waited to confront Khalil and Mansur during recess. She was also hoping to talk to Kareem.

They twins were sitting together on the stone bench that faced the basketball court feeling remorseful. That was where she found them. Both had a blackened left eye. Khalil's lower lip was split, and there was a cut above Mansur's right eyebrow.

"What did you do!?" Yasmeen accused. "I passed Kareem in the hall. He looks as bad as you two. When I asked him what had happened, he said to: *ask my brothers!*"

"We thought we needed to *talk* to him before school; it got out of hand. We didn't mean for it to become a knock-down-drag-out fight. We just wanted to *talk* to him. We know he's the one who gave you that bear." Mansur was unsuccessfully trying to justify their actions to ease their sense of guilt.

"Oh, I see," Yasmeen said sarcastically, "he *needed* to be taught a lesson and you two took it upon yourselves to be the teachers. I am to *understand* that you think I cannot take care of myself and that I *need* my two older brothers to *protect* me from someone you *suspect* gave me a stuffed bear? Do you realize how *stupid* that sounds? You were afraid that people would talk – so what do you do – *you go out of your way to make me the center of attention.* Don't you think the school is already buzzing with the news? *'Yasmeen's brothers and Kareem had a fight over Yasmeen. They must be boyfriend and girlfriend.'*"

Khalil and Mansur had the decency to look sheepish. "We just meant to look out for you," Mansur mumbled.

"I'm really disappointed in you. This is so *unlike you.* I've always looked up to you two. But right now, I am ashamed," Yasmeen said as she looked with eyes bright with unshed tears at the two brothers she adored. She turned around and walked away.

"We probably didn't handle that as well as we could have," Khalil said to Mansur. "We shouldn't have pushed him around and used our fists, even though he *did* hit us first. Yasmeen has a right to be angry," he said as he looked at his bruised knuckles.

Yasmeen searched the school campus and finally saw Kareem, sitting alone, on the steps of the Science Building.

She went up and sat beside him on the top step. "I want to apologize for my brothers," she started.

"You have nothing to apologize for," Kareem said studying the gravel in the path. "I probably would have done the same thing if it were *my sister*. They are just concerned about your reputation. I *do* understand that."

"I know they meant well," Yasmeen admitted. "But, it was still *wrong* – especially two of them against one!"

"You saw the way they looked," Kareem said trying to smile. "I gave as good as I got."

"I *like* you," Yasmeen said hesitantly, "but here –to *like* a boy - as a *friend* - is not really allowed. My parents wouldn't approve; my brothers pretend they don't understand it, though secretly probably wish they had your nerve. It would be misunderstood for me to talk with you or sit with you in the library. Part of the reason our parents brought us here is so we *wouldn't* be distracted by boyfriends and girlfriends." She paused and looked at Kareem, I know they don't want me, or my brothers for that matter, dating, but that didn't give my brothers the right to hit you."

"Is *that* what we have?" Kareem said looking intently into Yasmeen's eyes. "Are we boyfriend and girlfriend?"

Yasmeen looked back for just an instant. "It feels like it," she whispered so softly that Kareem wasn't sure he had heard her.

"Anyway, I *wanted* to tell you that we shouldn't email each other or talk on the phone," Yasmeen said as she got up from the step and brushed off the back of her school trousers. "That was what I *resolved* last night to tell you, but after the fight with my brothers this morning, I have changed my mind. I'd *like* it if we emailed – only delete my emails after you read them, as I do with yours. I won't call you, but I would *like* it if you called me. I won't sit with you in the library, or speak to you in the halls. I'll purposely avoid you. This will make my brothers think they have won, and will hopefully dampen any rumors that they created today. I realize this is a bit deceptive, but I like you and I would like it if we could be friends."

Kareem smiled, feeling his swollen lip with the tip of his tongue. "The bear *was* from me."

"Yes, I know," Yasmeen said briefly smiling at him.

Chapter 24

"So, what is this about you and Kareem?" Nadia asked as she leaned against Yasmeen's desk. "Having your brothers *defend your honor* is quite impressive."

"I don't know what you mean," Yasmeen calmly replied. "They certainly weren't *defending my honor*. They had some personal issue with Kareem I guess. It really has nothing to do with me," she lied.

"The rumor is that they saw you sitting with Kareem in the library and they think he is your boyfriend."

"That's absurd! I can't help where Kareem chooses to sit. He is certainly *not* my boyfriend."

"I saw you sitting with him on the Science Building steps," Nadia probed.

"Yes, you did. I had heard the same rumors you had, and sought Kareem out to apologize for my brothers."

"So, there is *nothing* between you? You can tell me, I can keep a secret," Nadia said hopefully, crossing her heart and hoping to die.

"There is nothing to tell, though I *will* let you in on a little secret; I *do* have a *friend* in the States – an *American* friend to whom I write."

"Your secret is safe with me," Nadia said already mentally making a list of whom she would tell.

Yes, I have an American friend to whom I write and her name is Molly, Yasmeen said to herself as she watched Nadia whispering in Hala's ear.

It was a grim Mohammad and Sarah who picked up the kids from school.

"I had a call from your principal this morning," Mohammad said surveying his sons' battered faces in his rearview mirror. "I can *see* you have been in a fight again."

"We had a *minor* encounter with one of our classmates. It's really no big deal," Mansur said.

"It was just a misunderstanding," Khalil offered. "Everything has been resolved."

"And the only way to deal with this *misunderstanding* was to use your fists?" Sarah looked back at them.

"We didn't fight on school grounds," Mansur said defensively. "We had promised we wouldn't, and we didn't."

"So, am I correct to assume that this involved your sister?" Mohammad questioned, trying to remain calm.

"Indirectly," Mansur said. "We mistakenly *assumed* that one of the boys in our class was sweet on her," he lied.

"I want to be sure I fully understand," Mohammed carefully enunciated. "This boy was *not* interested in Yasmeen?"

"No, we were wrong," Mansur continued embroidering the lie.

"So, the *two* of you attacked an innocent boy?" Mohammad said as his anger grew. "Do you think that *two* against one is fair?"

"We weren't thinking," Khalil mumbled. "To be fair, it did take the *two* of us. He is one strong SOB – *dude*," he hurriedly corrected himself as Sarah turned around to glare at him.

"Did you apologize?" Sarah asked.

"*I* apologized for them," Yasmeen said. "I went up to him on campus and apologized. It took all of three minutes."

"Do you *know* this boy?" Mohammad questioned.

"He sat at the same table in the library once while I was looking at a book on Palestinian costume." Yasmeen looked at Sarah. "He seemed nice. He mentioned that you and *Sitteh* should go and visit his mother and grandmother in their village. Apparently, they still wear embroidered dresses and have lots of patterns," she said lightly.

"And that is the extent of your contact?" Sarah questioned looking at her daughter.

"I *know* what you and Baba expect. That is the extent of our school contact. Thanks to Khalil and Mansur's actions today, people *think* that there is something more going on. There isn't."

Mohammad looked annoyed. "Well, for fighting – even though it was off campus – you two will relinquish your cell phone and computer privileges for three days. And I expect you two to apologize to this boy. Maybe we should drive out to his village."

"That isn't necessary," both Khalil and Mansur hurriedly said. "We'll apologize tomorrow."

"And as for you, Yasmeen, you are to have no contact with this boy at school. That will be the best way to put a stop to any rumors," Mohammad said as he caught his daughter's eye in the rearview mirror.

"I promise," Yasmeen truthfully said meeting his eyes in the mirror. "I will avoid him at school."

From that day on, Kareem called Yasmeen every night promptly at 10:30. Yasmeen anxiously waited for his calls. In the days and weeks their friendship blossomed, but to see them at school, no one would know it.

It was about this time that Sarah became acquainted with Basim.

Sarah liked to shop for fruits and vegetables in the *hisbeh* – the open-air market. Though it was obvious that she was foreign; she looked foreign and spoke fractured Arabic, she was friendly and kind and frequented the same vendors who came to know her and consequently gave her the *same* price they gave non-foreigners.

Sarah was watching the vendor weigh tomatoes. The scale was perfectly balanced, and yet he reached over and put another tomato in the bag."

"Why did you do that?" Sarah asked him in Arabic. "Allah says we will be measured by how we measure. I always put *just* one more in the bag. I know Allah is watching," the vendor laughed.

"May Allah bless your hands," Sarah smiled taking the bag from him.

Just then, one of the many boys who push grocery carts through the market stopped to ask if he could carry her purchases for her – of course for a price.

"I'll deliver them to your car, or take them to your house if it isn't too far," he smiled.

"Thank you," Sarah said placing her purchases in his cart. "What's your name?"

"I'm Basim," he smiled.

Basim was slight of build, spoke in a rather high-pitched voice for a boy, and had all-too-obvious feminine gestures.

"How old are you, Basim?" Sarah inquired as they wove their way between the crowded stalls.

"I am sixteen," he smiled as he swerved the cart out of the way of another cart, ignoring the comment that the pusher of the other cart hurled his way.

"Don't you go to school?" Sarah asked as she put potatoes into a plastic bag.

"No, *Khalti* (Auntie/ma'am)." My mother is a widow and I need to work. I have four younger sisters at home."

Sarah and Basim continued to carry on a one-sided, question-answer conversation as Sarah made her purchases and filled the cart.

"The car is just over there," Sarah pointed as they exited the *hisbeh*. Basim maneuvered the cart across two streets and parked it in front of the trunk to Sarah's car. Sarah opened the driver's door and released the lever that opened the trunk.

Basim dutifully placed her bags inside. "There you go, Khalti. That will be five shekels, if you please."

Sarah reached into her change purse and took out a ten-shekel coin. "Thank you, Basim," she said handing him the coin.

"I'm sorry, I don't have change, Khalti," Basim apologized.

"I don't want any change," Sarah smiled, "the rest is for you.

"*Shukran*. Thank you. I'm always here, Khalti," Basim smiled. "When you come again, I will be only too pleased to carry your bundles. If you want to shop for bread, or to go to the grocer's, I can follow you there as well," he said eagerly.

"I'll remember that," Sarah said. "Instead of calling me Khalti, you can call me Im Khalil."

"Thank you, Im Khalil."

As Sarah got in the car, adjusted the mirror, and maneuvered into traffic, she glanced back at the boy Basim. He was standing with one hand resting against his hip, one hand resting on the handle of the grocery cart. He seemed to sigh as he flipped his dark bangs out of his eye with a slender hand.

"How sad," Sarah thought. "No father, no school, having to work for five shekels here and five shekels there. And looking like he looks, he must get teased a lot. The boy, Basim, had touched her heart.

Basim hated being the way he was. He had to *consciously* think about the gestures he made, the way he walked, the way he talked. He wished that he was like the other boys, but he wasn't. *They* knew it, and *he* knew it.

He was picked on all the time. As he was pushing his cart through the different stalls, he tried *not* to hear the comments and the kissing noises from some of the other grocery-cart boys. They called him *girlie,* and *homo* – it was interesting some of the English words they had picked up from films. He hated the bus ride home to the camp. Invariably, a big, husky guy would sit next to him and rub up against him. He always attempted to sit next to an old lady, but it was not always possible.

If it had been possible, he wished he was *anyone* else.

Im Khalil was nice, he thought. *I wonder if it is because she is foreign. I wonder what it would be like to have a mother like her.*

Chapter 25

Imad had listened to his grandmother's comments about his proposal to have an *understanding* about Yasmeen but her words did not change his mind. That day at Friday prayers as he knelt and faced East with his head touching the mosque's worn carpet, he *thought* he heard the angel, Gabriel himself, whisper into his ear: *she is written into your life.*

Imad only half-listened to the Imam's sermon. Thoughts of Yasmeen and the *message* he thought he had received from one of Allah's angels married in his mind. *I will speak to Khali Mohammad today,* he said to himself with unshakeable resolve.

After the Friday mid-day meal, he called his uncle.

"*Khali* Mohammad, *Salam aleikum.* This is Imad*.*"

"*Aleikum as' salaam, Imad,*" Mohammad responded.

"*Khali,* if you are free, I would like to take you out for coffee. There is something I want to discuss with you."

Mohammad hesitated. He could guess what Imad wished to speak to him about. "Why don't you come to the house, *Khali?* We can have coffee there."

"Please *Khali,* I'd really like to take you out for coffee," Imad said hopefully.

"Alright, *Khali,* if that is what you would prefer. Why don't I pick you up at the entrance to the camp in about twenty minutes?"

"*Shukran Khali.* Thank you. I'll be waiting. *Salam aleikum.*

"*Aleikum salam.*"

"Who was that on the phone?" Sarah asked.

"It was Imad. He wants me to meet him for coffee. There is something he wishes to discuss with me in private."

"I suspect it is about Yasmeen," Sarah sighed. "What are you going to say to him?"

"I will tell him the things we have discussed. *I had hoped* that after Hasna spoke to him there wouldn't have been the need for this conversation. It is not *always* good to have things out in the open. It is bound to be awkward now, and is guaranteed to be awkward later."

Imad was standing at the entrance to the camp when Mohammad pulled the car to a stop next to him. They smiled and shook hands as Imad slid into the seat on the passenger's side.

"Thanks for meeting with me, *Khali.*"

"No problem," Mohammad said as he drove the relatively short distance to a hotel coffee shop that catered to tourists and thus was open on Fridays.

The waiter took their order and five minutes later returned with two cups of Arabic coffee *Osman'ee'ye* (Turkish-style) with just a little sugar.

"What's on your mind, *Khali?*"

Imad rubbed his sweaty palms against the pant legs of his jeans, cleared his throat, and looking his uncle in the eye began:

"You can probably guess what this is about. *Sitteh* Hasna told me what you said to Sidi Omar. She had given me the same arguments when I first talked to her about the subject. I know I should be listening, but..."

Mohammad started to interrupt, but Imad waved his hand in the air.

"Please let me finish, *Khali*. I'd like you to hear my side before you say anything."

Imad's coffee was untouched. He moistened his lips and continued.

"Everything you said is true: I am twenty years old; Yasmeen is only fifteen; we do come from very different worlds; my English is not so good, and I am a cousin. But the fact is, ever since I laid eyes on her, I believe that she has been *written into my life*. Today at Friday prayers, I *heard* the angel, Gabriel himself, whisper in my ear that your daughter has been *written into my heart*."

Again Mohammad started to say something, and Imad put up his hand to silence him.

"Please *Khali*. I am willing to wait for her until she graduates from high school. I am willing to allow her to go to college if that is what she wants. I am even willing to immigrate and live in the States if that would make her happy. Her happiness would be my primary concern. There is nothing I wouldn't do for her. All I am asking is a chance for her to get to know me – of course in the presence of her family – and hopefully, after she gets to know me a little, we could arrive at an *understanding*."

Imad looked hopefully at his uncle.

Mohammad toyed with his coffee cup, trying to think how to best phrase his thoughts.

"Imad, I am honored that you feel about Yasmeen as you do. She couldn't ask for someone better. You are a respectable, thoughtful young man. I don't doubt your determination – in fact, I admire that in spite of all that has been said, you are still convinced about how you feel."

Mohammad took a sip of his coffee.

"I don't want to repeat what has already been said to you."

Mohammad took another sip of coffee.

"Your Aunt Sarah and I feel quite strongly about cousins – even distant cousins – marrying. The reasons it was done in the past are no longer valid. Genetically speaking, it is not wise."

"But we are *not* close relatives, *Khali*. And the fact that *Mart Khali*, Sarah is an *American'nee'ya* is an important factor," Imad asserted.

"I like you, Imad. The points you raised today are all reasonably thought out, but I know my daughter. Yasmeen, if she *knew* we were having this conversation, would be appalled and rebellious. Your Aunt Sarah would never agree, and frankly, neither could I. In a different situation – if you weren't my sister's grandson – I would be honored with your proposal. If there weren't these blood ties between us ..."

"*I* am not acceptable," Imad sadly said. "I still think that *if* Yasmeen got to know me, the fact that we are distant cousins wouldn't matter. I know lots of first cousins who have married, and there has never been any genetic problem. The only couples I know where there have been children born deaf, or blind, or retarded is where there has been a history of intermarriage: the couple are cousins; their parents were cousins, and their grandparents were cousins. This is not the case here."

Mohammad listened and felt Imad's pain.

"I wish it were different, *Khali*, but it is not. You need to forget about having any *understanding* concerning Yasmeen. I am truly sorry."

"At least *think* about it, *Khali*. If someone had told you that you couldn't marry *Mart Khali* Sarah, would you have listened?"

Mohammad reluctantly smiled. "Of course I wouldn't have, but the situation was different. Your Aunt Sarah and I were not related, and we both wanted to marry."

"All I am asking, *Khali,* is that you *think* about it. *Think* about allowing Yasmeen and me the opportunity to get to know each other – not alone of course, but with you or *Mart Khali* or her brothers around. If, after getting to know me a bit, Yasmeen wouldn't dream of our eventually being together, I will remove myself from the picture," Imad pleaded looking expectantly, hopefully, at his uncle.

"Let me *think* about it, *Khali.* I'm *not* going to change my mind. I *don't* want to give you false hope, but I will *think* about what you said."

Mohammad took the last sip of his coffee. It was cold and some of the sludge at the bottom touched his lips. He hated feeling that he had somewhat *given in.* It was wrong to give Imad even this slender thread of hope, but he couldn't bear the disappointment in the boy's eyes. It was postponing the inevitable, but perhaps it was *kinder* to let him down gradually.

It's funny how old ways of dealing with unpleasant situations come back to you, he thought. *A person is already dead, and what do you tell the relatives when they call? 'He isn't too good, I think it will probably be tonight; you need to prepare yourselves'. There is this innate compulsion to soft-pedal bad news. You especially don't want to disappoint people you care about. I care about Imad, but I care more about Yasmeen.*

Mohammad dropped Imad off at the entrance to the camp. Returning to the house he threw the car keys in the brass dish on the table just inside the front door.

"So, how did it go?" Sarah asked.

"It was as we expected. He gave all the same arguments, adding only that he would be willing to immigrate to the States if that is what Yasmeen wanted."

"And what did you say?" Sarah inquired looking intently into Mohammad's eyes.

"I only stressed that we would never agree to a marriage between cousins because of the possible genetic problems; that since he *is* my grandnephew, that we would not even consider such an alliance. I tried to soft-pedal it..."

"Did he accept that?" Sarah asked taking a seat beside Mohammad on the sofa and tucking her legs beneath her skirt.

"No," Mohammad sighed. "He wants us to *think* about allowing Yasmeen to get to know him a bit – always in a chaperoned situation – and says that *if* after they get to know each other Yasmeen is unwilling, he will withdraw his request."

"And what did *you* say?" Sarah asked already *guessing* what he had said.

"I said that I wouldn't be changing my mind, *but* that I *would think* about it," Mohammad said guiltily. "I couldn't help it," he hurried to say taking Sarah's hand. "I know it was cowardly, but he looked so disappointed."

"You *are* a coward," Sarah said as she leaned over and touched her lips to his. "About some things you are an old softy. I like Imad too, but giving him even a little bit of hope is not going to make things any easier in the long run."

"Guess what I just heard," Khalil excitedly said to Mansur.

"I overheard Mama and Baba talking; our cousin Imad in *interested* in marrying Yasmeen!"

"You've got to be kidding!"

"Nope, Baba went and had coffee with him and he was reporting back to Mama what was said."

"Yasmeen would never agree; Mama and Baba would never agree!"

"They aren't agreeing. But Baba wants to let Imad down gradually."

"I wonder if we should say something to Yasmeen."

Chapter 26

Yasmeen kissed the blonde curls on Amr's head. He was nestled in her arms and intently looked at the pictures of the book she was reading. Though she, Khalil and Mansur *only* spoke to Amr in Arabic, they did *read* to him in English.

She closed the book on the smiling little train that *knew he could* and *did.*

"Kaman," (another one) Amr said looking at her lovingly and patting her cheek. *'Bess, wahad,"* he implored lifting one finger.

"Okay, *habeebee. Bess wahad* (just one more)." Yasmeen smiled as she hugged him and picked up another storybook.

By the time she had closed the book, Amr's eyelids were heavy and his long, blonde lashes fluttered against his cheeks like butterfly wings.

He was soon fast asleep in her arms.

Yasmeen hugged him close and began to tell him a story in English. She knew he was asleep; she knew he wouldn't understand even if he had been awake. She desperately *wanted* to tell someone.

"Once upon a time, not so very long ago, a girl of just fifteen – a girl very much like me -thought that she was in love. It had happened oh so gradually." Yasmeen situated Amr in her arms so his head was pillowed against her breast.

"The boy was not so very tall, but he had black raven curls, dark black eyes that seemed to sparkle when he smiled, and he was very, very strong. He was so strong that he could take on two boys at once." Amr stirred in his sleep and moved his hand so he could slip his well-sucked thumb into his mouth.

"He would write this girl every day and call her every night. It was like butterflies dancing in her stomach when – promptly at 10:30 - the phone under her pillow silently vibrated. At school, she had to *pretend* she didn't even *see* him, but she could *feel* when she passed him in the hall, and *sense* when he was in the courtyard."

Yasmeen adjusted Amr in her arms.

"She had never kissed him or even *held* his hand. Yet she *knew* she loved him."

There was a gentle knock at the door. Mansur turned the handle and ducked his head in the door.

"I'm glad you are still up. Khalil and I have something to tell you. Can we come in?"

Yasmeen smiled and nodded.

"Here, let me take that little guy from you and put him in his crib," Khalil said lifting the sleeping Amr onto his shoulder.

Amr nestled his head in the crook of Khalil's shoulder and automatically wrapped his arm around his neck. Khalil turned his head slightly and kissed his curls.

Mansur had removed the quilt from Amr's crib so Khalil could put him down. He drew the quilt up to Amr's shoulders, and bending over the railing, kissed the top of his head.

Yasmeen drew her feet up so her brothers could sit at the foot of her bed.

She waited expectantly.

"We weren't sure we should tell you but decided you have the right to know."

"Know what?"

"I overheard Baba telling Mama that *Amti* Hasna's grandson, Imad, is interested in you."

"What?" Yasmeen said in a startled voice. "He has to be twenty years old. He's a *cousin!*"

"Baba and Mama *aren't* considering his proposal. They know he is too old and they would never agree to you marrying a cousin."

"I'm not agreeing to marry anyone. I'm *fifteen!* I won't marry a cousin, and frankly, it is *my* business whom I marry, not Baba's and Mama's."

"Baba and Mama would agree with you. Imad has asked that they *think* about allowing you to get to know him. Baba wants to *let him down* gradually."

"I wish we had never come here," Yasmeen said. "I *knew* something like this would happen. It's *not* okay to *date,* but it *is* okay to get married!"

"They *aren't* saying that," Mansur said trying to soothe her anger. "I think they are as surprised as you are but are trying to be extra sensitive because Imad *is* a relative."

"Oh brother, what am I going to do?"

"We think you should talk to Baba and Mama."

"But how will I explain where I got the information?"

"It's okay to tell them that I overheard their conversation and told you," Khalil bravely said.

"I don't want to get you in trouble. Why don't *you* and Mansur go to Baba and Mama and tell them you accidentally overheard their conversation and think it is a bad idea to even *think* about allowing me to sit with Imad. It is perfectly natural for *brothers* to express their opinions over affairs concerning their sisters – as you so aptly proved when you thought that boy, Kareem, was interested in me."

Both Mansur and Khalil sheepishly smiled. "We admit that we over-reacted there. Maybe you're right. It *would* be better coming from us. You can pretend you don't know."

"I think Yasmeen is right," Khalil said to Mansur. "*We'll* tell Baba and Mama."

The boys got off the foot of the bed and headed to the door.

Mansur turned and smiled sardonically at Yasmeen. "Now, why couldn't you have worn glasses, had acne, been overweight and plain? Maybe then we wouldn't have to worry about a twenty-year-old cousin drooling over you and anonymous boys giving you teddy bears."

"Maybe we'll have to fight Imad, too," Khalil chuckled.

The next afternoon, after a late lunch, Khalil said, "Yasmeen, why don't you take Amr into the kitchen? We want to talk with Baba and Mama."

Both Mohammad and Sarah looked at the twins in surprise.

"It sounds ominous," Mohammad said raising his eyebrows and pouring another cup of coffee.

Sarah lifted her cup so he could refill it.

"So, what is this about?" she asked.

"Well," Khalil said as he searched for the words. "I happened to overhear your conversation yesterday about *Amti* Hasna's grandson, Imad."

"Were you eavesdropping?" Mohammad said frowning.

"Not intentionally," Khalil hastened to add. "I had gone to the kitchen for a coke and happened to hear Yasmeen's and Imad's names. I listened only for a couple of minutes. I know I shouldn't have – but I did."

"And you have an *opinion* I presume?" Sarah said.

"Yes," Mansur said entering the conversation. "We think that you should be straight with Imad and tell him that you won't even *think* about his proposal. It really isn't fair to give him hope when you know that no one, especially Yasmeen, would ever agree to it."

"And, we are to assume," Mohammad said trying not to smile, "that by *no one* you mean you two?"

"That's right," both Khalil and Mansur bravely said. "Yasmeen is our sister, and *we* would never agree to her marrying a cousin. It is really up to *her* whom she marries." Khalil looked questioningly at his father, "Isn't it?"

"Of course that time is a long way off," Sarah added. "And of course it will be her decision, as it will be yours when the time comes."

"We don't think that Imad should be permitted to sit with Yasmeen."

"So, you two have decided what your mother and I should do, have you?"

"We *know* you feel as we do, and we don't want you to think we are telling you what to do. We just wanted you to know that you have *our* support."

"Well, that's very good to know," Mohammad said trying to keep the smile out of his voice. "A father needs to know he has the support of his sons."

Khalil and Mansur both pushed their chairs back from the table. "That's all we wanted to say. We need to get started on our homework."

"*I am* sorry about the eavesdropping," Khalil said. "I promise it won't happen again."

"See that it doesn't. I will have to *think* about an appropriate punishment," Mohammad said at last not hiding his smile.

The boys walked through the kitchen on their way to their room. Both patted Yasmeen on the back as they passed her. "You were right; it *was* better coming from us. I think Baba is going to be straight with Imad."

They overheard their father laughingly telling their mother, "You've got to love those two!"

Chapter 27

Nijmeh slipped her arm into Sarah's as they walked toward the cemetery. "I'm so glad you are with me," she said to Sarah in Arabic. "I come once a year, always on the anniversary of Ahmad's death. It has been over thirty years. I *still* see him as the ten-year-old boy he was."

When they reached the low stone wall surrounding the Moslem cemetery, Sarah took a silk scarf out of her coat pocket and covered her hair. Nijmeh stopped at the entrance to the graveyard and raising her hands, whispered the prayer for blessing on the dead.

They wound their way among the graves until they came to Ahmad's gravesite. Nijmeh stooped down and brushed away the pine needles that had accumulated on top of the stone. Once again, she raised her hands toward heaven and whispered a prayer. As she finished she passed the palms of her hands over her face.

"You know the story, I am sure, of Ahmad and Khalil and how their grandmother, *Sitteh* Hasna, gave two-year-old Mohammad to the grieving Khalil to look after. Khalil was always like a father to Mohammad. The years that Khalil was in prison, Mohammad would wear one of his shirts to bed every night, *habeebee,*" Nijmeh smiled wiping the tears of memory from her eyes.

"Mohammad still feels about Khalil as a son feels about his father," Sarah said putting an arm around Nijmeh. "The bond between them is still very strong."

"*Illhumdillah*," Nijmeh smiled. "It is a blessing when brothers are close."

"I read once," Sarah said as they sought out *Sitteh* Hasna's grave, "that when one visits the graves it is like bringing *trays of light* to the deceased."

"Trays of light," Nijmeh repeated, "I *like* that. I *like* to think I have brought a tray of light to Ahmad and *Sitteh* Hasna.

"You know that *Sitteh* Hasna was more than my mother-in-law; she was my mother and my friend. I loved her dearly. What a wonderful storyteller she was, and how she could *scold*!" Nijmeh laughed.

Nijmeh continued to hold onto Sarah's arm as they walked out the exit and down the path toward the camp.

"I've wanted to talk to you, *binti*," Nijmeh said. "I am so glad that your Arabic is now strong enough to understand me," she smiled squeezing Sarah's arm.

"I know that Mohammad has told you about Hasna's grandson, Imad. Often one only *sees* with the eyes and doesn't really *see* with the heart. They are *too* different.

"He thinks they would be happy together," she continued. "They would not." Nijmeh paused and turned so she was facing Sarah. "Abu Omar has spoken with

Imad and told him there is no hope. I think he finally understands."

"You are very wise, *Mart Ammie,* thank you," Sarah said giving Nijmeh a hug.

This time Sarah took Nijmeh's arm. "I thought you all would be agreeable to an eventual marriage between Imad and Yasmeen."

"I want them both to be happy, and they would *not* be happy together. It is like when I thought Mohammad shouldn't marry you but should marry the girl I had picked for him. Once I met you, I knew that the two of you were *meant* to be together. Your Yasmeen, *habeeptee,* would not be right for Imad, nor he, for her.

"People have a better chance at happiness when they marry their own kind," she added as she stepped over the threshold into her courtyard. Of course, some are kindred spirits even when they come from different backgrounds; like you and Mohammad, Mansur and Zaleena," she smiled.

"So, who would be Yasmeen's kind?" Sarah asked, curious as to what her mother-in-law would say.

"Someone who is like her; a Palestinian Moslem who has been raised in the States as a child. Wouldn't it be grand *if* he had an *American* mother too?" Nijmeh smiled, her eyes twinkling, "And an old *Sitteh* who lived in a camp?"

Sarah looked at her watch. "We still have time for coffee before Mohammad comes to pick us up. I have something to show you – I had almost forgotten. You will be so excited."

Issa's wife Yasmeen came into the courtyard carrying Amr. "You are just in time for coffee," she smiled handing Amr to Sarah. "What will we be excited about?"

Sarah hugged Amr briefly before putting him down. "Go and play for a few minutes, *habeebee,* while Mama has coffee.*"*

Nijmeh had already arranged four stools in the last patch of sun hitting the courtyard wall.

"Set the tray down here, *binti,"* Nijmeh said to Issa's wife. *"Shu'kran sal'lem edaike, (*May Allah bless your hands)*"*

"What do you have to show us," Yasmeen asked eagerly. "We can't wait."

"It is this," Sarah said taking a manila envelope out of her bag. "One of my colleagues at work found a pamphlet when she was going through the agency's old files. The pamphlet was from 1948 and contained a number of pictures of refugees. She thought I would be interested in seeing the brochure since Mohammad's parents were 1948 refugees. I was skimming through the pictures when I turned to *this one!"* Sarah said drawing out of the envelope the enlarged print she had made from the photo.

She handed the print to Nijmeh. In the photo was a young refugee man. He was wearing an *umbaz* and had a *kuffiyeh* on his head that didn't quite cover his curly hair. He had a dark, shaggy mustache and was holding in his arms a curly-haired infant less than a year old. He was unsmiling; standing in front of a tent; his ill-fitting shoes were heavy with mud. He was handsome and looked like Mohammad had when he had been a boy, and very much like the twins looked now!

"Why *it's* Omar and Mansur!" Nijmeh said in disbelief. "This must have been taken that day I first went to work as a maid. Omar was so unhappy. A woman never worked outside her own home, but there was no work for the men, and we women could find jobs cleaning."

"I was just a little older than your Yasmeen," Nijmeh said wiping the tears that gently fell with the back of her hand. Abu Mansur was only a little older than the twins." She paused as she kept running her hands over the glossy print as though erasing the years and touching the cheeks of her young husband and infant son. She raised the print to her lips and gently kissed them as they had been.

"A lifetime ago," she sighed. "Mansur was the only one of our children born before we fled our village," she added knowing that her daughters-in-law knew this. "And now he is a grandfather! How the years roll on," she sighed.

Yasmeen took the picture and studied the image of her father-in-law. "His sons all certainly look like him, don't they?"

"Even his *grandsons* are handsome like him," Sarah added.

"This is a real treasure," Nijmeh tried to smile through trembling lips. "May I keep this?"

"Of course, it is for you, *Mart Ammie*. I brought you a frame for it too," she said drawing a picture frame out of her bag. "I thought you might like to hang it on the wall with the other photos."

"Thank you, *habeeptee*" Nijmeh smiled taking the frame. "I will save this for another picture – perhaps you have a picture of the children? This picture," she said again running the tips of her fingers over the image, "this picture I will keep in a safe place where I alone can look at it. It brings back so many memories that I have kept locked away in my heart. Memories of my mother and sisters, of Omar's father and brothers – of all those people who are no more, of a village we will never see again."

"I am so sorry, *Mart Ammie*. I wasn't thinking. I was so taken with how much Mohammad and the boys look like *Ammie* that I didn't dream how painful it might be for *you!*" Sarah could feel her eyes filling with tears. "How thoughtless I have been."

"Don't be *sorry, binti*. No, I *am glad* to have this photo. It is *good* to remember those we have loved. It is good to see how young and handsome my Omar was," she smiled at last and touched Sarah's knee with her work-worn hand.

"What do you have there?" Omar asked as he came in the door.

Nijmeh handed him the photo.

"Ah, I remember this. A foreigner was snapping pictures. I didn't want my photo taken, but he took it anyway. This was taken on the day you first went to work in the city. I didn't want my *shame* pictured!"

Omar chuckled as he addressed his daughters-in-law. "This was the first time that a woman in our family had ever worked outside the home, and I thought by allowing Im Mansur to go I was less a man. How young and foolish I was – though *quite handsome,* don't you think?" He said winking at them.

"You are *still* handsome, *Ammie!*" Sarah and Yasmeen laughed. "Your sons and grandsons get their good looks from you, *mashallah.*"

"It just proves the old saying," Nijmeh smiled at Omar, further lightening the mood, "that I loved you more than you loved me!"

Sarah and Yasmeen both burst out laughing when Omar said, "And *who* do our daughters look like, the *jee'ran* (neighbors)?"

That evening Sarah told Mohammad about his mother's reaction to the picture.

"Our association with the picture is naturally different than hers. For us, it is an interesting bit of history. It has captured a moment in the youth of my father. For us, it is interesting to see how his sons and grandsons resemble him. For *Im'me* it has captured some of the horrible pain of being uprooted from her village, the death of their neighbors and families, the terrible uncertainty into which they were thrust." Mohammad paused and took Sarah's hand. "I can understand her not wanting the picture framed and hung with the others, but you have given her a very valuable *gift*. She can look at that picture and remember more clearly all those she has loved and look back and see: *there was where they started* and *here is where they are.*"

"What do you mean?"

"My parents survived! They had ten children; their sons have all been educated and are professionals; their daughters have all made good marriages; they have dozens of grandchildren and great-grandchildren; their family survived!"

Mohammad continued holding Sarah's hand. "In many ways, the picture is a picture of *hope* that no matter what happens: *it will all be well in the end.*"

Chapter 28

Sarah couldn't seem to get the boy, Basim, out of her mind. She had told Mohammad about him.

"I really feel sorry for him. I wish there was something we could do to help him."

"What could we possibly do? We can't change the way he is. We can't change the way people will treat him. There is little tolerance in our society for boys who are like you say he appears to be."

"Even in the West," Mohammad added, "where there *is* more tolerance for people who are different – people like that are not truly accepted by their families."

"I can't believe you said that."

"It's true. Think about the small town in which you grew up. Did you know anyone who was *openly* gay?"

Sarah had to admit that she hadn't.

"It was only after you went to college and began to see a variety of people that you really came into contact with openly gay individuals. Here, it is *just* not accepted. People tend to look at it as they did in the West fifty years ago – a *sickness* that could perhaps be treated with hormone therapy, or *prison*. In cities like Amman, men, who are like this boy seems to be, are stigmatized as prostitutes."

"*Prostitutes?!* You've got to be kidding!"

"I recently heard of a young man – openly gay – who tried to cross the bridge into Jordan and was turned back on the Jordanian side. He was told *Amman already had too many prostitutes and didn't need any more.*"

"Where did you hear that story?"

"Someone from work was talking about it."

"That only seems like one more reason that we should help this boy."

"What *kind of help* do you have in mind?"

"Maybe we could pay for him to attend a trade school. Surely he can do something more than push a grocery cart through the *hisbeh.*"

"He needs, as you said, to support his family. Are you suggesting that we also support them while he is in a trade school?"

"We *could.* Doesn't the Quran state that it is one's *personal responsibility* to help those who need help? It could be part of the *zakat* (alms) that we give every year."

"You really feel quite strongly about this, don't you?"

"There was just *something* about that boy that touched me. I really can't explain it. He's about the same age as our children, and he is working to support his mother and sisters by pushing a grocery cart through the market! We can afford to help him, and we should!

Doesn't God put into our path the people we are *meant* to help?" Sarah said smiling.

"You have really thought this through," Mohammad smiled back. "Okay, you win. The next time you go to the market I'll go with you, and if the boy is there, I'll have a talk with him. If after talking to him I am as convinced as you, we will see what we can do to help him."

"That's all I want. You can judge for yourself."

Sarah leaned over and kissed him, "I am so glad that I married you."

"It's because I'm a *pushover,*" Mohammad teased. "Isn't it?"

Three days later on their trip to the *hisbeh,* Sarah ran into Basim. As soon as he spotted her he wove his cart between the shoppers, venders, and other boys pushing grocery carts.

'Im Khalil! Can I help you today?"

"Yes, Basim. I was hoping to run into you. I need to make the rounds and buy fruits and vegetables. I also want to go to the bakery and get some bread; swing by the butcher's and also the chicken place for chicken and eggs, and the place that sells fish. I've parked the car in the parking lot right across from the old *Hashameya* School. Do you know where that is?"

"Yes, Im Khalil," Basim smiled.

They carried on a running dialogue as Sarah made her purchases. Basim was quick to advise her. *Don't buy from that vendor, Im Khalil. He cheats foreigners. The vendor three booths up has better bananas than those, Im Khalil.* Whenever she made a purchase, Basim was quick to take it from her and place it in the grocery cart.

He waited patiently outside the butcher shop while she made her purchase, taking the packages of meat from her and depositing them in the cart. It was the same at the bakery and the place that sold chicken. Basim waited patiently on the sidewalk in front of each shop.

At last, when she had finished the purchase of three kilos of fish fillets from Denmark, he walked sedately behind her to the parking lot across from the old *Hashemeya* School.

"That's my car over there," Sarah pointed to a white vehicle with UN painted on the side. "That's my husband, Mohammad, waiting for us. I was telling him about you and he wanted to meet you."

"You told him about me?" Basim halted. "Why does he want to talk to me?"

"There's nothing to worry about," Sarah smiled. "Come; it's alright."

Basim hesitated, but he pushed the grocery cart to the back of the car.

Mohammad had opened the rear doors so Basim could place the various packages inside.

"How much do we owe you?" Mohammad asked.

"I charge 10 shekels, Ammo, for going to other places besides the *hisbeh* and delivering the groceries to the parking lot."

"Seems very reasonable," Mohammad said handing Basim a ten-shekel coin.

"I wanted to talk to you for a moment if I might," Mohammad said.

Basim didn't know what to say.

"We can go and get a cold drink if you like." Mohammad offered.

Basim just shook his head.

"I understand from Im Khalil that your mother is a widow and that you are taking care of her and your sisters. Is that right?"

Again Basim just nodded his head. He was clearly uncomfortable.

"If you don't mind me asking, *Ammo,* how much money do you usually make a day?"

"It depends," Basim said softly, "on how many customers I have. There are lots of boys with carts in the *hisbeh.* Sometimes, on a good day, I can make 50 shekels. Most days it is not that much."

"And that is enough for you, your mother and sisters to live on?"

Basim just nodded his head; his eyes not meeting Mohammad's.

"I gather that you don't go to school because you have to work?"

Again, there was just a slight movement of his head.

"How far did you get in school?" Mohammad asked.

"I finished ninth grade."

Mohammad looked over at Sarah.

"Im Khalil and I would like to arrange for you to go to the trade school in Deir Debwan. They offer a two-year program in training boys to be metal workers, electricians, plumbers, carpenters. At the end of the two-year program, the boy sits for the government *tawjihi* exam and the school arranges for employment of its graduates."

"I can't go to a trade school, Ammo. I need to support my family. How would they live while I was going to school? I wouldn't have the money to pay to go to a trade school. I wouldn't even have the money for a seat in a taxi to go to Deir Debwan every day."

"I know of agencies which would supply the tuition for the trade school, give you 50 shekels a day with which to support your family, and also enough each week to cover the cost of taking a seat in a taxi."

Sarah looked at Mohammad questioningly when he mentioned *agencies*.

"Why would you do this for me?" Basim asked, trying to keep his eyes from tearing. "I am no one to you."

Mohammad reached out and put his hand on Basim's shoulder.

"Our three older children are just about your age. Im Khalil likes you and thinks you have potential. It is something we would really like to arrange. Think about it."

Basim looked away and blinked his eyes rapidly to remove the tears. He pressed his lips together to stop their quivering.

"I don't know what to say?" he mumbled. "No one has ever been so kind to me." He finally looked Mohammad and Sarah in the face.

"Are you sure you want to help someone like me?"

Both Sarah and Mohammad smiled and nodded.

"Think about it, Ammo," Mohammad said. "And tomorrow at this time, I will be here for your answer. If you decide that you want to do this, you can take me to meet your mother and I will talk over with her what we are suggesting."

"Thank you Abu Khalil," Basim said.

"By the way, Ammo, where do you live?"

"I live in the camp just south of town."

"Yes, I know that camp," Mohammad said. He didn't tell Basim that it was the same camp *he* was from. "And what is your family name?"

"I am Basim Ibn Naseef."

"Until tomorrow then, Basim Ibn Naseef."

"So what do you think," Sarah asked as Mohammad drove out of the parking lot and headed toward their apartment.

"He seems like a nice kid. It is interesting that we are from the same camp. I will ask my father indirectly about him. If he does decide to accept the offer, I will go to the training school in Deir Debwan and talk to the principal – tell him a bit about Basim."

"Why did you say you knew an *agency* that would help him?"

"He will feel better if he thinks the money is coming from an anonymous agency than if he thinks it is coming from us."

Chapter 29

"Yes, I know of Basim Ibn Naseef," Omar said. "His father, *Allah yer'hum'o,* has been dead for about two years I think. The boy has no uncles, no older brothers, and no male cousins. There is just Basim, his mother, and four younger sisters. The boy has suffered because he has had no male role model."

Mohammad took another sip of his coffee. He and his father were sitting on a pallet on the courtyard tiles, their backs against the concrete wall, enjoying the last of the afternoon sun.

"If you have seen the boy, you know what I am talking about," Omar said wiping some of the wet coffee from his mustache. "Unfortunately, his father was very much like Basim. I can remember the father as a boy. I think he and your brother, Khalil, were in the same class in school."

Omar took another sip of coffee. "The boy has *never* had someone in his life to teach him *how* to be a man. Why the interest in him?"

"Sarah met him at the *hisbeh* and something about Basim touched her. She felt sorry for him, and thought we should indirectly help him."

"Help him, how?"

"Sarah thinks that he should be taught a trade and not just push a grocery cart through the market. She was touched by how kind and thoughtful he was; impressed that he was working to support his mother and sisters, and thinks that we should arrange for him to go to the trade school in Deir Debwan."

"And what do you think?"

"I met the boy yesterday. I think he *should* be taught a trade. As far as *the other,* there is nothing we can do about that." Mohammad drank the last of his coffee and set the cup down on the sun-warmed tiles. "What do you know of his mother?"

"That you will have to ask your mother about. I think she knows her. Nijmeh!" Omar called.

Nijmeh came wiping her hands on her apron.

"You know Im Basim, don't you?"

"*Mean* (who is) Im Basim?"

"Im Basim Ibn Naseef. Her son works in the *hisbeh.*"

"Ah, that Im Basim. Yes, I know her. Why?"

"Mohammad is interested in helping her son and wants to know something about his mother."

Nijmeh pulled up a stool next to the pallet.

"Im Basim has had a hard life. She was married off to a man she didn't want. He died shortly after the birth of her fifth child. She only has the one son, Basim, who must be the age of your Yasmeen," she said looking at

Mohammad. "Abu Basim, *Allah yer'hum'o,* was never one to work much. He liked to hang out at the coffee shop and play *tric-trac.* When he died, Basim quit school and pushes a grocery cart in the *hisbeh,* I think."

"That's where Sarah became acquainted with him," Mohammad said. "She thinks we should help him."

"It would be a kindness," Nijmeh said. "The boy hasn't had much help in growing up and has had too much laid on his shoulders at an early age. And sadly," Nijmeh sighed, "he isn't like other boys."

"We have made him an offer. He is supposed to see me tomorrow to tell me if he accepts our suggestion. If he does, I would like you, *Yum'ma,* to go with us to see his mother."

Nijmeh smiled. "Of course, *Yum'ma.*"

The next day Sarah and Mohammad waited in the parking lot across from the old *Hashameya* School. Basim didn't show.

Mohammad had put the car into reverse and was backing out of the parking spot when Basim – pushing his grocery cart – arrived.

"I am sorry that I am late. I had to deliver things for the lady at the Grand Hotel. It took longer than I thought it would. I am really sorry," he said in his rather high-pitched voice.

Mohammad and Sarah had gotten out of the car.

"Have you thought about what we talked about yesterday?" Mohammad asked.

"Yes, *Ammo.* I talked with my mother and she would like to meet you. I would like to go to the trade school, but *Im'me* wants to talk to you first. She was wondering if this afternoon would be possible."

Sarah looked at Mohammad and nodded. "This afternoon is fine," Mohammad said. "I would like to bring my mother along as well."

"Your mother, Ammo?"

"Yes, my parents also live in the camp. It seems that my older brother, Khalil, went to school with your late father, *Allah yer'hum'o,* and my mother knows your mother."

"Your parents live in the camp? I thought you were *med'da'knee'ya* (city folk)."

"Only on the surface," Mohammad smiled. "Inside I am a *fellah and a la'je* (a peasant and a refugee)."

"Would five o'clock be a good time?" Sarah asked.

"Yes, Im Khalil" he smiled. "Five o'clock will be fine."

"You will need to look after Amr for an hour or so," Sarah said to Yasmeen and the boys. "Your father and I have a five o'clock appointment. We shouldn't be too long."

"Where are you going?" Mansur questioned.

240

"We're going with your *Sitteh* Nijmeh to visit a lady in the camp. Her son works in the *hisbeh;* your mother became acquainted with him and would like to help him finish his studies."

"Works in the *hisbeh?*" Khalil asked. "Is he one of the boys who has a grocery cart and carries things for people?

"That's right," Sarah said. "I think he must be around your age. He carried my groceries for me a couple of times and we struck up a conversation. He had to drop out of school to support his family when his father died."

"We sometimes pass that way and have seen the *shabab* who push the carts. Which one is he?" Mansur asked.

"He's about your height: black hair, slender, polite."

"You *don't* mean the *fag?*"

"I beg your *pardon,*" Sarah scolded. "I'm surprised at you, Khalil, and disappointed."

"I didn't mean anything by it, honest. It's a term the guys at school use to describe one of those boys at the *hisbeh.* The boy they are referring to always acts feminine and has a high-pitched voice."

"I'm really surprised at you," Sarah said. "You must have known gay kids at school."

"There were kids that may have been, but it was different," Mansur said.

"I don't want you using stereotypical terms to describe people. People are just people. They shouldn't be *labeled* because of how they *look* or how they *might* seem. When you use a term like the one you just used, you are labeling someone without knowing anything about him."

"It is like when someone uses the term *Moslem terrorist* – not knowing anything about the individual or the situation," Mohammad added.

"It's *hardly* the same," Mansur said under his breath.

"The *point is*," Mohammad said a bit sternly, "the term is used as a label and consequently a *judgment*. I don't want any of you ever *judging* someone before you know their circumstances..."

"*Before we have walked in their shoes*," Khalil said.

"Yes, that's right: *before you have walked in their shoes*. We never can really know why someone behaves the way he or she does until we have been in their place."

"So, *is* the boy you are talking about, *that* boy?" Khalil persisted.

"He is probably the same one you are thinking of," Sarah finally said.

"We're not going to have to have any contact with him, are we?" Mansur asked.

"I don't see why you should," Sarah said unsmilingly, "though I am not happy with your attitude."

"We're sorry, Mama. We know you are right; it's just that *we* have reputations too. It's *good* that you want to help him, *really it is,* but please don't make him one of the family."

Sarah was taken aback. "You need to get to your homework," was all she said.

Khalil and Mansur both kissed her on the cheek.

"Please don't be angry with us, Mama."

"I'm not angry," she smiled and patted both boys on the cheek, although inside she was deeply disappointed.

"I'm not really surprised at the boys' reaction," Mohammad said as Sarah refilled his coffee. "Being gay, even *associating* with someone who is thought to be gay, can be damaging to a kid's reputation *here.*"

"I am just surprised," Sarah admitted stirring half a spoonful of sugar into her coffee. "Our boys are such great kids – so open-minded about a lot of things."

"Unfortunately, in this society people who are gay have to be good at hiding that part of themselves in order to be accepted, even in order to survive."

Sarah thought of Mohammad's beloved brother Khalil and his friend Amr but said nothing.

As they prepared to leave the apartment to go to meet Basim's mother, Khalil and Mansur handed Mohammad two large plastic bags.

"We put together a few things that we don't really wear anymore. They'll probably fit the kid. We feel bad about what we said earlier. It's just we already *stand out* here, Mama. We are really trying to blend in." Khalil and Mansur both gave Sarah a hug. "But, whatever you decide to do is alright with us."

Sarah smiled ruffling their curly hair and kissing them on both cheeks.

When their parents had left, Mansur turned to Khalil. "We really did mean what we said, I just *pray* that they don't want to make him our *foster* brother, but I can see that happening when Mama gets involved." And the boys couldn't help grinning.

Chapter 30

Im Basim's house in the camp was quite small. It was like the house Omar and Nijmeh had first lived in before they built the second story: a courtyard, a closet-sized kitchen, and two rooms with a tiny bathroom under the stairs leading to the roof.

Im Basim, who must have been only in her thirties, looked as though she was fifty. Many of her teeth were missing, and when she spoke she tended to keep her mouth covered with her hand.

"Please come in, please come in," she motioned with her one free hand, directing them into the sitting room/bedroom. There were a few metal straight chairs, a daybed, and an old TV on a not-too-sturdy-looking TV stand.

Basim sat beside her, his four younger sisters kept peeking in the door.

Nijmeh, Sarah, and Mohammad all sat on the daybed.

"Im Basim," Mohammad began. "My wife, Im Khalil," he said nodding toward Sarah, "became acquainted with your son a few weeks ago and was impressed with how polite and kind he was. She told me about him and I had the opportunity to meet him a few days ago."

Im Basim looked at her son and then back at Mohammad.

"We are involved with an agency that helps orphan boys like Basim. This agency is interested in sponsoring – that is *paying for* – deserving boys to complete a training course like that offered in Deir Debwan so that they can find good employment. "

"We know," he continued, "that boys like Basim are supporting their families and this agency is willing to *pay* the boys to go to school – an amount similar to what they would have earned when they work. They are willing to do this for up to a period of two years."

Im Basim continued to just look at them.

"Im Basim," Nijmeh interrupted. "What my son wants to know is if you would allow Basim to take part in such a program. The agency of which he speaks would pay Basim to go to school. He would still be earning what he earns now." Nijmeh had purposely emphasized that it was an *agency* that would be paying. It was a stretching of the truth but Im Basim was a very simple woman and Nijmeh wanted to make sure that she didn't think the money was coming from Mohammad and Sarah – though it was. Thinking that the funds came from an agency somewhat removed the feeling of *obligation* that Basim and Im Basim might feel, and made Mohammad's and Sarah's charity somewhat anonymous as they wished.

"I don't know what to say," Im Basim said wiping tears from her eyes. "You know how hard things have been for us, but *nush'kur Allah* (thank God) we manage. It would be good if Basim were to be trained to get a real job. I don't know how to thank your son and his wife for this opportunity."

"If you are willing, my son will speak to the principal of the training school about Basim and make all the arrangements."

"Of course we are willing. I just don't know how to thank you," she said close to tears.

Mohammad nodded at his mother. "My son wants to be sure that you understand that the money is *not* from him. He is just the spokesperson for the agency."

"God bless you," Im Basim said. "We are very, very grateful."

"That is settled then," Mohammad said moving as though to leave. "I will make the arrangements and contact Basim."

"Please, you must have coffee. It is ready. Heba! Bring the coffee, *Yum'ma.*"

They sat dutifully and drank coffee.

Basim walked with them back to Omar and Nijmeh's house. "You must come and visit us, *Sitteh,*" Nijmeh said to him.

"Oh, I almost forgot," Sarah said hurrying into the courtyard. "These are a few things that my sons thought you might have a use for," she said handing Basim the two plastic bags of clothing. "It is nothing really."

"Thank you, Im Khalil. And thank your sons," Basim said not meeting her eyes. "I don't know what to say. You are being so kind to me."

Basim shook hands with Mohammad. "*Shukran, Ammo.* I will work very hard and not let you down."

"I know you will, Ammo. I will speak to the principal and bring you word in a day or two. Let me walk a little ways with you," Mohammad said.

"Ammo, when you shake hands grab the other person's hand in a strong grip – like this," he said shaking hands once again with Basim. When you speak to someone, look them right in the eyes and lower your voice just a bit."

Basim felt the blush that inflamed his cheeks. "The boys at the training center are going to make fun of me," he whispered. "The boys always make fun of me."

"You are going to be fine," Mohammad assured him. "Look them straight in the eye; shake hands with them, and *if* they push you around – *push back!* That's all there really is to it. Boys only tend to push around those boys they *think* can be pushed around. *Push back.* If anyone even *says* anything to you, get right in their face. They'll back down."

"That *doesn't* really work, does it?" Basim said with the shadow of a smile.

"Sure it does. My father always said '*take the offensive.*' And people are often so *startled* that it works!"

"My father never gave me any advice," Basim said studying the pebbles in the road.

"Anytime you need advice just come to me or stop and see my father, Abu Mansur. He has lived over seventy years, raised five sons and numerous grandsons. He'd be pleased to give advice to another 'grandson'," Mohammad laughed.

"Even a grandson like me?" Basim said still looking at the pebbles.

Mohammad reached down and raised Basim's chin. "What do you mean *even a grandson like you?* There is nothing wrong with you, Ammo. Remember that. Believe that!"

On impulse, Basim took Mohammad's hand, kissed it and raised it to his forehead. "Thank you, *Ammo,* for everything."

"How did it go?" Sarah asked when Mohammad returned to his parents' house.

"I'm really glad we are going to do this," he smiled. "It was such a good idea you had!"

"I *do* occasionally have a good idea," Sarah smiled. "Your mother has tea ready in the sitting room."

Omar was sitting on the daybed with his shoes off, his legs folded under him, and his bare feet peeking out from under his *umbaz.*

"*Yaba,* I told Basim that when he needs advice he should come to you; that you had raised five sons, and numerous grandsons, and would be pleased to have another grandson to teach."

"I *never* have enough grandsons," he smiled taking a glass of tea from the tray Nijmeh put in front of him. "So few people *ask* for my advice, it will be good to have someone interested in what I have to say."

"We are *all* interested in what you have to say," Mohammad laughed. "Basim was worried that you wouldn't want a *grandson like him.*"

"There is nothing wrong with him," Omar said gingerly taking a sip of the scalding tea. "He just needs to talk occasionally to an old man like me. We are the way Allah in His wisdom has made us. He throws into our paths people who need us, and whom we need."

"How did you get to be so wise *Yaba?*"

"I learned whatever wisdom I have from your mother," he chuckled looking lovingly at Nijmeh. "One cannot be married to her for over fifty years and *not* become wise!"

"*Inshallah* I will be able to say the same thing," Mohammad smiled at Sarah, "after you and I have been married for over fifty years."

"You mean you can't say these seventeen years together has taught you wisdom?" Sarah joked.

"Of course, *habeeptee,* but I want to be as wise as my father."

"In that case," Nijmeh laughed, "I think you need *six* more children."

"*If* that's the case," Sarah countered, "I think he needs three more wives."

Mohammad burst out laughing, spraying tea all over his trousers. If I even contemplated bringing a second wife into the house you would kill me and the police would find my disfigured body in a dumpster."

"And *I* would help her put it in the dumpster," Nijmeh said winking at Sarah.

"*Yum'ma!*" Mohammad exploded.

"You couldn't find a better wife than Sarah," Nijmeh said looking affectionately at her daughter-in-law. And she *has* given you three sons!"

"Ah, there's the rub. Now, if you had given me daughters only I would have a legitimate excuse to take a second wife," Mohammad said pretending to sigh. "But alas, the first time – what did you do but present me with *twin boys!*"

"It's too bad that Islam doesn't permit four *husbands,*" Sarah joked.

"*One* husband is *more* than enough," Nijmeh laughed nodding toward Omar. "What would we do with another one?"

By this time they were all laughing.

"We *are* very blessed to have each other," Mohammad said seriously.

"Yes we are," Nijmeh, Omar, and Sarah nodded in agreement.

Chapter 31

It was a perfect spring morning. Summer was certainly in the air, the almond blossoms had all fallen and were replaced with the hard, green prelude to almonds. Basim had been in the trade school in Deir Debwan for several weeks and, after the initial adjustment, was loving it, or so he had told Mohammad. Khalil, Mansur and Yasmeen would soon be going to the States to spend the summer with Grandpa Ken and Aunt Martha:

It was the kind of morning that Omar loved. He trudged up the rocky slope toward the stone wall he was repairing and thought of how blessed his life had been. He and Nijmeh had been married fifty-five years; they had had ten children and had thirty-six grandchildren, thirty-seven if one considered Basim, (and Omar did), and thirty-six great. *Subhan Allah* (Praise God).

I can neither read nor write, Omar thought, *but Mansur is a doctor; Khalil is a lawyer, Mohammad is an agricultural engineer, and Issa is a well-known artist. And if you consider Amr a son, which I do, he is a wealthy businessman. My daughters are all happily married, illhumdillah. I have much for which to be thankful.*

The sun was warm on his back as he placed stone upon stone, filling in the gaps with small rocks and pebbles. He was an artist of sorts – a real craftsman. He liked the feel of the stones in his hands; their texture was rough and they smelled of earth and *time. They have been here long before me and will be here long after I am gone.*

He had been thinking of his mother, Hasna, the last few days. He had even been dreaming about her. He could clearly see her in his dreams as she had been in her youth – red hair, blue eyes, and freckles. He recalled how she had danced in the street – tears streaming – when the British jeep had driven through the town with the bodies of her two brothers stacked like cordwood among the dead.

How angry she was when I told her I had seen a girl at the well. He chuckled remembering her words. *How angry my father was when he found out I had spoken to Nijmeh. Subhan Allah, how thankful I am that Nijmeh has been written into the days of my life. I can still see her face that evening when I lifted the wedding veils from her face; how her tears had caused the kohl with which she had outlined her eyes to make muddy trails over her cheeks.*

I can still see Nijmeh smiling at me as she held our first child, Mansur. I can still hear her words echoing in my heart, 'He looks just like you.'

Omar placed another stone on top of the one he had just laid.

I can still feel her anguish and grief when I lifted her weeping form off of Ahmad's body the day he was killed. Some memories never leave us, he thought, as he wedged a small, pointed stone under the rock he had just laid so that it lay flat and unmoving.

The sun was warm on his head as he sat leaning against the stone wall and took out the sandwich that Nijmeh had prepared for him: slivers of goat cheese and cucumber. He unfolded the bit of white cloth in which she had wrapped the bread. His hand trembled a bit. *I must be getting old,* he smiled. Sometimes of late his breathing had been a bit labored and he had found himself wanting to take deep breaths.

Omar felt sleepy. *The warmth of the sun has made me drowsy,* he thought. *I'll just close my eyes for a moment and then finish the wall.*

Omar closed his eyes and slipped into heaven.

"I wonder why Abu Mansur isn't back yet," Nijmeh said to her daughter-in-law, Yasmeen. "It is almost dusk. He should be home by now."

"Issa, your father isn't home yet," Yasmeen worriedly said to her husband. "Do you know where he was working today?"

"Saji knows," Issa replied. "I'll go and get him and we'll meet *Yaba, inshallah,* on his way back."

Issa and Saji hurried over the rocky terrain with Sami and Imad. The stars were already out and there was a full moon.

"*Sidi* was working up there," Saji said pointing to a stone wall half-way up the rocky slope.

They found him sitting on the ground; his back leaning against the unfinished stone wall; his head resting against his chest as though he was sleeping.

"*Sidi,*" Saji whispered falling to his knees beside the silent form of his grandfather. *Sidi!*"

Issa too dropped to his knees and grasped his father's hand. *"Yaba, Yaba,"* he wept.

Sami, Imad, Saji, and Issa carried the lifeless form of Omar down the rocky hillside. At the bottom of the hill, they placed him in the backseat of the car, his head rested in Saji's lap.

Nijmeh was waiting at the entrance to the courtyard when the car came to a stop in front of the metal gate. Issa went up to his mother and wrapped his arms around her. "*Yaba...*" he started to say and couldn't get the words out.

Nijmeh slumped in his arms as her legs gave out. Yasmeen came running. One look at Issa's tear-stained face and she knew the truth. She saw the same grief mirrored in the faces of Imad, Sami and Saji.

"I'll go and get my mother," Saji brokenly mumbled, "and I'll call *Khali* Mohammad."

Within half an hour the house was filled with people. Hasna, Imad, and their sons were there; Mohammad and Sarah were there.

"I'll call Amman and have them call America and Dubai," Mohammad said, trying to keep the tears out of his voice.

Mansur picked up on the third ring.

"*Salam aleikum,*" he said as soon as he heard Mohammad's voice.

"*Aleikum salam,* brother," Mohammad murmured. "I have bad news," he paused. "*Yaba a'talk om'roh,* (Father has given you his years), he said using the age-old Arabic phrase. He was unable to keep the tears from his voice.

"What?" Mansur cried in disbelief, "*Yaba mat!? (Yaba* is dead?!)"

"He was repairing a wall and just fell asleep," Mohammad said brokenly. "The funeral is tomorrow. Please try to come. We need you to call Mona and Manal in America and inform Azeezeh and Najla in Dubai."

"*Inshallah* Khalil and I will be there tomorrow," Mansur said, sorrowfully. "*Allah ma'kum.* (God be with you)."

Omar's body was carried into the sitting room and placed on the dining table.

"Leave me a few moments with your father," Nijmeh whispered brokenly placing her hands on the arms of her sons. Once the men had washed the body and prepared it for burial custom dictated that she would not be allowed to touch him. Her goodbyes would have to be said before the men washed the body.

So it was that Nijmeh was left alone, for the last time, with the man she had loved for over fifty-five years.

She gently closed the door behind her. Tears were streaming down her face as they had that first night when Omar had lifted her veils. She had been a girl of fifteen then, now she was seventy. She gently ran trembling fingers over his face and mustache, willing them to *remember.* In her mind she saw him as the youth of seventeen he had been. She could barely recall the years of hardship, all she seemed able to remember were the years of love. They had never slept apart in fifty-five years – not even for one night.

"Ya Omar," she said brokenly as she ran knowing hands over him. "We should have gone together. How can I live on without you, *roh'elbe* (my heart's spirit)? Wait for me, *habeebee;* I won't be long. I won't be long."

Nijmeh kissed him on the forehead; she kissed his cold lips – his mustache brushing her cheek for the last time; she kissed his hand and placed it against her heart.

She went and quietly opened the door. 'You may go in and wash him now, *Yum'ma,*" she said to Issa and Mohammad.

A weeping Hasna, Yasmeen, and Sarah guided her to a chair in the courtyard; they murmured words of comfort that Nijmeh did not hear.

So it was that his two youngest sons and three of his grandsons washed his body for the last time. The men unashamedly wept as they bathed Omar, talking to him as though he could hear their words.

"Just think, *Yaba,* today you will be with Ahmad. How glad he will be to see you," Mohammad cried as he washed one of his father's hands.

"And all your brothers will be waiting to welcome you," Issa wept as he bathed his father's feet. He smiled as he washed his father's toes and saw the wisps of wiry black hair. "Remember," he said brokenly to Mohammad, "how *Im'me* used to say that all she had seen of *Yaba* before they were married was the hair on his toes when he had stopped to talk to her at the well?"

Saji wept as he washed his grandfather's other hand. "Remember, *Sidi,* how, after the soldiers and settlers had beaten me, I refused to leave the house unless you were holding my hand? You always made me feel safe." Saji said kissing his grandfather's hand for the last time.

Mohammad went to the door and took from Hasna the sheet in which Omar would be swaddled.

A pallet was spread on the floor and Omar's wrapped body was placed on it. His body was then covered with a blanket. All that was left exposed was his face.

The dining table was moved into the courtyard. "The women may come in now," Mohammad said.

The men went into the courtyard as the women filed into the sitting room. Some of the women sat on plastic chairs while others sat on the daybed under the collage of pictures. Nijmeh, her daughter, Hasna, and her daughters-in-law, Yasmeen and Sarah, sat on the floor. There was no wild grief as there had been when the child Ahmad had been killed, for Omar was an old man. There were tears nonetheless.

Mona and Manal called from America, "Let us talk to *Yum'ma,*" they wept on the phone to Mohammad.

"She won't leave *Yaba's* side," Mohammad told them.

"Tell her we are catching the first available flight and that we will be there, *inshallah,* tomorrow night," Mona said. "I know it will be too late to see *Yaba,*" she cried, "but we will be there for *Yum'ma.* Najla and Azeezeh should also be in the West Bank tomorrow night. Mansur and Khalil hope to be there tomorrow morning in time for the funeral. Amr was not given a permit to cross the bridge, but he wanted me to tell you that he sends his love."

"I will tell *Yum'ma,*" Mohammad said his voice breaking.

At 8:30 the next morning a taxi pulled up in front of the metal gate and a weary Mansur and Khalil got out. They had been given a three-day permit to enter the West Bank and attend the funeral of their father.

The metal door had been left partially opened for people to come and go. A long line of chairs was just inside the door. Some of the men had gone home for a break, only Mohammad, and Issa, unshaven, sat to receive mourners. They had risen automatically when the two men crossed the stone threshold. When they saw their two brothers they fell into each other's arms.

The four men hugged each other and wept.

"Come and see *Yaba*," Mohammad said through his tears. "There is no one in the sitting room but *Yum'ma*, Hasna, Yasmeen, and Sarah."

Mansur and Khalil entered the room in which they had all slept as children. There on the pallet lay their father's body covered with a wool blanket. Only his face was exposed; his head was wrapped in a new, white *kuffiyeh.*

"*Yum'ma*," they whispered kneeling down to put their arms around their mother. Nijmeh patted their faces and kissed them on both cheeks, unable to speak, her tears mingling with theirs.

Mansur and Khalil knelt over their father's body and kissed him on the forehead. They looked into the wet, swollen faces of their sister and sisters-in-law. They sat for a few moments with their family until other women began to arrive.

"*Yallah, Yum'ma*," Nijmeh tried to smile through her tears. "Go into the room with the men."

The brothers sat in order of age: Mansur, Khalil, Mohammad, and Issa, and then came Hasna's husband Imad and their sons. The line of chairs went around the walls of the courtyard filled with grandsons and great-grandsons. Mohammad's and Issa's sons had chairs at the very end of the long line.

Among the women were the wives of Omar's grandsons as well as his many granddaughters and great-granddaughters. Yasmeen sat among her female cousins with little Amr in her lap. Out of respect for her grandfather, like the other women and girls, her hair was covered as was that of her mother, Sarah.

At ten the *sheikh* rose and nodded to Mansur that it was time. He and his brothers went out into the street and waited for their father's body to be brought out of the house and placed on the wooden stretcher that would carry it to the mosque and the graveyard.

Hasna's sons had gone into the room of women and lifted the body of their grandfather onto their shoulders. The room was filled with the wailing of the women as they cried their farewells to Omar. Nijmeh, breaking with custom, followed her grandsons out of the room. She went into the street and saw Omar's body placed on the wooden stretcher. She watched as her grandsons lifted the stretcher to their shoulders. She saw her four handsome sons, their arms linked, prepared to walk behind their father's casket. For a moment it flashed through her mind how much they looked like Omar.

Stepping in front of them she rested her hand on the wooden box. "Wait for me, *habeebee.* I'll be coming soon. It won't be long. It won't be long," she wept.

Surprisingly, it was Sarah who came out of the metal gate and put her arms around Nijmeh. "Come, *Mart Ammie,* Ta'aali (come)" she said gently, the tears dripping off her chin.

They stood to the side as the procession moved through the narrow alley. The line of men was almost out of sight when Nijmeh looked at Sarah. Silently Sarah nodded and the two women, their arms around each other's waists, followed the men.

They stood discreetly outside the low wall of the graveyard and watched the line of men file toward the open grave. They stood quietly as Omar's body was removed from the box it was laid in and lovingly handed into the arms of two of his grandsons who placed it in the grave. They stood silently and listened as the *sheikh* said the graveside words; they listened as the men raised their hands and recited the *Fatiha*.

Before the workmen began to sling the dirt into the grave, Mohammad glanced over at the two women standing some distance away and slightly shook his head. Sarah understood. He didn't want his mother to listen to the dirt being shoveled onto Omar's body.

"Ta'aali, Mart Ammie," Sarah said turning her mother-in-law away from the cemetery.

"Shukran, binti, shukran," (Thank you, my daughter, thank you) Nijmeh whispered as they slowly wove their way back.

Chapter 32

Nijmeh, in the seventy years of her life, had *never* slept alone. As a toddler and child she had always slept with one of her sisters, and from the time she was fifteen, she had slept with Omar. She stretched her arm across the pallet and encountered only emptiness. It matched the emptiness in her heart.

The house was once again filled with children – *her and Omar's* children. That evening Mona and Manal had arrived from the States, and Najla and Azeezeh had crossed the bridge from Amman.

It had been Mohammad's suggestion that they spend this first night, as they had as children, all sleeping in the same room. He had talked it over with Sarah and she had been too choked up to speak. She nodded her head and hugged him tightly.

"We should be with *Im'me* tonight," he had said to his siblings. They had all readily agreed.

"What a wonderful idea," Manal had said kissing him, wetting his cheek with her tears.

Pallets had been spread on the sitting room floor.

"You should definitely sleep on the daybed," Khalil said to Mansur. "After all, *you are the most educated of us all*," he joked remembering *Sitteh* Hasna's insistence that Mansur sleep on the daybed as he *could read and write and was going to Russia to study to be a doctor.*

The same naked light fixture dangled above their heads, gently swaying in the late spring breeze that seeped around the ill-fitting window.

"The last time we all slept in this room," Hasna said, "was over thirty-six years ago. Ahmad, *habeebee,* was still alive, and *Sitteh* Hasna, and of course *Yaba, Allah yer'hum'o,*" she said with a catch in her throat.

"We were only children then," Mona said. "Look at us now. Some of us are grandparents!"

"I don't know about you," Manal said, "but I *feel* just the same inside. I *may* look forty-eight, but there are days when inside I am still *twelve!*"

"That is how I like to remember you best," Nijmeh said out of the darkness. "In spite of everything, those were happy days."

They talked long into the night, the darkness poignant with reminiscences of their childhood, punctuated with some of *Sitteh* Hasna's humorous stories; the pauses filled with loving reflections of their father.

Finally, they all slept; that is, they all slept but Nijmeh. She lay awake long after her children had fallen asleep. In the moonlight filtering through the slats of the shuttered window, she looked at the silver wedding band on her finger.

Omar placed that ring on my finger fifty-five years ago, she remembered. *It has never left my finger. It is no longer possible to be slipped off,* she smiled to herself – her lashes heavy with tears. The gold bracelets, gold necklace, and the pair of gold earrings she had been given on her wedding day had been sold that first year when they fled their village. All that had remained had been the silver wedding band. *It hadn't been worth much,"* Nijmeh said to herself *since it wasn't gold. I would have sold it anyway, but Omar would not allow it,* she thought with the tears falling unhindered over her cheeks.

The children had not slept well. Each, in his or her turn, had awakened during the night to the muffled sounds of their mother's weeping. Their own grief was great, but hearing the sound of their mother's grief broke their hearts.

Following tradition, the women of the family went to the grave just before dawn the morning following the burial. Mohammad had gone to get Sarah at 4 in the morning and had brought her back to the house in the camp. Since it was pre-dawn, he accompanied his mother, his five sisters, his sister-in-law, Yasmeen and his wife to the cemetery. He sat on the low stone wall that separated the cemetery from the street and waited.

"In the name of God, the Merciful, the Compassionate..." the women began their hands raised and open to heaven. There was no violent weeping, but their tears flowed freely, unashamedly. Mohammad was touched that even Sarah had raised her hands toward heaven and had repeated the words of the *Fatiha* in Arabic.

Mona had brought a Quran and read a Sura. She passed the Quran to Manal, who also read. Each of the sisters and Yasmeen read a few verses over Omar's grave. Sarah recited a short Sura that she had memorized.

Nijmeh looked at her five daughters and two daughters-in-law. "Come, my daughters. It is time that we went," she said as she led them out of the cemetery through the gate to where Mohammad waited.

There would be three days of official mourning where people would come to pay their respects. Bitter, sugarless coffee would be served along with dates. The women would wear somber clothing and no jewelry. The men of the family would not shave or wear scent.

The Imam came every afternoon and sat with the men.

"Death is a welcomed part of life," he said. "We mourn the person's passing as we shall miss him, but we would not wish him back. What is earth compared to heaven!"

Nijmeh, in the room with the women, listened to the words the Imam spoke. She sorely missed Omar and she selfishly *would* have wished him back, but she *knew,* deep in her heart, that he was in heaven with Ahmad and she could not wish him back from there.

Yasmeen had emailed Kareem to tell him of her grandfather's passing. He had immediately phoned that night and they had talked – it seemed for hours – about her grandfather. Yasmeen had found comfort in Kareem's call. She *wished* she could see him – *touch* him. She wanted so badly to feel his arms around her. She wanted to lay her head on his shoulder. They had never even held hands.

Basim had learned of Omar's passing from his mother. In the several weeks he had known Omar, he had come to look upon him as a grandfather. He had often gone to *chat* with him. He wanted to go and pay his respects but was hesitant.

On the second day of mourning, both Basim and Kareem arrived at the metal gate leading into the house at exactly the same time. They both had been somewhat hesitant to come. Basim wanted to come because he had grown to feel great affection for Omar. Kareem wanted to come for Yasmeen – even though he wouldn't be able to see her.

They shook hands with the men. When Basim reached Mohammad he *firmly* gripped his hand. There were tears in his eyes. "I am so sorry, *Ammo, Yislam ra'sak.*" (May your thoughts be at peace.)

Mohammad drew him into a hug and kissed him on both *cheeks.* "*Allah yisal'mak, habeebee.*" (May Allah bless you, my dear.)

Khalil and his brother, Mansur, were at the end of the line. Basim reached them first. He said the traditional words and shook hands with the twins. Kareem also shook hands with them and was somewhat surprised when Khalil and Mansur leaned in to kiss him on both cheeks.

Both Khalil and Mansur moved from the line of mourners and went to sit beside Basim and Kareem.

"Thank you for coming," Khalil said.

"We appreciate that you came," Mansur added.

It was awkward, but it was a beginning.

Basim and Kareem sat for about fifteen minutes and then got up. Once more they shook hands with Khalil and Mansur, and as they reached the door, once again with Mohammad and his brothers.

When Kareem was shaking hands with Mohammad, he glanced into the room where the women sat and caught Yasmeen's eye. She did not nod or outwardly show that she had seen him, though her heart did a little dance.

On the third day of mourning, Sarah just happened to be sitting next to Nijmeh. It was still quite early and not many women were present. Nijmeh took Sarah's hand and said, "*Binti,* it came to me last night that Abu Mansur continues to live," Nijmeh paused when she saw the startled look in Sarah's eyes. "He lives, *binti,*" she continued holding Sarah's hand in a strong grip, "in each of my children, grandchildren, and great-grandchildren. I look at your husband, Mohammad, and I see a bit of Omar. I look at Mansur and Khalil and I *see* Omar. I look at your sons, *binti,* and I see Omar as he was at seventeen. Omar is there in each one of them."

Sarah's tears fell gently as her heart understood what Nijmeh was saying.

Nijmeh smiled, though the lashes on her own eyes were heavy with tears. "I can look into the faces of *eighty-one* people and see Omar. I can listen to the things they say, and catch bits of the things Omar has said. *He* continues to live in each one of them. And," Nijmeh paused and looked directly into Sarah's eyes, "he will always live in my heart and mind, just as Mohammad will always live through *your* children and through *you.*"

The morning of the third day Mohammad's brothers, Mansur and Khalil, had to return to Amman. As they hugged their mother goodbye, she smiled at them. "Do not worry, *Yum'ma,*" she patted their cheeks with a rough hand. "I am fine. I will never forget a word, a look, a gesture. I have been dearly loved for over fifty-five years and I know," she said wiping a vagrant tear from her eye, "that he loves me still. I am at peace."

And they knew that she was.

That night as Sarah rested her head on Mohammad's chest she whispered something. He was not sure he heard her correctly.

"*What* did you say?" he asked raising her head from his chest so he could look into her eyes.

"I said that I want you to make an appointment with the Imam. I am ready to convert."

"You're *ready to convert?*" Mohammad repeated the statement not believing what he had heard.

"I have been thinking about it for a very long time, but after sitting with your mother and listening to her words," Sarah paused in thought. "I want what she has. She told me that your father continues to live in her heart and mind," again Sarah paused and raising her head looked into Mohammad's eyes, "just as the children and *you* will always live in my mind and heart. I know she is right. By embracing Islam, I am also embracing you, and her, and all your wonderful family. I no longer want to be on the outside."

Mohammad was too overcome to speak. He tightened his hold on Sarah.

"I have talked with our Yasmeen, and once I have spoken to the Imam, she and I are in agreement that we will wear *hijab.*"

"You don't need to do that," Mohammad finally got out. "You don't need to do any of it."

"I know," Sarah said. "You know me well enough to know I would never do anything if I wasn't convinced. It has taken me seventeen years, but *I am convinced.* This *is* the right thing for me, and ultimately for our children."

It took Mohammad a long time to fall asleep. He was so overwhelmed with love for the woman he held in his arms.

Chapter 33

Khalil and Mansur were *shocked* at their mother's decision to convert.

"What are Grandpa Ken and Grandma Martha going to think?" Khalil said in disbelief.

"Don't forget Mama's parents," Mansur said to his brother. "Their worst fears will have come true!"

"Yasmeen was saying that she and Mama are going to wear *hijab!*" Khalil added in a shocked voice.

"You're kidding! They wouldn't!" Mansur was astounded. "Mama is *too independent* to conform in such a way."

"What am I too independent to do?" Sarah said coming into the boys' room with a load of folded laundry.

"You're too independent to wear *hijab,*" Mansur said. "I can understand Yasmeen doing it so she won't get hassled in the street, but I can't see *you* covering your hair."

"You've always been a bit of a rebel, Mama," Khalil added. "We can't see you conforming like this. Aren't you giving into *gender stereotypes?* Isn't that the phrase you sometimes use?" Khalil teased.

Sarah put the folded clothes in the boys' wardrobe.

"I suppose it can be viewed as *conforming*," Sarah said sitting down on one of the beds. I see it as becoming part of the community – a part of the extended family. Covering my hair doesn't change who I am, in fact, it is almost *liberating*."

"How is it *liberating?*" Mansur questioned.

"I can express my *rebel ideas,* as you so aptly phrased it," Sarah smiled, "and some folks will see that even *observant* women who wear *hijab* are intelligent, thoughtful individuals who have modern ideas." Sarah paused. "I think people will be even *more* interested in listening to what I have to say when they aren't immediately labeling me as a westerner with *foreign* ideas, but seeing me as a woman who appreciates the value of tradition and custom, as well as being broad-minded and liberal."

"Are you saying that you aren't really *convinced?*" Khalil asked. "That you are converting for the sake of appearance?"

"No, I *am* convinced. I look at your *Sitteh* Nijmeh and see what an intelligent, thoughtful, caring individual she is. She can't read or write, but she is one of the most intelligent women I have ever met. I look at her and see how she has greeted all the hardship and adversity in her life, and how her *simple* faith has molded her into the amazing woman she is. I *want* that. There is something to be said about *seeing God in everything – of accepting both good and bad equally as the 'will of God' and submitting to the 'will of God'*".

"But wearing *hijab?*" Mansur persisted. "Isn't that giving into male domination?" he said with a twinkle in his eye. "The next thing we'll see is you walking ten paces behind Baba and keeping your eyes on the floor tiles."

"Your father isn't *forcing* me to wear *hijab,*" Sarah laughed. "He knows better than that. In fact, he sort of tried to talk me out of it. It is *my* decision. I will certainly *not* be walking ten paces behind him and studying the patterns on the floor tiles, or counting the cracks in the pavement. I think there is value in not wanting to flaunt one's appearance."

"But some of the girls who cover their head do *just* that," Khalil argued. "They *call* attention to themselves with their fancy scarves and the way they tie them. Some girls even attach a beehive-thing under their scarf so their heads looked deformed. If you decide to wear a scarf you would no longer be you."

"I will *always* be me," Sarah said giving her sons a hug. "A scarf won't change who I am."

The boys looked skeptical.

It was easier becoming a Moslem than Sarah had thought. All she had to do was declare her belief that *'there is no God but God,* and *Mohammad is a prophet of God'* – not the *only* prophet, but *a* prophet. *There is still a place for Jesus* she thought. *Jesus is in the Quran, as is his mother Mary.*

She hadn't realized that when she had stood at the gravesite of her father-in-law the morning after his burial and raised her hands to heaven and repeated the *Fatiha,* that she had already declared herself a Moslem.

"You mean that is all there is to it?" she asked Mohammad. "I don't have to have instruction, or take a course, or stand before a congregation, or at least an Imam, and declare my faith?"

"Nope," Mohammad smiled. "You have always fasted Ramadan with me; you give *zakat* to the needy and less fortunate; you always strive to be kind and thoughtful to others – look what you are doing for Basim; you have read the Quran in English and a number of books *about* Islam. If you are interested, my mother or Issa's wife or Hasna can instruct you as to how to pray, but all you really needed to do was what you did in the cemetery.

The biggest surprise was the reaction of her older children, especially Yasmeen.

"I am *so glad* that you have decided to become Moslem like the rest of us," she said.

"What do you mean, *like the rest of us?*" Sarah asked in surprise.

"Well, Khalil, Mansur, and of course, Baba and I, have always been Moslem. We have always prayed every day facing East; we have fasted since we were twelve, and we were certainly *raised* Moslem. Oh, we did go to church with you on Sundays, and we *did* enjoy the social contact in Sunday school and youth group; it did make us feel more like our classmates. Also, it is great celebrating Christmas with Grandpa Ken and Grandma Martha, but we *knew* inside that we were Moslem."

Nijmeh's response to Sarah's announcement was one of tears and smiles.

"Oh, I am so glad," she cried as she hugged Sarah. "I was so afraid that you would not be with us when we died. I have daily prayed that you would be drawn to Islam."

"Not be with you?" Sarah questioned, a little perplexed.

Nijmeh tactfully ignored Sarah's question. "It does my heart good to know that we will all be together, *Subhan Allah,* Nijmeh sighed. "I have a gift for you. It is a prayer shawl and skirt, and a prayer rug," she said spreading before Sarah a colorful head covering and a matching skirt. The prayer rug was a deep blue trimmed in black. "Mohammad suggested that we teach you the Moslem form of prayer."

Sarah diligently wrote down the words of the formal prayer and made note of the different positions her mother-in-law demonstrated: how to hold her hands, how to kneel, how to place her forehead on the rug. She had observed these things when Mohammad had prayed and when he had instructed the children as to how they should pray, but now it was somehow different because it was *her.*

I am not sure that I had bargained for all of this, Sarah thought, *yet it still feels right.*

Chapter 34

The first morning that Sarah and Yasmeen wore their headscarves, Mohammad, Khalil, and Mansur were speechless. Even Amr had stopped playing with his blocks and stared at his mother and sister. No one knew what to say.

"Is it that bad?" Yasmeen asked.

"You look so *different,*" Mansur said. "Who are you? And what have you done with our sister?"

"It's still me, though I have to admit that when I first looked at myself in the mirror I *did* wonder who that girl was peering back at me."

"And Mama," Khalil said, "I just don't know what to say."

"Well, you can say 'Gee, Mama it looks great,' or 'Gee, Mama, you should have done this before," Sarah joked.

"Well, *I* think you both look great," Mohammad said first kissing Sarah's cheek, then Yasmeen's. "I can't wait to hear what comments you get today."

"I am a little shy about what the kids at school will say," Yasmeen admitted as she scooted into the backseat.

"And I imagine there will be a few *raised eyebrows* at work," Sarah said as she adjusted her scarf. "Folks are certainly going to be *surprised.*"

"I don't think *surprised* is quite the right word," Mohammad smiled as he backed out of the driveway. "*Astonished or shocked* is more like it. I would like to be that proverbial *fly on the wall* or *mouse in the corner.*"

Mohammad was right. People were *shocked.*

When Yasmeen walked through the gate at school between her two brothers, heads turned, mouths dropped open, and people stared.

Mahmoud, the guard, left his guard station to come out and congratulate her.

As they lined up outside according to class, all of the girl classmates gathered around her.

"Yasmeen, I can't believe you are wearing *hijab!* Did your dad force you?" Heba asked.

"It really looks nice," Hala said. "*Mabruk* (congratulations)."

"It makes you look so *different,*" Jumana said. "*Different* in a nice way."

Yasmeen felt awkward and embarrassed. During the first recess, she hid out in the library. It was there that Kareem found her sitting alone at one of the tables, close to the stack of reference books and dictionaries, at the back of the library.

Kareem went to the back of the tall shelving and pretended to look at one of the encyclopedias. He looked over at Yasmeen and *willed* her to join him. Yasmeen got up and pretended that she also wanted to check a reference.

They were standing side-by-side apparently *absorbed* in the books on the shelf.

"I think you look *beautiful,*" Kareem whispered. His hand briefly touched Yasmeen's and she felt as though she had been burned.

He looked at her and smiled before picking up his book bag from the floor and leaving the library.

The women with whom Sarah worked were literally speechless – at least at first.

Marion said: "You are the *last* person I would have thought would do something like this, not that it doesn't look good on you," she hastened to add, "It does. I'm just *surprised.*" Marion lowered her voice. "Did Mohammad force you?"

Sarah laughed, "Mohammad couldn't *force* me to do anything. I made the decision and am *convinced* that this is the right thing for me. It doesn't change who I am. I am still me!" she laughed.

"It seems to me like you are going *native,*" Heather remarked. "You know people are going to treat you differently, don't you?"

"They may take me a bit more *seriously,*" Sarah said. "I think when we are working out in the field some of the local staff will feel more *comfortable* talking to a woman wearing *hijab*."

"Dream on, girl; they'll think you are *putting on airs* – after all, *you're American,*" Heather continued.

"Yes, but I am married to a Moslem, my children are Moslem, and my husband's mother, sisters, nieces, and sister-in-law all cover their hair. I think of it as a sign of *respect,*" Sarah said somewhat defensively. "When it comes down to it, it is a very *personal* decision, and one I shouldn't have to defend."

"You're right," Marion said. "I personally think you look great."

Rather than helping her *blend in,* wearing *hijab* was causing Yasmeen to *stand out.* "It's kind of having the *opposite* effect," Yasmeen confessed to Khalil and Mansur. "I'm sure in the street the boys will ignore me, but here at school, I am one of a handful of girls who wear *hijab.* Maybe I didn't give this enough thought." Then Yasmeen played over again in her mind what Kareem had said about her looking *beautiful.* "I guess it will just take some getting used to, for them *and* for me," she said to her brothers.

That night Yasmeen emailed her friend, Molly, about the funeral and about deciding to wear *hijab.* She also wrote a line or two about her second cousin, Imad.

The women and girls all sat in one room with the body. I was sitting in the back holding Amr. Sitting right next to me was my cousin, Imad's, **new wife!** *Remember I had* *emailed you about him being interested in marrying me when I turn eighteen? According to my mother, my grandfather- God rest his soul- convinced him a while ago that there was no chance. Then a month later Imad married his mother's eighteen-year-old niece!*

The biggest news is that my mother and I have decided to wear hijab – that means to cover our hair when in public. Today was the first day. You should have seen the reaction of the kids at school! It has made me stand out rather than blend in as I had hoped. I'll have Khalil take a picture of me with my hair covered on his cell phone and I'll email it to you.

Molly wrote back immediately.

I can't believe you are covering your hair! Will you be wearing a long black robe and covering your face like those Moslem girls we see on TV?

Yasmeen typed her response.

Of course, I won't be wearing a black robe and covering my face! When you actually see a picture of me, you'll realize I am the same person. It may seem a little weird at first, but I think it makes me look quite attractive – though that is NOT the reason I decided to do it. When Kareem saw me today he thought I looked BEAUTIFUL. Will email tomorrow. Luv, Yasmeen

Basim was having yet another sleepless night. Ever since he had met Khalil and Mansur he had not slept well. He had never seen Ammo Mohammad's sons before. Meeting them at the *aza* (wake) had been a bit of a shock. They seemed to be everything he had ever wished he could be. Basim wondered what it would be like to be them.

He rolled onto his left side and punched the pillow to get it just right. It didn't help.

I have to work on my image, Basim thought. *I am learning skills that will make me employable, but no one is going to hire the 'me' they see.*

He rolled onto his right side. He had listened to all that crap about *role models* and *male influences* and *hormonal imbalance.* All the role models, male influences, and hormone treatments in the world wouldn't *change* the way he felt inside. He *was* the way he *was,* and he fervently *wished* he wasn't. *I'd give anything to be like everybody else,* he said out loud as hot tears stung his eyes. *I hate being me! I hate the way I look; the way I walk; the way I talk. I'd be better off dead.*

It was with that last thought in mind that he finally fell into a restless, *thankfully* dreamless, sleep.

The next morning, as he boiled coffee for his mother and himself, he looked around at the barrenness of the room. A heaviness descended on his spirit. For a fleeting moment, he looked at the blue flame of the primus and thought how *easy* it would be to set it on the floor and feed the bottom of his *dish-dash* into the dancing flame. *It would be agonizing for a moment, but then it would be over.*

He physically shook himself. The Quran strictly *forbade* suicide. He would have to wade through these waters that – at times – seemed to engulf him. *As much as I want to be like Ammo Mohammad's sons,* he thought, *I never will be. But I am only sixteen and I can take every opportunity to make my mother's life better; to provide for her and my sisters. My life will not be in vain.*

Basim covered the coffee *brek (*pot) with a chipped saucer. He put two handless coffee cups on the tarnished tray and carried the tray to his mother.

"*Ta'ffud'da'le Yumma* (Please help yourself, mother)*,"* he said offering the coffee to his mother.

"*Shukran, ibnee,* (thank you, son)*"* she smiled her gapped-tooth smile at him. She sipped the hot coffee, making a slurping sound. His youngest sister crawled into his lap, making it impossible for him to drink his coffee. He was afraid he would spill it on her.

Sarah and Yasmeen joined Mohammad, Khalil, and Mansur for the pre-dawn prayer. Sarah had memorized the words that Nijmeh had taught her. She had a wonderful sense of *well-being* as she performed the ritual. It was all *speaking* to something deep inside her.

She caught a glimpse of Amr when she was performing the last part of the prayer. He had gotten out of his bed, walked into the sitting room dragging his *Winnie-The-Pooh* blanket behind him. Seeing his parents and siblings kneeling in prayer, he had spread the blanket on the floor beside Yasmeen and had put his head down like she was doing. His little butt was raised in the air and he was looking sideways to see if he was *doing it right.* He looked so cute!

When the others raised their heads and caught sight of him, they couldn't help but smile.

"So, Baba, you got up to pray too!" Mohammad said pulling Amr into his lap and giving him a hug. "We'll have to get you a prayer rug of your own, habeebee!"

Amr smiled and rested his head on Mohammad's shoulder and contentedly sucked his thumb.

Chapter 35

Aunt Martha and Uncle Ken had not come at Christmas as they had planned. Three weeks before the planned flight, Martha had fallen and broken her leg. It was one of those freak things that one assumes *will never happen to me* and does. She had been coming out of the grocery store, somehow missed the curb and fell in *just* the *wrong* way that she fractured her right leg in two places. The trip was out.

"I don't know who is more disappointed," she had said to Sarah on the phone, "Uncle Ken, the kids, or *me!*"

"Not *just* you and the kids, but Mohammad, and *me!*" Sarah had said.

"I'm marking off the days on the calendar until you all are here," Martha had said. "I know you and Mohammad only have a month's holiday, but we are *counting* on the kids for all summer. We would gladly have Amr too, though I suspect you wouldn't be able to stand *all* the kids being gone."

"You are certainly right about that," Sarah laughed. "You'll have your hands full with the three older ones."

"We're getting summer jobs lined up for all three," Martha laughed. "They are going to have to *work* for their keep!"

"They are so looking forward to the summer with you," Sarah said.

When Sarah had emailed about Omar's death, Uncle Ken and Aunt Martha had called. It was on the phone that Sarah broached the subject of her and Yasmeen wearing *hijab.*

"You're going to be covering your hair?" Aunt Martha asked. "For pity's sake, why?"

"It's something I have thought about for a long time," Sarah said. "It just seems *the right* thing to do. It not only will make me feel more part of the family, but I feel there is something *inside* pushing me. I guess I can't explain it as clearly as I want. Being that my father and Uncle Ken are Jewish and you and my mother are Christian I have always been comfortable with the idea that there are many paths to God. I feel like Islam is the culmination of this. It brings it all together for me, somehow."

"It sounds like you have given it a good deal of thought, love. You know that your Uncle Ken and I support you in whatever you do. You know your dad and mom – your mom especially will feel this is *the last straw.* All her imagined fears will have come true."

"I *do* know that. I'm not doing it *purposely* to hurt her. In fact, I wouldn't wear it in front of her, or dad, or you. One only has to wear it in public, not in front of the family."

"You mean you would wear it even here in the States?" Aunt Martha asked.

"We are not taking the decision lightly, nor are we taking it casually by wearing it only when it is convenient. It is a serious commitment."

"I'm sure you know best, love." Aunt Martha said the words but was not *really* convinced of the wisdom of wearing it in the States; especially in the small farming town where Sarah had grown up.

Martha had just hung up the phone when Dave popped in for coffee.

"I was just on the phone with Sarah," Martha said. "She sends her love."

"How are she and the kids doing? That includes Mohammad too of course."

"They are fine. I told you that Mohammad's father passed away," Martha said as she handed Dave a cup of coffee. "Sarah was saying that she and Yasmeen have given a lot of thought into wearing a scarf to cover their hair," Martha said testing the waters.

"What do you mean *wearing a scarf to cover their hair?* Do you mean like those Moslem women on TV?" Dave asked incredulously.

"Yes, that is what I mean," Martha said blowing on her coffee. "Sarah said that they wouldn't have to wear it around family, but would wear it in public when they went out."

"You mean she and Yasmeen would wear it in the street! Wear it when they went to the store? You surely don't mean that they would wear it *here* when they come to visit?!"

"Not *here* at the farm, but I guess *here* if you mean in town," Martha said taking a sip of her coffee.

"I can't believe that Sarah would do this. You *know* what this news will do to Emily?" Dave said setting his coffee cup down.

"Don't tell her. What she doesn't know for the moment will not hurt her," Martha said. "When she does see Sarah and Yasmeen this summer, they probably won't be wearing it. Maybe she will not find out."

"You can bet your last nickel that if Sarah and Yasmeen are seen in town with their hair covered the news will reach Emily before one turns the truck ignition and puts one foot on the gas."

Dave absentmindedly played with his cup. "I can't believe that Sarah would do something like this. Wear whatever she wants there, but here – here where she was raised – she shouldn't be throwing in our faces how different she has become."

Dave pursed his lips together. "I really like Mohammad, and he is a good father to those kids and a good husband to Sarah, but part of me – *a big part of me* – wishes Sarah had never met him!"

"When you think like that, Dave, remember *Sam*. Compared to him, Mohammad is a saint. Sarah couldn't have done better than Mohammad. So, she is going to cover her hair. It's really no big deal. I'd rather have her do that than do some of the other things she could be doing."

"I can't imagine what you are thinking about," Dave said perplexed.

Martha was *trying* to think of something. "Well, she could be having an affair, wearing tight pants that showed the crack in her butt, bleaching her hair, wearing low-cut blouses that showed cleavage, and tons of makeup – any number of things."

"Do you *know* any women in town who do that?" Dave asked starting to smile.

"Not off-hand," Martha smiled. "I'm just trying to put things into perspective. Wearing a scarf on one's head is really *no big deal*. Nuns do it!"

"We don't have any nuns in town. In fact, there isn't even a Catholic church in town," Dave said starting to chuckle.

"I'm just trying to make a point here. We *do* have *Amish* and not only do they cover their hair, but they wear dresses that touch the top of their boots, and don't have buttons on their clothes."

By this time both Martha and Dave were laughing. "It could certainly be a lot worse," Martha sputtered between laughs. "Maybe you should tell Emily that Sarah and Yasmeen are going to wear long, black coats *and* black veils over their faces. Then, if she sees them wearing only a headscarf, she will be so relieved that she will think nothing of it."

"I will keep that in mind," Dave said.

That night over supper Dave told Emily about Martha talking to Sarah.

"Mohammad's father passed away. He was only seventy-two," Dave said. "He hadn't been sick, just keeled over."

"Would you have some more potatoes?" Emily asked passing them to Dave.

"Sarah was saying that she and Mohammad only get a month's holiday this summer. They will come for the month but have promised the three older kids that they can stay all summer. Martha was saying that Ken has lined up some summer jobs for them."

"Would you have some more meatloaf?" Emily asked.

"You aren't *listening* to anything I am saying, are you?" Dave asked in frustration.

Emily looked Dave straight in the face. "When you say something in which I am interested, I will listen."

"Well then, Sarah and Yasmeen have decided to wear long black coats down to their ankles, to cover their heads, and to wear a black veil over their faces so that only their eyes show. And everything will be *pinned* in place."

Emily's mouth dropped open and no words came out.

"What's for dessert?" Dave asked. "Maybe I *will* have another slice of meatloaf. Pass me the ketchup."

Chapter 36

The school year was rapidly drawing to a close. They would soon all be going to the States. The boys couldn't wait! Baba and Mama would go for a month but the boys and Yasmeen would be staying for two months with Grandpa Ken and Grandma Martha. Grandpa Ken had emailed that, true to his word, he had kept the pick-up in running order for them. He had written that he thought *Kalb* – the mongrel – could *sense* that they were coming. It promised to be a great summer!

Their first year had been better than they had expected. Oh, there had been a lot of rough patches, but all-in-all it had been a good year. They were popular – especially with the girls. They even had a few male friends among the 'Arabic-Speaking' kids. It had helped, they felt, that they were so good at basketball and wrestling – their soccer was not too bad either thanks to the Friday afternoon games with their cousins in the camp.

"We only have one more year to go," Mansur said, "and then it is the States for college!"

The IB program at the Friends was strong. Kids were applying to some prestigious ivy-league universities and getting in. Khalil and Mansur had always been good students. Next fall, when they were in their senior year, they were going to apply to Yale, Princeton, Harvard and MIT. The college prep teacher had told them they stood a pretty good chance of getting in! Other graduates of the Friends had gotten in.

Mohammad and Sarah were hopeful.

"Imagine," Mohammad said, "what it will mean if the boys get into one of those ivy-league schools. It kind of blows one's mind to think that their paternal grandfather was an illiterate peasant and their maternal grandfather a farmer with a sixth-grade education."

"The amazing thing," Sarah said, "*is* that they have a good chance of getting in!"

"And then the year after, it will be Yasmeen's turn. She is already saying that she is going to apply to Swarthmore, Haverford, and Brown," Sarah added.

"I'm pulling for Brown. If the boys get into Harvard and Yasmeen gets into Brown – they are only an hour's drive away. It is an easy bus commute on a weekend. I'd like them to be handy to one another. I *do* have reservations about Yasmeen living in a dorm but if her brothers are only an hour's drive away, they can easily check on her and it wouldn't be quite so bad," Mohammad said.

"You – in your heart-of-hearts – would be happy to get her married off when she is eighteen," Sarah joked. "Admit it."

Mohammad gave her a sheepish grin. "I will admit the *thought* crossed my mind, but I want to give her the same opportunities as the boys. She is smart and capable and knows where the parameters are. *If* she wasn't so level-headed and if I thought that we couldn't trust her I *would* try to get her married off before college."

"The kids have really done exceptionally well adjusting, all things considered," Sarah reflected.

"Yes, they have," Mohammad nodded. "And so have *you, habeeptee,*" he said reaching across the table and taking Sarah's hand. "Though every time I catch you with your sunglasses perched on top of your *hijab,* I do a double-take," Mohammad laughed. "What a picture of the collision of East and West!"

Sarah laughed, "I told you that wearing *hijab* would not change me."

Surprisingly, no one at school really *knew* how Yasmeen and Kareem felt about each other. Some may have *suspected,* but the two had done a fairly good job in hiding their true feelings. At school, they were *casual and indifferent acquaintances* – Yasmeen had read that line in a book and it seemed to fit their situation. Their relationship seemed to be grounded in emails and those nightly phone calls. They certainly weren't *typical* teenagers. They had never *made out;* they had never kissed; they had never even held hands.

"It is as though we are in a 19th-century Gothic romance," Yasmeen had once written to Kareem. "Loving each other secretly and from afar," she had wistfully added.

"I *do* love you," Kareem had typed. "One day we will, *inshallah,* be together. And I will be able to shout it from the rooftops: *I love Yasmeen!*"

Kareem, like Khalil and Mansur, was hoping to study in the States. His grades were good; he was a hard worker; he was guaranteed outstanding references from his teachers, and he had an uncle on his father's side who was a well-known doctor and an alumnus of Yale. His uncle had told him that he had *connections* and would see that Kareem got into a top notch school.

When they had *talked* about their future plans – about the goals they had individually set – Yasmeen confided she had always wanted to be a writer! "I have such an abundance of stories to tell," she said. "I have stories about my great grandmother Hasna who had red hair, blue eyes and freckles and how her mother kept telling her that the only man who would marry her would be: *old, blind,* or *slow.* Then there are the stories of the life my *Sitteh* and *Sidi* lived: the *nakbe,* life in a camp, the tragic death of my Uncle Ahmad, the imprisonment of my Uncle Khalil, my Uncle Issa becoming a political cartoonist during the *intifada.* Their story is like a film! Or one of those Turkish soap operas that my Amti Hasna loves."

"You mustn't forget your parents," Kareem had written. "Now *there's* a love story: a Moslem man from a camp going to study in the States and falling for with a Mid-Western Christian."

"Or the story of my Uncle Mansur, going to study in Russia and falling in love with a beautiful Circassian," Yasmeen added.

"You *do* have a wealth of stories, and maybe one day you can write about *us*," Kareem typed. "Write the story of two Arab-Americans who were brought back to Palestine, went to a private Quaker school, secretly feel in love and..."

Yasmeen interrupted, "...and lived happily ever after. That's the way *I* would write the story."

"That's the way *I'd* write it too!"

Epilogue

Yasmeen stood in the long line of students signing up for their freshman courses.

"Can I help you find your classes, Miss?" the handsome upperclassman asked. "Let me see your schedule. Ah, you are taking introductory writing with Professor Rosenfeld. You'll like him. I think that's his assistant working at the table right over there," the boy said pointing behind her.

"I *could* use some help," Yasmeen smiled. "It is all so new, and a bit bewildering."

"Might I say that you look quite pretty? Your *hijab* brings out the blue of your eyes."

Yasmeen blushed. "Yes, you *may* say so," Yasmeen said dimpling as she slipped her hand into Kareem's.

www.ingramcontent.com/pod-product-compliance
Lightning Source LLC
Chambersburg PA
CBHW061541170626
46811CB00001B/48